I0637071

love, lace, and minor Alterations

V. JOY PALMER

WhiteFire

This is a work of fiction. All characters and events portrayed in this novel are either fictitious or used fictitiously.

LOVE, LACE, AND MINOR ALTERATIONS

Copyright © 2016, Vanessa Joy Palmer
All rights reserved. Reproduction in part or in whole is strictly forbidden without the express written consent of the publisher.

Scripture quotations are from the ESV® Bible (The Holy Bible, English Standard Version®), copyright © 2001 by Crossway, a publishing ministry of Good News Publishers. Used by permission. All rights reserved.

WhiteFire Publishing
13607 Bedford Rd NE
Cumberland, MD 21502

ISBN: 978-1-939023-76-6 (digital)
        978-1-939023-75-9 (print)

Dedicated to Sam, Mom, and Rie.
You three believed in me from the very beginning.
I love you guys!
(Imagine approximately eighty-seven thousand exclamation points and heart emojis.)

Chapter One

When a bride finds The Dress, there is joy, laughter, and on some occasions, even spontaneous dancing.

There is none of that right now.

The bride wails like her firstborn son has been promised to Rumpelstiltskin. I stare in horror at the once beautiful dress. Formerly perfect, sparkling with promise, and, well, now it doesn't.

"What are we going to do?" the bride asks, knocking me back into reality.

Um...I'm not sure there is anything we can do for that dress now. Her undergarments show, courtesy of the torn train, but I'll attempt to take a more positive route.

"I will have a seamstress look at it and see what she can do, but just in case, why don't I bring in some other gowns for you to browse through. Just in case," I add so she doesn't think all is lost with this gown. Even though all is totally lost with this gown.

"What do you mean, look at other gowns? This is The Dress. Are you crazy? This is *the* dress!" She screams right into my face, eyes bugging out of their sockets.

"Well, I know that, and you know that, but a bride should always be prepared for whatever happens. She should always have a backup dress. I was going to mention that to you when you came in today for your fitting," I say this casually while I take a step back. I'm not completely lying. I fitted a bride once who had *five* backup gowns. When I asked her about it, in one of her fifty fittings, she just called it being well prepared. I called it neurotic, but to each her own. I was going to mention it today for laughs, but you use whatever you've got to in a crisis.

"Really?" The bride looks at me in complete desperation. Her hazel eyes are wide and unblinking as she waits for me to fix her world with a single word. I have power.

"Really." I give her my best reassuring smile. "So why don't you change out of this dress while I go get some others? Do you want to try some in this same style, or maybe a different one? You would look divine in an empire waist gown." I keep my voice as sweet as maple syrup.

She takes the bait, and soon an empire waist gown that screams gorgeous drapes from her shoulders. Lace covers the bodice, and a big satin ribbon emphasizes the waist. The lace, covering a chiffon skirt, flows to the floor. It starts off covering her whole waist but gradually narrows at five points around the skirt, very similar to a star shape. When it reaches the hem, there are just five little dots of lace. It's even more beautiful than the dress her flower girl ruined. A few minutes later, she schedules another fitting and then disappears out the door.

Just another day's work at Ever After, the bridal boutique in Keene, New Hampshire, where I work.

My name is Isabel Vez. Yes, I love my job. No, the bridal boutique is not named after the movie *Ever After*. No, I'm not married yet. No, I don't let the fact that I work with annoyingly perky brides every single day rub salt in my raw single wound. And yes, I still love my job despite all that. Usually.

"That woman would make a model candidate for *Bridezillas*," my best friend and Ever After's one and only seamstress, Kaylee McGrurd, whispers with a giggle.

"No kidding." I pretend to straighten a couple bridal catalogs long enough to debrief her about the last customer. "I thought her head was going to explode when she saw the dress. Her eyes were twice the normal size." I try to imitate her expression for Kaylee's benefit.

"What happened to it?" Kaylee asks.

"The train had been partially ripped off the dress, and clung to one side of the gown by a single, jagged piece of fabric." Kaylee makes a face, and I hold up my right hand. "Don't ask me how, but if you get a train that long, it's going to come with some risks. I imagine it has something to do with the flower girl, who was playing with it, but then hid behind her mother when the bride started to hyperventilate."

"Good job with that client." My boss, Lilly Marshall, suddenly appears by my side. It's spooky how she does that.

I quickly straighten. "Thank you." My boss does not tolerate slouches at work. She says it brings disgrace to our gowns. Lilly went to an all-girl school from kindergarten to twelfth grade. Etiquette lessons were required each year, or you didn't move on to the next grade. This especially means that if she catches me slouching, she will give me a five-minute lecture about good posture. I know this speech by heart, in case you were wondering.

"Such a pity her other dress was ruined like that," Lilly mutters.

"Yes, it is a pity, uh, such," I say.

Kaylee starts to laugh at my bad grammar, but covers it with a cough when my elbow lands in her ribs. "Yes," she says, "It's such, such a pity," Kaylee says this with a straight face.

My boss stares at us for a few minutes. I really want to howl with laughter. Drat Kaylee and her ability to keep cool under all circumstances! Lilly snaps back to reality and smiles. "Well, back to work, girls. Those gowns won't find their brides all by themselves."

Um... okay. Creepy statement.

I look at my friend as our weird boss walks away. "Will you stop doing that?" I whisper. "The woman is not stupid. She's going to figure out you're mocking her."

"If she hasn't figured it out yet, then I don't think she's going to anytime soon," Kaylee says. "So, The Chow Man after work? I'm craving a good crab Rangoon."

"That sounds great," I say. "Do you want to eat there?"

"No. I'll pick it up on my way home. I just want to crash in front of the TV tonight."

"Oh, so your usual nightly routine?" I smile at her as she rolls her eyes at me and sticks out her tongue. We may be twenty-five, but we still act like we're thirteen with each other. You know, as long as no one is looking. Then we act like the mature young women they think we are.

They really have no idea.

"See you at home. I've got some errands. I'll pick up the Chinese food." Kaylee smirks. "Have fun with the nut cases."

"They are not nut cases. They are just stressed. Planning a wedding can be very stressful." I say this in a monotone, as I recite this line to sobbing, spazzing, and emotional brides almost every day. Some of them *are* total nut jobs, but I can't tell Kaylee that. I hate losing in any way, shape, or form.

"Whatever. I'll see you later."

Kaylee waves as she shoots out the door, her long, red hair flying out behind her like Wonder Woman's red cape. Kaylee is beautiful. She's five-foot-ten with long, sleek red hair and bright green eyes. Literally, her eyes are the color of a fresh kiwi. She has a fabulous fashion sense, witty humor, and a love of football, baseball, and various other sporting endeavors.

What? I don't like sports. I once forgot whether the Red Sox were a baseball or football team. Basically, Kaylee is every man's dream. She even cooks.

I am the opposite of every man's dream. I'm short—five-foot-two—with extremely curly, dark hair. I already covered the fact that I don't know baseball from football, and I do not cook. I can't even make mashed potatoes right. My roommates call the fire department every time I bring home groceries. You have one little incident with a fiery stove, and nobody trusts you anymore.

I walk around the bridal boutique. The front windows boast mannequins dressed in our newest gowns, but sheer curtains partition them off from the rest of the store. The front section of the store has popular dresses on display. The left and right walls are wall-to-wall mannequins dressed in bridal apparel, as well as a few random mannequins that stand throughout the greeting area. I stop to straighten the hem of one before going to stand behind the front desk, which is framed by a door on each side. One leads to the stockroom. The other leads to the offices.

The bell over the door chimes, and another bride walks inside the store. She takes a seat on one of the three couches arranged like a giant "U." They face the storefront, but that doesn't stop this blond chick from turning around to stare at me with the classic, "When is it my turn?" look.

Candace Matthews, the other consultant, comes out of the offices. "Is my two o'clock appointment here yet?" She tucks a strand of black hair behind her left ear.

I gesture to the girl who is still staring at us. How can you miss that?

Candace steps next to me and pretends to busy herself with some paperwork on the desk. "Her name is Precious. Precious Treasure."

I snort, and immediately start coughing to cover it. "Yeah. You have fun with that."

"Thanks." Candace rolls her eyes, and then walks over to the bride to introduce herself.

I get back to work, busying myself with some paperwork for the brides who have ordered gowns and are coming in for fittings, rather than buying off the rack. I don't have any other appointments scheduled for my shift, and before I know it, it's time for me to leave.

Once I walk out the front door, I turn left down the strip mall sidewalk. Ever After is right in the middle, with a shoe store and a trendy clothing store on the right. On the left, there is a bookstore and café called Whipped Cream.

I open the door to Whipped Cream, and am greeted by Grant Thurrs—the owner, as well as the man who thought of the corny name to this café.

"Hey Izze!"

I take a step back. Not sure why, but it's my first response to such an enthusiastic greeting. "Hi, Grant. Been a slow day?"

"I was so bored that I arranged the mugs by color." He gestures to the shelf to his right.

"And what color dominated?" We have a long-standing argument that he needs to get a variety of different colored mugs, not just blue mugs. He always says that the "mugs" on the customers are different enough for him. I say that's rude, and blue gets boring after a while. And on it goes.

He sighs. "Izze, do we really have to go there again?"

My lips curl in a smug grin. "Yes." I bat my eyelashes at him.

He mumbles in a low voice. I balance on my tiptoes to hear him. "Glue," he says. Yeah, that's what I heard, too.

"Glue? Do you glue you're mugs together? Does the health inspector know?"

"What? No. B-L-U-E. Are you deaf from all the shrieking brides?"

"I'm not deaf. You just mumble. Take a speech class," I say as I settle onto a barstool in front of the counter. "I'll take an iced

mocha with a shot of caramel and an extra shot of espresso. Pretty please." I add the pretty please for good measure. After all, I did insult his speech abilities.

He rolls his eyes. "No extra mocha shot this time?"

"I thought that was understood."

"Coming right up." He turns to get it ready.

I look around the café. It is dead in here. This strip mall is located in the middle of town. This is Keene, New Hampshire. No, it's not New York City, but it's not exactly a little stick-in-the-mud town in the middle of a state nobody remembers exists. Normally business is pretty steady.

Grant owns the café along with his sister Miranda, who chooses that moment to enter. Grant and Miranda happen to be my second cousins, so I get a discount on coffee.

"Hey!" she yells.

I blink. These people are not normally so starved for human interaction. "Uh...hi!" I respond, also yelling.

Now she blinks at me.

I decide to change the subject and spare myself from looking like an idiot. "So how are you doing, Miranda?"

"I'm good. It's been so slow today. It's making me sleepy. I can't wait until closing." She yawns.

Grant comes back with a to-go cup filled with my icy mocha treat. "What are we talking about?"

"Your sister just told me she's going to club you over the head, lock your body in the shed, and become sole proprietor of this establishment." I figure potential murder is definitely free of boredom. "Oh, and she's going to buy more mugs."

Grant rolls his eyes as he hands me my coffee. I take a sip of the sickly sweet but delicious drink. Grant almost gags as he watches me.

"How can you drink that much sugar and cream on top of

chocolate?"

"I have a strong heart."

"Whatever."

I grin. "Bye, guys. I'll see you tomorrow."

"Bye," they both echo.

I take a deep breath at the door. Iced coffee in the middle of winter was not a bright idea. I take another sip. Who cares? I open the door and run the rest of the way to my car.

⌒♥⌒

I pull into the driveway at my house. Yes, I said house. It's a four-bedroom house that Kaylee and I rent with two close friends from church, Apryl and Courtney Burns.

Sisters.

Twin sisters.

I'm sure you can imagine the joys that brings our lives.

It's a small, uh, good house. Really, it's a rundown shack. The paint is peeling. The shutters are falling off. The stove doesn't bake properly. The hardwood floors creak. The railing leading upstairs is broken. In fact, we kicked down what was left, rather than keep dealing with it.

On the plus side, there are four small bedrooms. Four small, small bedrooms. Barely big enough for a bed. That may be a slight exaggeration, considering I have a dresser, desk, and chair squeezed into mine. But I love this house. It's beautiful in a falling-apart-on-an-old-back-road-with-lots-of-sunshine-and-nature kind of way.

I get out of my little blue car. Sweet! I'm the first one here.

As I walk in the front door, I kick my shoes off in the foyer, hang my coat on the rack, and set my Coach purse, a Christmas present from my parents, on the decorative table where we all

keep our purses.

I walk the agonizing ten feet to the couch where I immediately collapse without bothering to change out of my skirt and blouse. Bring on the wrinkles, because only a chicken running through my living room screaming, "The sky is falling!" is getting me up and off this couch.

And if that happens I'll be going to get a psych evaluation.

About half an hour later Apryl and Courtney get home. I can hear them yelling from the car all the way in here, on the couch, with the volume on the TV turned up higher than necessary.

"Are you crazy?" That's Courtney and her familiar, high-pitched scream.

"Listen. I'm going to say this to you one more time. This is my job. I love to do it. And it's my head. If I dye the whole thing magenta, that is my right! It's your job to love me regardless of how I look!" Apryl screams back.

I pause the movie. I might as well listen without any distractions.

"But when you dye my whole head magenta, it's another story!" Courtney shrieks at a decibel appropriate only for dogs.

"Then don't bring up my hair color choices." Apryl huffs. Apryl has had some interesting hair colors. Currently, her hair is jet black, shoulder length, with a ton of layers—at least it was this morning. "And I did your tips. The very ends of your hair. Get over it. You said you wanted something different, and this is different. Besides, it looks great on you." Apryl sounds like she is trying to speak calmly, like she is trying to reason with her.

Yeah right.

"I'm a law student." Courtney says. "I'm going to be a lawyer. I can't have magenta tips! It's undignified. I was thinking blond highlights or even red. But this is frightening!"

"Listen, undignified works for you. King David was undignified.

I think lawyers are too stuffy. Live a little. Add some color to those gray suits." Apryl says all this in a bored tone. I bet they've been going at it for a while.

The door slams open and they walk inside the house. Courtney practically runs through the living room, up the stairs, and presumably into her room, because I hear another door slam. Apryl just stands there and looks at me. Probably because I'm lying on my back, legs flung over the back of the couch, and feet hanging off the edge. Also, I'm in a skirt.

Could be embarrassing if there were any guys here.

She drops her purse on the floor, kicks off her shoes, and belly flops onto the loveseat.

"Did you see her hair?" Apryl asks.

I fiddle with the remote. "She took off running too fast for me to see it. Flash would have been proud."

"It looks great on her. I'm not dyeing it back. She can go to some other hairstylist and pay for it if she's going to be like that." She huffs, sending her bangs flying.

I keep my mouth shut. I don't really want to deal with it. I just want to watch *Letters to Juliet* and eat my bag of Oreos.

Yes, I am going to eat the whole bag by myself. It's been a long day. Don't judge. I'll work it off.

Or I'll skip breakfast tomorrow.

"I love this movie," Apryl murmurs. "What are you watching next?"

"*My Fair Wedding*. Somebody's doing a wedding with sky diving or ocean creatures or something like that." I answer.

"What?" Apryl asks after a moment.

I don't know what was so hard to understand about that statement. I open my mouth to start over again only slower this time. "I said *My Fair Wedding*. The episode is about—"

"Not that, dork. I don't see how you went from sky diving to

ocean monsters. They are worlds apart." Apryl rolls her deep-set, blue eyes.

"Oh," I say. "I'm not sure where a lot of those ideas for weddings come from, but I've seen some weird stuff. I just remember it looked interesting."

"I see," Apryl says and then falls quiet again.

Thirty minutes later, a herd of elephants tromps up our porch stairs. Kaylee comes through the door seconds later.

Guess I was wrong about that herd of elephants.

"Hey guys." Her hands are full of Chinese takeout. "What are we watching? Where's Courtney?"

Apryl says, "*Letters to Juliet,*" the same time I say, "In her room."

"Oh, I love this movie!" She sits down and passes around the takeout containers and chopsticks. "Why?" She casts her eyes upstairs.

But she already knows.

We often go through this scenario with slight variations. First, one of us gets home and flops on the couch with the television blaring. Next, the rest of us start to find our way home. Then, Apryl and Courtney begin to argue about anything from haircuts to whether or not Congress would pass a law stating that socks cannot be worn with sandals. Later, after much "discussion," Courtney will storm to her room. Finally, Courtney, feeling convicted, will return to apologize, and we will enjoy a lazy evening in front of the TV.

I know my life. Boring for some, but not to me. I have a problem when I don't know what's going to happen next. Repetition is good. Change is distressing.

Apryl sets the small container of rice on the floor and rolls over. "She didn't like the dye job I did for her hair. It's too wild for her."

Kaylee just nods in an Oh-I-see way. This is an argument as old as time.

We sit in silence for about fifteen minutes before I hear Courtney come down the stairs. She walks over to the couch, stopping in front of us. Her hair looks great, actually. The magenta looks really good with her wavy, mahogany-colored hair. I pause the movie again and close my eyes.

"I just wanted to say that I'm sorry for freaking out. You're right. This is different. And that's exactly what I said I wanted." Her voice is soft, humble.

Even with my eyes closed I can still see the scene in our little living room. I smile.

"It's okay, Court. I understand." I open my eyes as Apryl passes a container of Lo Mein to her as a peace offering.

And all is well.

"Who's up for *My Fair Wedding*?" I ask.

I love my life.

It's a beautiful morning. The sun is shining bright, and the sky is blue.

Just like my mood.

I'm sure this has happened to you. You have an amazing dream. Then you wake up. The dream felt so real, probably because you wanted it to be real. And now that it's over you just want to go back to dreamland. Where life is exactly how you want it.

Not the best way to start the day. I roll over in my bed and stare at the wall. I'm just like any other single woman. Sometimes I just want to be loved. For me. I had a dream that I met Mr. Wonderful, Sweet, Smart, Hot, AND Sensitive. We were engaged and I felt so in love. I felt so full, so happy. How can you do that? Feel in love in a dream, I mean? It all felt so real, but better. I've dealt with reality, and let me tell you, living a dream is much better.

There's a verse in the Bible that talks about lifting your eyes up to the hills and about how your help comes from God. I think I'm going to give it a try. But since there are not a lot of hills in Keene, I roll onto my back and lift my eyes to the ceiling.

What is that nasty looking gunk all over my ceiling?

I am so getting up now. It looks like a giant dust bunny that's planning to eat me in my sleep.

Thirty minutes later I'm showered and hitting the coffeepot. I'm not dressed in my work clothes yet. Instead, I'm wearing a sweat suit that has seen a better millennium.

I go back to my room for a minute and return with my Bible and a notebook. Devotional time.

I head to the sunroom toward the back of the house. It's not the warmest part of the house in the middle of winter, but it is the most beautiful room no matter what season. The big bay windows show our whole backyard, and thanks to Kaylee's green thumb, our backyard is beautiful with its big maple trees, stone benches, and flower beds. This time of year, it is like a winter wonderland. A giant snow glob, if you will.

I sit on a little loveseat that Courtney dismissed because it didn't match any of the furniture we have. It's fuchsia. With blue flowers. I don't know where Apryl bought this, but I can't help the giggle every time I look at it.

I open my Bible and stare at the words, finding it hard to focus this fine day. My heavy heart definitely isn't helping matters. I haven't really been reading in a particular book lately, so I close my eyes and open my Bible, flinging the pages to see where they land. Hey, nothing's a coincidence.

I land in Luke chapter thirteen. I read. I still don't feel like anything sticks today. Like nothing applies.

The first part of verse thirty-three catches my eye. It says, "In any case, I must keep going today and tomorrow and the next day...."

Apparently God doesn't want me to wallow in this, but to trust Him to bring the right guy in His time, and in the meantime, to move forward in life and in Him.

Easier said than done.

Okay. I'm going to try it. Maybe it will help that weird, dull ache in my heart that just wants to be loved.

It's usually easy to ignore this ache. I think about the past, and about the terrible memories there. Then I just bury myself in friends, family, work, and church. But sometimes I'll watch a bride find The Dress and talk about her perfect fiancé, and that ache will come back with a raging vengeance.

But today is not a day for wallowing. It is a day for... uh, going on.

❤

I've gone on to the bookstore.

Ah. I love coming to the bookstore. Cause it's awesome.

I take a deep breath. Inhale. Exhale. I love the smell of books. Of paper. Of coffee. Of coffee and paper. It's poetically beautiful.

"Hey, Izze. How are you doing today?" Todd is roughly around my age. He has worked here since the beginning of time.

"I'm great! How's business? No crazy old ladies trying to pick you up again?" I grin as he sighs. Todd's a cute guy. The older generation adores him. The old ladies will even pinch his cheeks. I went on a couple dates with him a few years ago, but by the second date we knew there was nothing there.

I walk over to my usual section. Today I'm on a mission. I'm looking for something light-hearted, romantic, and fun. And I will not leave without it.

A wall of books towers over me. I wonder if anyone actually

uses the ladder they have hooked to the bookshelf wall. Maybe it's just for looks? Or does everybody just go without the books on the top shelf? Maybe the top shelf is reserved for all the books nobody likes.

Out of the corner of my eye I see a guy looking at me. He is really looking at me. He's not checking me out, or looking at me like he's trying to place who I am. He's just staring. It's weird. Obviously, his mother never taught him that staring is rude.

Ten minutes later I've got it narrowed down to two books. However, that guy is still staring at me. He's hardly moved from his spot. This is ridiculous! I am getting agitated now.

"Excuse me, can I help you?" I say in a polite voice. Polite but annoyed. At least I use my manners.

He looks at me as if I was the one who was staring. "No," he says, and then he turns and walks away.

"Grrr. People can be so rude sometimes." I grumble to myself. I can't decide which book I want, so I head over to the in-store coffee shop. There I can sit with a hot cup of some delicious coffee while I get better acquainted with these books.

I always feel a little weird taking something to read into the coffee shop in this store. Like what if I don't like the book, but I spill coffee on it because I'm a klutz? Then I'll feel obligated to buy it because I ruined the merchandise, and hindered their chances at a sale. If I hadn't drunk the coffee while reading, it never would have been ruined.

Maybe they shouldn't let people read anymore while drinking their coffee. Maybe they shouldn't let people read the books because they'll be less likely to buy them if they can just come to the store every day to read them. You know that saying about the guy who won't buy the cow if he's getting the milk for free? Well, it applies to more than just relationships. I like to think it applies to all aspects of life. Even book buying.

I stop dead in my tracks once I'm in the open coffee shop. There in the middle of the line is Rude Guy. Seriously? I am so not happy right now. He's not looking this direction so I slip quickly into line.

Yes! I don't think he saw me. I start doing little fist pumps in a muted victory dance.

"Uh, Miss, can I take your order?" The barista gives me a funny look. That's okay—I deserved it that time.

"Hi, uh, I'd like a large caramel latte with whip cream on top," I say, working to keep my voice normal. No need to freak her out any more.

"Whole milk or skim milk?"

"Whole milk with a ton of sugar, please." I glance up the line.

She scribbles on my future coffee cup. "Anything else today?"

"Just those fake glasses with the bushy eyebrows and oversized nose so I can discreetly lay low," I say.

The barista doesn't even crack a smile. She's like sixteen! She should appreciate my joke. Or at least be polite and smile.

The manner system in America is failing us.

I hand her the money and then move down the line to pick up my drink. I face the glass display case and pretend to be engrossed in studying the desserts, but out of the corner of my eye I watch Rude Guy to see if he's noticed me. He's looking at the paperback in his hand as he waits for his coffee.

As the line moves, I stealthily make my way down a little farther.

I feel like a spy.

Rude Guy gets his drink now and turns to leave. This time I don't do any fist pumps, but I can't help the sigh that escapes my lips.

I reach the end of the line, pick up my drink, and look for a semi-clean table. The first one I sit at is coated in some slimy, tan-colored substance. I move toward a table by the window and

sit. Ah, perfect.

I take a sip of my drink and open the first book.

Suddenly, a shadow falls over me.

I look up, and who do I see?

That's right. Rude Guy.

"You're sitting in my spot."

"I beg your pardon." My mouth hangs open.

"It's perfectly fine. I'd just like my seat back."

"Uh, no, I think you misunderstood me."

He raises his eyebrows at me, and I notice his striking blue eyes for the first time. "You're not going to move?"

"Yes. I mean no. I mean yes."

His eyebrows creep higher at my stuttering.

I take a breath. "I mean you misunderstood when I said, 'I beg your pardon.' I meant it like, 'I don't understand what you're talking about.' So, no, I am not giving you the seat back because you were not sitting here. To answer your last question."

His eyebrows have taken a flying leap to the moon by the time I finish. Which makes his rather gorgeous eyes that much more obvious. Oh, I really hate that I notice this.

"Okay." He sets his coffee down and takes the seat across the table from me.

Bad. Bad. *Very* bad.

This isn't going to end well. I can feel it in my bones.

"What are you doing?" I snarl. Politeness gone. Out comes Snot Face.

"I'm sitting."

"I can see that, but why? This is my table. Go get your own." My sneer would make any middle-school kid proud.

"Well, I say it's my table, but you clearly think it's your table. So you're not going to budge. Correct?" He holds my gaze and nods when I don't answer. "That's what I thought." He sips his coffee,

sets it down, and folds his hands all lawyer-style as he waits for me to refute his logic.

Oh, I'll refute it all right.

"I don't know you. And I'm not sharing a table with someone I don't know." Ha! Take that.

"I'm James Miles Clayton, but my friends call me Miles. And this is my spot." His smug grin reveals an even row of teeth. "And your name is?"

"None of your beeswax." Great, now I'm reverting back to myself at age five.

"That was a good, mature comeback." He smirks. "You don't have to tell me your name, but it would sure go a long way in getting to know you." His expression is somewhat charming. And insanely aggravating.

"You could be a stalker."

"I assure you I'm not."

"I'm sure that's what all stalkers say. Especially when the restraining order is placed."

"I sit at this table every time I come to this bookstore."

"I bet the other tables would like to make your acquaintance. Share the joy."

"I'm a one-table-for-life kind of man," he shoots back.

"Look, you weren't sitting here when I sat down. It looked like James had left the building." I purposely don't call him Miles because I am not his friend. This man is crazy.

His eyes sparkle. Uh-oh. "Now, why did you think I had left?"

"Um, because I didn't see you."

"If you didn't see me, I would think you would have said something like you didn't see me. You said it looked like I had left. Meaning you saw me. Possibly even *watched* me."

"Uh..." Sigh. I cannot tell a lie. "Uh, I wasn't watching for you. I saw you and ducked."

"Why is that?" He leans forward.

"Because you were staring at me earlier. And that bugs me."

He doesn't deny staring at me. He just doesn't address it.

"Did your mother ever teach you that staring is rude?" I ask.

"My mother raised me to be quite the gentleman."

I snort. Like a lady. "On the contrary. Gentlemen don't stare."

James the Rude Guy shrugs. "Think what you'd like, but let's get back to you. You were watching me after you ducked. To see if it was safe to sit or run."

I refuse to comment. Hey, if he can do it, I can too.

He chuckles. "Looks like between the two of us, you're the stalker."

"I am not!"

Heads turn our way and someone shushes me. Great.

"I am not," I say again, this time just above a whisper.

"That's what they all say."

"Argh!" My head drops to the table. "Can I please just have my table?" Might as well try polite desperation.

"Nope."

I raise my head. "Why? Why sit here and bug me? Why not get another table?"

He looks me square in the eyes, and it almost takes my breath away. "Because I like this spot. And the company intrigues me." He stands up. "But I'm afraid I have to go pay for this book. I hate reading a book in a coffee shop that I haven't purchased yet. Until next time." He winks and walks away.

This time I make sure he walks out the door.

Chapter Two

Miles walked as fast as a man of his size could walk without looking like he was running away.

From a girl no less.

Thankfully, his long legs made that pretty easy, and he found his orange car quickly. After unlocking the door and getting in, he dropped his head to the steering wheel. He tried to slow his breathing, but his heart betrayed him and kept thundering.

Miles had been minding his own business in the bookstore, trying to find his mother a book for her birthday. His mother liked sappy romance novels, so there he was in the bookstore, awkwardly pawing through Karen Kingsbury, Susan May Warren, Rachel Hauck, and Janice Thompson books like a good son. Really, what single, twenty-eight-year-old male would do that? He deserved an award.

Then she walked into the bookstore.

Instantly, Miles's eyes had been drawn to her. She was the most beautiful woman he had ever seen. Dark, mocha colored curls that bounced around her shoulders, creamy colored skin...and she had these dark eyes. Oh, those dark, killer eyes! Even from a distance, they pierced his soul, leaving him breathless.

Then he realized that he had seen her before.

He blamed his photographic memory. It came in handy in

high school because it meant he never had to study for a test. He never spent days trying to remember what movie an actor was in last. He was one of those awkward people who would go up to someone saying, "Johnny! How are you man? It's me, Miles. We had chemistry together in junior year."

Her picture was in a little golden frame on the wall labeled "Ever After's Employees." The realization had stunned Miles, and turned him into a flabbergasted idiot.

Today, his gift became a blessing and a curse.

A blessing because he had this joy in his heart from knowing he would get to see the beautiful brunette from the bookstore again. What could possibly be better than that?

A curse because he was pretty sure that she thought he was some kind of deranged freak.

An hour and a half later I pull into my parking spot at work. The books I purchased today are sitting in the front seat in their plastic bag.

I couldn't pick just one.

I grab them and wrap the plastic bag around the books for a more protective covering. Then I stick them under the driver's seat.

What? When books sit in a hot car, in direct sunlight all day, the covers bend funny. I know it's weird, but it bugs me.

I moan and groan to the listening ears of my car. I am so not a fan of closing. I just like getting to sleep late. At the end of the night we have to inventory all the gowns and veils and shoes and notepads. Yes, even the notepads. We have to make sure all the dress orders from that day have been submitted, and then tidy the place up. Even though we close at eight, it takes almost two hours to do all these tasks.

Sometimes sleeping in is not on the greener side of the fence.

I drag my lazy body out of the car and toward Ever After. Upon entering, the madness inside the boutique seriously makes me consider turning around and leaving.

A ton of people are crammed into every corner of this place. Don't get me wrong. Ever After is fairly big. It can hold a good amount of people before the fire marshal gets mad. But so far I've counted seventeen women and nine men.

Every one of them is talking. Or maybe shouting is a better word. Yep. Pointing, waving their arms, and shouting. Most of the mob faces the front desk. Lilly stands behind the desk, trying to type on the computer and waving some papers for the mob to see. She looks like all she wants to do is duck behind the desk and scream for someone to save her.

There is no saving her now.

Lilly sees me just then and starts to holler my name. At least I assume it's my name. I can't hear to be sure, but if I lip read, it looks like my name. I push and squeeze past a couple of women and make it to the desk.

That in itself was a miracle of God.

Now how do we get rid of all the bodies?

"Man, this is a bad day for Candace to be off. Who are these people?"

"This"—Lilly swirls her hand in the air to indicate the general chaos—"is the O'Malley family. They are planning a triple wedding for their triplet daughters, Tara, Jane, and Mary. The wedding is in three months. All three girls have very different tastes in wedding gowns, and that is a problem. The theme of the wedding is based on the movie, *My Big Fat Greek Wedding*, so they are trying to get gowns that sort of match as well as go with the theme."

"Why are there so many people here?"

"They each brought their bridesmaids and future mothers-in-

law."

"And all the men?" I'm up to a twelve count on guys now.

"Father, uncles, and brothers. Listen, you take Mary and Jane. Mary's easy going. Jane will like pretty much anything, she's just so happy to be getting married. Tara is the big bossy one. I'll take her. I was thinking we'd get them all into big ball gowns with some Greek goddess theme to it." Lilly's voice takes on a drill sergeant quality. "Any questions? Okay. Good. Now, go!" She claps her hands like a sports coach.

"And break!" I yell.

"Wait one second!" A shrill voice assaults my left ear.

"Ahh!" I grab my ringing ear. "Can I help you, ma'am?" The woman, who shows no signs of remorse for making me deaf in one ear, is tall. Scary tall. The blond hair piled elegantly upon her head just adds to the way she towers over me. And she wears a scary expression that just makes the scary tallness worse.

"The theme is not *My Big Fat Greek Wedding*! That is so been there, done that. The theme is ancient Greece. And I want flowing, Greek goddess themed dresses. Got it?"

I'm scared. "Uh, Lilly, did you hear that?"

"Yes, my mistake, Tara," Lilly replies politely.

My turn to yell. "So Mary and Jane, if you guys could come into dressing room two, we'll get started." Heads turn my way.

Right, look at me like I'm the weird one.

I lead Mary and Jane into the second appointment room. I try to stop and turn around. Try. Mary and Jane almost take me out. I spin awkwardly out of the way and sidestep twice before coming to a stop. Deep breath.

I think they were running. From their dictator sister.

Sorry, God. I'm not being very nice. Again.

"So...how do you guys feel about these Greek goddess dresses?" The two sisters exchange a look. "We like the idea, but..." Jane starts.

"But we don't want Tara to have the last say," Mary finishes.

Jane's lip quivers. "She wants us all to wear diamond white, and I look terrible in straight up white!"

I believe it. Jane just does not have the complexion to wear diamond white.

"We just wanted to ask that you pick gowns with that theme in mind, but pick ones that won't look terrible on us." Mary states her declaration of independence.

Yeah! These girls don't want to suffocate under Tara's dictatorial wedding rule.

Drat! I'm doing it again.

I place my right hand over my heart. "I, Isabel Vez, do solemnly swear that I will pick gowns complimenting your Greek goddess theme, while at the same time complimenting your own unique styles."

Jane grins.

"Do we need to sign anything?" Mary asks very seriously.

I laugh.

I hope she's kidding though.

There is going to be a war in Ever After.

Tara glares at Mary and Jane.

And me. Gulp.

All three sisters have come out into the main room in their favorite wedding dress to show the impatient army of waiting family and friends. The minute Tara turned around and saw them, I swear her eyes turned red. Mary and Jane cower behind me, all their earlier bravado gone.

It's up to me.

I need some superhero music.

"What"—Tara points an accusing, talon-like finger at her quivering sisters—"are those gowns doing here?"

Lilly shoots me a "What on earth are you doing?" look.

I send her a "Defending the just!" look in reply. Then I meet Tara's scary expression. "These bridal gowns are in keeping with your Greek goddess theme. I think they really compliment their individual looks as well," I answer calmly.

"We all agreed on white dresses. And that mine would have sparkle. And that all three would be strapless." She comes over and fingers Mary's one-shoulder Grecian dress. It's an off-white color and gorgeous against her skin tone. There's a touch of sparkle on the shoulder. The back is dramatic with twisted fabric and drapes, flowing, all the way to the bottom. "This dress is everything we said we wouldn't do."

Seriously. The touch of sparkle on Mary's dress is so small it's ridiculous. She's upset about this?

"And Jane's dress is..."

"And Jane's dress is what?" Jane steps out from behind me. "You don't like my spaghetti straps? Or the sweetheart neckline? Or the empire waist with the crystals showcasing it? Or the fact that it's not the boring little peasant dress you demanded I wear? Well, what is it?"

You go, girl!

Jane has been so quiet and calm throughout this appointment. I thought if anyone got into a fistfight, it would be Mary and Tara. Looks like I was wrong.

Hehe.

Jane doesn't even let her get a word out. "We like these gowns, Tara. It's my wedding, and it's Mary's wedding, too. And if you don't like the gowns we're wearing, even though they are perfect with your stupid Greek theme, then you can go have your own wedding, and Mary and I will have a double wedding!"

Mary takes a step closer to Tara and points a finger at her. "That's right, sis. So, what will it be?"

Tara is speechless.

Hehe.

Thankfully, Lilly swoops in on autopilot to finish the appointment with three big purchases before it really does turn into a bickering bridal brawl.

I can't help my relief when the party leaves. I close my eyes to enjoy the pleasure of golden silence.

"What are you doing?"

I open my eyes with much difficultly to see Lilly standing there. "Praying for Mary and Jane. They will need some divine help to survive that engagement."

Lilly smirks. "Well, when you're done, come out back. Your aunt just got here. We're having a meeting to discuss some big news."

I love my aunt Jill. She owns Ever After. She used to work here full time, but when I moved here, she took over buying the dresses and advertising, instead of working in the store full time. Lilly took over as store manager.

Big news from Aunt Jill could mean anything. She's pretty unpredictable. I'm not worried though. Big news from Aunt Jill is almost always a good thing.

I open the door to the offices, which is really just one big room divided by cubicles. In my humble opinion, cubicles are just a way for everyone to pretend they have a private office, when in reality it's just a desk and a chair squeezed in between fake walls.

I walk into Lilly's cubicle and hug my aunt.

"Hello, hon. I've missed you, too."

"Hey. So what's up?" I ask while settling into a chair facing Lilly's desk.

Aunt Jill takes a deep breath. "Well, there's no easy way to say

this. I'm retiring. I'm not young anymore, and I find that I just want to be around my family instead of working. Lilly and I have been talking a lot about this, and...I'm selling the business to Lilly."

I blink.

Lilly pipes up then. "We decided to tell you before Candace since, well..."

I can fill in her hanging sentence in my head. Since this is like a family business for me.

Lilly continues. "Everything will be like it is now except I will take over Jill's job on top of mine. Which brings me to some news of my own—I've hired someone to help me with marketing, advertising, taxes, and expenses. He has a master's degree in business and comes highly recommended from his previous employers."

I think I'm going to puke.

This is too much. It doesn't sound all that bad. But it's just so weird. So different.

There're going to be changes.

I don't like changes.

"He is going to be here any minute, Izze, so that you and Jill can meet him. I've meet him once before." Lilly re-straightens the neat papers on her desk. "It's important to me that you get along with him because he is going to be very involved here."

"So be nice, honey." Aunt Jill gives my shoulder a squeeze. "Don't take your shock out on him."

"And for goodness sake, stop slouching. That is not a good first impression."

Someone knocks on the wall then. Kaylee sticks her head inside our cubicle. "James Clayton is here." Kaylee's face is neutral, so I can't get any details or clues. He's probably a middle-aged man who makes way too many jokes about numbers. That describes most finance guys, right?

Wait a second!

Kaylee's head disappears. In her place a very good-looking man walks into our circle.

A good-looking man with blazing blue eyes and a very familiar —and very annoying—smirk on his lips.

James Miles Clayton is James Rude Guy.

Lilly smiles at him like he's Patrick Dempsey. I mean, sure, he's got the hair, but he's no movie star.

Is it getting hot in here? I fan myself with both hands, and Aunt Jill shoots me a weird look. My eyes are probably bugging out right now.

What do I do?

There are times in your life when, frankly, you don't want to act like the Christian you are. This is such a time for me because I would love to unleash my fury on every single person in this room about what can only be considered a sick joke.

Instead of letting my enraged warrior side consume my entire being like the Hulk, I respond like the mature Christian woman I am.

"This is a joke, right?"

Almost.

Lilly gasps and Aunt Jill shoots me a look that would thaw a polar ice cap. James just smirks.

"Izze," Lilly says through clenched teeth. "This is no joke. James is our new employee."

"I, uh, I'm sorry. I didn't mean it like...um, that." So eloquent. "I just, uh, met Mr. Clayton earlier...today." I am the reason grammar school exists.

I glance at James for a little help. He grins wildly as he leans against the desk with his arms crossed over his broad chest. If the width of your smile were directly proportional to winning, you would think he just had a billion dollars dropped in his lap.

Oh, swell. He's not going to bail me out at all. I really don't like this guy.

Aunt Jill raises one eyebrow at me, in a way that says *I smell something fishy.* "I see." She looks at James with a smile, and I want desperately to stick out my tongue, but my aunt has eyes in the back of her head, and I gave up acting childish this morning.

Remember, it didn't work.

"James will be our new financial advisor," Lilly says with a proud smile.

"What are your qualifications?" I ask.

Lilly gasps yet again. "Izze, must you harass the man?"

"No, it's quite all right." James's voice is velvety smooth. It's a little more refined than this morning, meant to impress, I presume. "I have a master's degree in business, with a minor in accounting. I'm afraid I can't impress you with the name of a famous school, as I graduated from a Christian college with only a hundred graduates. But I had a four-point GPA, and I took a job with a firm in Virginia after graduation. Have you ever been to The Lemonade Stand?"

The Lemonade Stand is on his résumé? Impressive. Best blueberry lemonade and honey barbeque on the east coast. The company went national last year. Soon America will be dotted with these restaurants from here to Oregon.

"Yeah."

"She means *yes.*" Lilly, the Queen of Proper Grammar. One day, she will say, "Yup," and there isn't a mountain high enough or an ocean wide enough to stop me from being there to hear it.

"I worked on the financial team for The Lemonade Stand."

"Impressive for someone so young." Aunt Jill has officially been lost to Rude Guy James and his charms.

Clearly I have no pull here.

Lilly smiles much too brightly.

Oh, wait! Maybe, just maybe, his current firm is taking this account on as well. So hopefully, he will not be working here, but just running the numbers and calling Lilly. I can deal with that.

I smile. "Congratulations, I'm sure your new firm is pleased that you have picked up this account."

"Well, once I moved to New Hampshire, I left the firm. I've been working for myself. I haven't built up a large clientele yet—right now I only have one other account, which does not require the same level of involvement." His eyes twinkle in a way that tells me he knew exactly what I was thinking.

This is my fate. An old family saying comes to mind for situations like these: Fake it till you make it! "Lilly, I am thankful you gave me the chance to meet James. This decision will really benefit Ever After. I apologize for the inappropriate way I received the news." I swivel my head toward James. "It was a pleasure to meet you."

Lilly beams. Aunt Jill raises an eyebrow at me. She knows when I'm faking it. After all, she taught me how to fake it after a dozen or so of my father's failed attempts at cooking.

Aunt Jill pipes up, "Lilly, Izze needs to leave early tonight for dinner with her parents. She arranged this a while ago."

She's on to me. It's not the goodness of her heart that motivates her to get me out of this awful meeting—and closing.

"That's right! You may leave. There are some details that we will need to discuss tomorrow. Also, I am teaming you up with James. James, anything you need, any questions you have, take them to Izze."

Oh, joy.

"Thank you. Excuse me." As soon as I cross the threshold, I walk-run.

I can almost feel Aunt Jill breathing down my neck.

"Izze!"

Ack!

Her hand clamps down around my left shoulder just moments later. I never participated in track, in case you were wondering.

"Hey, I was just getting ready to go. I have to stop at the store first." Having totally spaced dinner at my parents'. "I'll meet you there?" Please don't corner me. Please don't drill me right now. I'm not even sure what I'm feeling, but I don't want to get into it. I beg her with my dark eyes to just drop it.

She raises an eyebrow at me. Her dark lashes frame her chestnut colored eyes. "What was that?"

I sigh. "I don't know." I massage my temple with my right fist. "I met him earlier today, and he was just rude. Also, a little crazy. He kept staring at me, and wouldn't leave me alone. He sat down at my table—uninvited! Then he gave me a hard time for taking his table! Who does that?"

She looks at me like my coffee is a few espresso beans short of a bag. "So, he sat down at your table. Naturally, here at work, you had to be rude back."

"No, he just threw me for a loop. I was surprised. That's all. Honest."

"So what do you think of him then?"

"He's swell," I say through clenched teeth.

"Uh-huh. Don't you think it was smart of Lilly to hire someone to help with the finances and advertising?" She tilts her head to the side, her wavy red hair following her.

"I think that all financial and advertising guys are rude, arrogant, and strange, so it's great that he fits the description. Means Lilly's getting her money's worth."

Aunt Jill snorts. "Izze."

"It's true. I'm not crazy. It's all true."

"That is judgmental."

"It's true though. Every one of them runs around with arrogant,

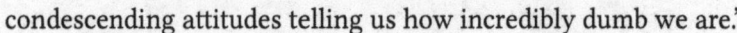

condescending attitudes telling us how incredibly dumb we are."

"Careful, Elizabeth. Mr. Darcy may be more than he appears."

"Do not put a *Pride and Prejudice* spin on the situation! You only get one shot at a first impression. He already blew it with me."

"Izze, that story is an amusing anecdote to tell your parents over dinner. It is not a reason to hate someone."

"I don't hate him. I just want him to leave me alone," I mumble.

"Well, that's not going to happen. Lilly has hired him, and I've washed my hands of all your crazy shenanigans." She pretends to wash her hands, dry them off, and toss the towel away. "So you need to make peace with the man." With that, she turns and walks away.

"Now, get going. You don't want to be late," she calls over her shoulder.

The Rude Guy and the Bridal Consultant.

Every little girl's dream.

"Mom, let go. It hasn't been that long."

"Ah, sweetheart, it feels like an eternity. Besides, don't you love me? Just let me hug you." Her grip tightens around me, crushing my ribcage in all the wrong places.

"Don't you love me? Right now it feels like you're trying to squeeze the life out of me." Seriously, I can't even gasp for air right now.

"Stop it. I brought you in to this world, and trust me, I can take you out." Mom pulls away with a grin on her face.

Air rushes back into my body.

"Is that Izze?" Breathe quickly. "Izze, dear! We missed you so much!" My father charges me with open arms.

"Dad," I choke his name into the blackness that starts to

overtake my vision.

"Benjamin, stop choking your daughter." Aunt Jill's voice echoes from somewhere behind the fog.

"Oh, I'm sorry, honey!" Dad lets go, and I can feel my lungs physically praising God. Oh, it's good to breathe.

My parents stand there smiling at me.

I scrunch my eyebrows. "Why are you guys staring at me?" I rasp out in a smoker's voice.

"We missed you. That's all." Mom looks misty eyed. She playfully slaps my father's arm. "Come on, Ben. Let's go set up the table." Dad winks at me before following my mother into the dining room.

Aunt Jill comes over and rests her hand on my back. I jump at her touch, ready to run if anyone tries to hug me again. "Can you breathe yet?"

"I will never take air for granted again."

"They've been pretty excited for you to get here. They miss you."

"I haven't been living here for seven years. I would think they would be used to it by now."

"Honey, you're their only child. They love you more than anyone. You could also try to call them more during the week." She pats my back in a way that says, *I reprimand you because I love you!*

After the week I've had, I find this more annoying than helpful. I shrug away from her. "I've been busy. Work's been crazy, you know, with the owner selling, and the new owner hiring rude people, and all." I give her a pointed look. One that says, *The current problems of my world are your fault.*

She holds her hands up in surrender. "Hey, that was not my fault."

"You sold the store to her. So by default, or association, or whatever, I count you guilty." Round Two: Izze one point.

Aunt Jill rolls her eyes. "Sweetheart. Grow up. It is what it is.

Are you going to quit your job?" I glare at her. "I didn't think so. Get over your grudges so that you can work to the best of your ability. This only weighs you down spiritually, and believe me, that damages your work attitude."

Let me tell you about something I hate: I hate being reprimanded. I've been reprimanded twice tonight. And it only makes me angrier that she's right. On both counts. I can't even look her in the eye.

She rubs my back as I stare at the ground. "This hurts you more than anyone else. Just trust God. I may have shocked you, and Lilly may have thrown you a curve ball, but none of this came as a surprise to Him. Tend to your heart and your own attitude, and trust God for where these changes will lead. Okay?"

Aunt Jill was a youth pastor for eleven years. Can you tell?

I wipe a tear away. I hate that I'm such an emotional girl. "Yeah, you're right."

Round Two: Aunt Jill wins.

She grins at me. "You are so much like your mother."

"How so?"

"You both cry every time you get a spiritual slap in the face."

I snort. "Yeah, we all have our downfalls, don't we?"

Mom comes back into the living room. "We're ready to eat, you guys. Come sit down."

We follow my mother into the dining room. My mouth waters. I didn't realize how hungry I was.

Dad helps Mom sit down, and then takes the seat next to her. "I'll say grace tonight."

Aunt Jill and I sit across from my parents. Dad reaches out and grabs Mom's hand. They each hold open their free hand for someone to take. In this family, on thankful or truly holy occasions, we hold hands when someone says grace. Apparently, my dinner visit falls into one of those categories. Then again, it has been at

least a month since I was last here...

I have never felt more like the prodigal son.

"Amen," my dad says.

I look up in a slight panic. I didn't hear any of that! I chide myself on my awful prayer-listening abilities.

"Izze!"

"What!" I look at Mom with wide eyes.

"I asked you to pass the butter. Three times."

"Sorry," I mumble. "Here you go." I will resume my personal scolding at home in the safety of my room.

She takes the butter from me, and it almost tips into Dad's lap. Once it's on the table, she butters some French bread for Dad and then some for herself. As soon as she sets the knife down, she resumes holding my dad's hand. She notices me watching her and winks before dragging their hands under the table, out of eyesight.

I love that my parents are so in love.

I'm just not sure I can stomach it over dinner.

"Izze, do you know what Lilly's plans are for Ever After, now that she's the owner?" Dad asks.

I shovel another bit of pizza casserole into my mouth and finish chewing before I answer. "She hired this rude guy who is supposed to be a business consultant or something." Aunt Jill kicks me in the leg under the table. I bite my tongue to keep from yelping. "He'll work with Lilly to advertise the store more. He will also be looking into our budget, maybe find a few corners for us to massacre."

"Why do you say that like it's a bad thing?" Mom asks while carefully keeping her focus on measuring the amount of Caesar dressing pouring onto her salad.

"Lilly will not be on the floor as much, so I'm just a little apprehensive about that. Could make things difficult." I wipe my mouth with a napkin. I feel like red sauce is smeared all over my face. I probably shouldn't have eaten so fast.

"She's got a lot of new responsibilities. Hiring that guy sounds like a very wise move on her part." Dad heaps more casserole onto his plate. "Delegation is a very important thing for a leader to master. You try to do too much, and you'll get bogged down faster than a cheetah landing his prey."

I am the cheetah. My prey is pizza casserole and French bread. Roar.

A cell phone chimes at the table. We all look at one another, trying to figure out whose phone chirps like a bird in an air compressor. When I was a kid, we had one landline, and Mom would gripe about me using the phone all the time. Now we all have cell phones that we hardly ever use.

Aunt Jill stands up. "Excuse me," she says as she leaves the room.

My parents and I are talking about, of all things, West Nile Virus when she comes back into the room. She is as white as a fresh layer of snow on the top of Mount Washington in the blinding sun.

"Jill, are you all right?" Concern laces Mom's voice.

She looks at her in a daze. "What?"

"Are you all right?" She stands up. "You don't look too good. Here, you'd better sit down." Mom motions to Jill's abandoned seat.

Aunt Jill comes out of her daze, and shakes her head almost vehemently. "No, Sandy. I'm fine. My stomach hurts though. I think I'm just going to head home. I'm sorry to call it an early night."

"Maybe I should drive you home. In case you get sick on the way," Dad tries.

"No." She fakes a smile. "I'll be fine. Just enjoy your evening with Izze. Have a good night. Love you guys." She rushes from the room, and the front door slams at her departure.

I have never seen her rush.

I've never even seen her speed walk.

"What do you think that was about?" Dad asks as he shovels

more casserole onto his plate.

Mom stands glued to her spot watching the smoke shaped version of Aunt Jill dissipate. "I have no idea. But I'd be willing to bet it was that phone call."

Something is fishy here.

I have never wanted to kick back my chair, run from the room screaming, "Wait one second!" and tackle someone to the ground more than I do right now.

Chapter Three

Miles typed on the computer set up on the little, rickety card table in his cubicle corner. His "office" at Ever After. The dinky folding chair groaned beneath his weight. He was seriously starting to doubt whether it would hold him for much longer. Would a broken tailbone be in his future?

Someone knocked on the cubicle divider.

A pretty redhead poked her head into his cubicle. "Hi," she said.

He recognized her from yesterday but couldn't remember her name. "Good morning."

Her smile was friendly, but the glimmer in her eyes was downright curious. "I'm Kaylee. You're James, right?"

"Call me Miles." He stood up and extended his hand. Did girls shake hands?

Thankfully she saved him from looking like a total idiot and took his hand. His mind whirled like those characters from science fiction movies. Everything he had been told or read about this young woman downloaded into his mind. "You're the on-staff seamstress," he said, refraining from repeating his database of facts like a robot.

"Yes." She grinned. "I'm also Izze's best friend and roommate."

Great. Just stinking fantastic. He understood her curious look now. She wanted to see the guy her best friend had put on the

top of her hit list. Maybe she even wanted to take a verbal swing at him herself.

Kaylee laughed. She must have read his expression. "Don't worry. I'm not here to fight Izze's battle. She can be a little stubborn once she's made up her mind about something."

The corners of his mouth lifted. "A little stubborn?"

She tucked a stray strand of hair behind her ear. "I wouldn't call it a flaw exactly. More like a growing opportunity."

"For who? For her or for those who have to deal with the stubbornness?"

Kaylee pretended to glance around the room and lowered her voice before answering. "For us. An opportunity to grow our patience!"

Miles snorted.

"I'm actually here because Lilly asked to me reschedule Izze's appointments this afternoon because she's going to be working with you."

There it was again. That strange jumping beat that happened any time he heard her name or pictured her face. "Uh, yeah," he stuttered, tongue-tied. The last time he remembered feeling this way about a girl was in tenth grade when he doused himself in two bottles of truly terrible cologne in a futile attempt to gain her attention with his manly smell.

Actually, that weird feeling might have been more from the smell of the cologne than the girl herself.

"I just wanted to give you a little tip about Izze."

Miles perked up, ready and waiting.

"Get her coffee."

"Coffee?"

"Coffee. She loves people who get her coffee."

This peaked his interest. "Really?" He tried not to sound too eager.

"Her cousins own a coffee shop in this strip mall. Whipped Cream. Go there and ask Grant or Miranda to get you Izze's usual."

"Okay."

Kaylee smiled. "Good luck." Then she left.

Miles waited for the door to close before he got up and grabbed his sports jacket from the back of the world's worst chair. Time to win this woman over.

∼♥∼

I don't want to do this. I don't want to do this.

I really don't want to do this.

How, I repeat how, did I get to be the one stuck going over the inventory with James?

It wasn't fair. Lilly blindsided me, asking me to help her, special emphasis on *her*, with the inventory so that James could get a good idea of how much we spend on gowns, and how often. What was I supposed to do? Say no to the boss? Let me tell you, that does not go over too well. I learned that one a long time ago.

If I weren't a Christian, I would think all the elements of the universe were out to get me.

I can't help but imagine God on His throne, laughing hysterically, and saying, "You need to play nice."

No.

I'm sitting at my desk, in my cubicle.

Thud.

I've been banging my head on tables a lot ever since I met James.

I rub my eyes. "Why God? Can't I make Kaylee do it?"

"Nope." I look up to see Kaylee standing in the "doorway" of my cubicle.

"I will do your laundry for the next year if you do this for me."

I am not beyond begging and bribes at this point.

"No again."

"What about Candace? Where is she?"

"She has the day off."

"Argh," I growl.

Kaylee rolls her eyes. "Izze, you need to give the guy a chance. He seems rather charming. I bet you'd like him once you got to know him."

Why do people keep telling me this? "I know. I know. It's just... something about him rubs me the wrong way."

She gives me a doubtful look. "Right." She sounds so convinced. "This is because he was staring at you at the bookstore. Grow up. Move on. He probably thought you were pretty."

"Thought?"

"Then he had to deal with you, and that's enough to send any man running."

I shake my head. "With friends like these..."

"You are your own enemy, Izze." She loses the light and teasing tone of voice, and her eyes take on a look as old as time. It's almost like she understands a secret that is lost to me, and one that I desperately need to know.

My eyes sting with a rush of emotion. Why do I keep getting this lecture? I really don't understand. I'm a Christian. I'm nice to people. I read my Bible every day, and I talk to God. Why does it seem like I am suddenly failing so much? I just don't trust the guy. The fact that I don't trust a lot of people is not the point. Besides, the one time I trusted a guy with my heart...let's just say it didn't end well for me. And as much as I want love, I don't want to experience that again. "I'll give him another chance." The words barely escape my clogged throat.

"I'm sorry. Are you okay?"

"I'm fine." Just go away. The painful memories are coming

back in a chaotic blur, and I need to—I *must*—get control of my emotions. "Really. I just need to get this done before James gets here." I pretend to start working on a pile of paperwork.

"Okay." I ignore Kaylee, but out of the corner of my eye, I can see her hesitate. I feel awful, but the idea of talking about this anymore makes me want to stand and scream at the sky in a horrifying, arched position. Thankfully, her private debate ends in my favor, and she leaves.

I drop my head back to my desk. "I will try to be nice, God."

"Well, that's a relief."

Splendid.

I leave my head on the desk and squeeze my eyes shut. "Do you need a list of the gowns or anything like that?"

"Yeah."

"Okay." I lift my head and rub my still-closed eyes. "Give me a second."

"Would coffee help?"

"Probably."

"Here."

I open my eyes to see James, in all of his annoying perfection, holding out an iced coffee in a to-go cup. From what I can tell, it looks light and sweet.

"You got me coffee?"

"Kaylee told me that you love the people who get you coffee." He grins like Timmy Thompson in second grade. He chased me around the playground with a frog in his outstretched hands. When the teachers finally caught him, he just grinned unrepentantly. It looked just like the grin James wears now.

My mouth waters. The coffee addict in me takes momentary control of my body. "Is there cream and sugar in it?"

"Eight creams and eight liquid sugars, and by the way, that is disgusting. Way too sweet."

"You're not the one drinking it."

"Thank God."

I look at the coffee. I look at him. I look at my desk. I look back at the coffee, and stretch my hand out, accepting his peace offering. "This doesn't mean I love you."

"All in good time."

My head snaps over to look at him. He winks at me.

My face is on fire now.

"Um, I'm going to...um, print off some papers, and stuff, we can...um, uh...use. For the inventory." This is so awkward! "It will take a couple of minutes."

"No problem." He pulls the fold-up chair off the wall, and sets it up. "I'll just sit and wait until you're ready to conquer the case of the mystical inventory."

I bark a laugh. "Was that supposed to be a Sherlock Holmes pun?"

"Maybe."

"That was awful."

"Like you could do better." His chin rises in a challenge.

Bring it.

If there's one thing I can do, it's sarcastic and witty, with a pinch of verbal warfare thrown into the mix.

"James, Izze, and the wedding gowns of doom."

"That definitely has some potential." His smile sends shivers through my body. "I'd make one small adjustment."

"And what is that?"

"You should call me Miles. That's what my family and friends call me." His look is warm and inviting, beckoning me to accept his token of friendship.

Man, is it hot in here? Suddenly it's hard to breathe.

Stop it. Stop it. Stop it!

The sparkle in his eye promises too much. It promises exactly

what I know isn't there. And all the implications, the underlying meaning to everything that has happened...it's making me extremely nervous.

Was Kaylee right?

Does he like me? *Like me*, like me?

The question keeps rolling around inside of my head. My brain feels like a surfer. This disturbing question is the wave, giving me what could be the ride of my life.

It doesn't matter what that man feels because I feel absolutely nothing for him.

I force myself to concentrate on printing the information we'll need. The machine sucks the papers into its mechanical body, and spits them back out with new tattoos. For some reason the mechanical orchestra helps calm me down.

I avoid looking at James.

I completely ignore the spark of heat in his eyes and instead mumble some stuff about the papers and inventory instead, leaving no room for him to comment or question.

It's silent.

Not a creature is stirring. Not even a mouse.

I swallow around the lump in my throat. "I'm ready. Are you all set?"

"I've been waiting my whole life for this," he drawls. I'll give him points for his sarcasm.

"Funny."

I lead him out of the office area, back into the main room of Ever After, and through the door into our stockroom. Our procession comes to a grinding halt. The room is pitch black. The kind of thick darkness that latches onto your soul and feeds off it, leaving a horrified person lying in the fetal position on the floor.

I hate the dark.

I flip the light switch and hear the familiar pop and sizzle that

precedes the dim light. I will not move until the light warms up. I don't know if you've ever been in a stockroom before, but I've had nightmares about them. I can't explain it. Some people are scared of elevators. I am petrified of the common American stockroom.

"You don't like it in here, do you?"

I wish I wasn't so easy to read.

"I despise it in here. Especially when I have to wait for the light to warm up." Who ever heard of such a thing? I know that it's pretty common, but seriously. This is America! We should be able to manufacture light bulbs that turn on blindingly bright. I, for one, have had enough of the light bulbs that *warm up* to the standard dim, eyesight-destroying model.

Anyway. "So I printed a list of the gowns we have in-stock." I wave the list in front of him.

"What does that include?" He looks at me intently, and his glasses magnify his blue eyes.

"This includes purchased gowns that we have ordered and will be coming in soon, as well as gowns waiting to be picked up. There will be a little side note after each serial number saying whether it is an in-stock gown, a purchased gown, or an incoming order. I printed another list of the gowns we do not have in-stock, but can order per request, and how frequently we order them. I assume you'll need that later."

"Thank you. You've done a lot of organizing for this."

"Not really. All I did was hit the print icon. Lilly made sure these programs were set in place. She's very organized."

"I got a glimpse at that the other day when I came back from the bathroom and my makeshift desk was completely rearranged."

"She could win an award for her organizational skills...or be put in a mental institution." We share a grin. I feel something squeeze my heart as his blue eyes hold mine. I resist putting my hand to my chest like the faint heroine from an old western movie.

I shift into information mode again. "We frequently use gowns from five different designers. We have all of their gowns, two of every size. We keep three gowns from the most resent trunk show in stock from another five designers, specialty designers like Vera Wang."

James looks a little overwhelmed. Who knew there could be so much information about wedding dresses?

"The gowns that we keep in stock are for the brides to try during their appointments. It's very rare that a bride purchases one of those gowns. Most of them want a gown made specifically for them with as few alterations as possible."

And I think I have officially lost him. I recognize that stumped look.

"Do you have any questions so far?"

"How do you identify each gown?"

I grin. This is one of my favorite parts of the job. "By sight."

He chokes. "What?" His voice is incredulous. His baby blues have a look of sheer panic whirling through them.

I laugh. "I recognize them by sight. I have inventoried these gowns a lot. I know a lot of them by name, and that includes the serial number and the designers' name for the gown."

"So how would you like to do this?"

"Well, like I said, the in-stock list has the serial numbers. I figure you can take one side of the room, and I'll take the other side. We'll meet in the middle."

That's an annoying coincidence. Considering that is just what I told God I would do with the man himself. I'm a firm believer that annoying coincidences are messages from God. His way of saying, "Yeah, I heard you!" He's decided to remind me that I will not be able to back out of my promise to be nice to James now.

"I assume you have your own list?"

"Yup."

"And I assume that because this is Lilly's store, that there is some kind of organization to this stockroom?"

"You assume correctly, young Jedi. The horizontal rows in front of us are for the gowns waiting to be picked up, refunds, or orders that have been recently canceled. The vertical rows are all the gowns we have in-stock."

He nods in understanding, then points at the racks. "What are the big numbers standing out in the middle of the racks?"

"Starting with rack one, they are organized from smallest to largest size, by the last name of the designer, and all of his gowns are grouped together based on year and serial number."

"So it's like A to Z, small to big, year by serial number, left to right." His blue eyes are wide now.

"Yes."

"Man, this is impressive." I glance at him. He really seems to mean it. I can't explain why, but his being impressed at our operation means a lot to me.

"Let's get started. I'll start from the right."

We work for a few minutes in silence. Uncomfortable silence.

I will break the silence in half. "Why did Lilly want you to do this with me, instead of just giving you the lists to look at yourself?"

"She wanted me to see what you have, and what you go through. She thought inventorying the gowns with you, and then comparing your numbers and lists from last month would give me the information I need. She also said something about how it would give us bonding time."

"Of course she did," I mumble.

"What was that?"

"That makes sense," I yell.

I flip to the next page. I look at the item number then use my right hand to shove the gowns I haven't inventoried back about a foot. I slide into the space and use my body to hold back the gowns I have inventoried. As I reach for my pen, my weight shifts just enough to send the wall of gowns cascading toward each other, sealing me in their cocoon.

"How long have you been working here?" I strain to hear his voice from my position inside the gown rack. Thankfully, the echoes help me figure it out.

Ah, the small talk begins. Such fun.

"Seven years." The smell of heavy plastic assaults my nose. Possibly branding itself there forever, so that all I smell for the rest of eternity is heavy plastic.

"That's awesome. Was your aunt working in the store then?"

I beat my way out of the gowns before answering. "For a little while, but that's when she started to cut back and started hunting for gowns. She helped train me and would work to cover vacations that first year, but mostly she just handled the finances and the ordering."

"Sounds like she trusted you guys to run the store without her being there watching your every move."

"Yeah, I guess so. She would still check up on us from time to time, always with pointers, things to improve."

"Ah, good old life. It can always be improved." He sounds closer now. I'm going at lightning speed through these racks. A second person sure does make this lengthy process a much quicker event.

"So, you were praying earlier."

Not a question. "Yeah."

"You're a Christian."

Also not a question.

"Yup."

"Church."

Was that a question?

"Yeah."

"Yeah what?"

"I don't know. You said, 'church,' so I said 'yeah.'" Another row of dresses body slams me. Using my elbow, I fend off the attack. Thankfully heavy plastic means I can claw my way out without ruining the gowns.

"I meant where do you go to church?" He pops around the corner of the rack. His rolled copy of the list sticks out of the front pocket of his jeans. The sleeves of his dress shirt are rolled up, revealing tan arms and dreamy-looking hands.

I don't like the way my heart rate speeds up. There is a very real part of me that wonders what those soft hands would feel like framing my face. How would it feel to be wrapped in his arms?

Focus. Focus on something negative.

My eyes wander to his tan arms again.

I dislike people who have tans in the middle of winter, whether real or spray-on.

Hopefully that worked.

I struggle to focus on something else. Anything else. I don't need to look at him while he talks. I don't need to see those amazing blue eyes. Or those cute dimples. Or those luscious looking lips. Oh, I wonder...

I am weak. I can't help but gaze dumbly into his eyes.

He raises his eyebrows at me.

What was the question again? "Huh?" I sound so smart and sure of myself. I look back at the gowns and shove them back for no reason, huffing at myself. What is wrong with me? What happened to my ability to function like a normal human being?

"Where do you go to church?" Once more for the suddenly dumb folks.

"I go to the church just outside of town. The Potter's Church." Give me a hand, folks. I spoke like one who has fully functioning faculties.

"I've seen that church. That's a cool name. It's based off the verses that God is the Great Potter and we are His clay to be molded the way He chooses, right?"

"Yeah, Pastor Dean says that he struggled with the idea of moving here and starting the church. He was comfortable with his life in Florida. He read his Bible one day, and these verses completely convicted him. He realized that he was the clay. If God shaped his clay to be a pastor in New Hampshire, then what could he do but be molded into that?" I keep working as I talk, growing comfortable with the familiar subject. That increasing comfort may also come from the fact that I haven't looked at him since I started sharing the history of my church.

"Does he have any regrets about leaving Florida?"

"He misses the hurricanes. Says he would take those over thirty below zero winters."

"Thirty below?"

"Rethinking living here?"

"I'm warm blooded."

"Pastor Dean and his family love it here, and all of them will tell you it was the best decision for them. He says he only wishes he had gotten his act together sooner. He's not shy about telling anyone that this was a huge leap of faith for them. It pushed them and tested his family in ways he had never experienced. But he is adamant that being pushed out of their comfort zone made them stronger, made their love for God bolder."

"It's funny how God has a way of doing that."

"Doing what?"

"Pushing us out of our comfort zone, into a season of change. In hindsight, we always see the blessings it brings into our lives. I always think to myself, 'If you had just trusted God from the beginning, then this would have been a much smoother process.'" We reach the end of the last rack, but we both stop there.

Conviction makes his voice sound bolder. He means it. Every word. I look at him. In his eyes I see something new. This man loves his God.

I feel a little bit uncomfortable.

Like God is talking to me through James.

I don't appreciate being pushed out of my comfort zone. I don't like change. I am that Christian who screams bloody murder at God when He brings me into those seasons. And they always come. My life never goes how I plan it. People come and go and make a mess of my plans. God always rocks my perfectly prepared boat.

Once upon a time, I had this season of my life planned. And I was not single. And James was not the man who sent tingles down my spine.

I blink. Don't go there. Do not go there with James standing right there. I can feel his eyes on me. Deep breath. Fake smile. There we go. "Yeah, I know what you mean."

His eyes turn a darker blue, as if the white gowns are amplifying their color. And the conviction and passion he feels about God shines in them. He watches me intently. He notices the change in me, and his eyes ask what he does not. They ask to know the secrets that I am hiding.

I ignore the look. I barely know James. I will not burden him with my past. I will not see that familiar look of pity grace his eyes.

"When does church start?" His voice is softer. It caresses my ears, and the tenderness in it settles down into the wounds of my heart, burning like rubbing alcohol.

"Ten."

"I will see you then."

"All right."

We walk toward the door, and as I turn off the pathetic excuse for lights, I can't help thinking that my next uncomfortable zone will be James at my church.

For entirely new reasons.

❦

I am washing my hands in the church rest room for the third time.

Elderly Mrs. Sherman cornered me as soon as I got to church because her granddaughter just got engaged. As she discussed whether or not a strapless gown was the best choice for her granddaughter's ample bosom, I spotted James talking to Pastor Dean and his wife, Carla. My plan had been to casually ignore his presence, if and when I saw him. However, within minutes my hands had turned into a leaky faucet. Unfortunately, Mrs. Sherman then decided to grab my hands in hers. Her wide eyes and not-so-subtle gasp provided the perfect opportunity for my escape.

And now I am hiding.

I huff. I am a Grown Woman. A *confident* woman. I do not need to hide in the bathroom when a boy makes me nervous, when I see someone I don't like, or when my hands sweat. I am not fifteen anymore. Time to prove that I can act like a calm, nonchalant adult.

I pull my cell phone out of my purse. Five minutes until worship starts. Coast should be clear now.

Don't judge me.

I nonchalantly stick my head out. Only latecomers and chatty people haven't gone to claim their seats in the sanctuary. I don't see James, so I stroll on toward the sound of guitars strumming.

I slip into the back row. This is good. Now I won't be distracted.

"Good morning, everyone." Pastor Dean gives a little wave from the front of the room. "Let's worship God this morning."

I stand as the worship team starts to play. I get lost in the music, and apparently forty minutes passed in a blink.

"Everyone, please find your seats, and then we will dig into

the Word."

I blindly grope for the seat behind me, landing partially in the next seat to me, knocking my purse and Bible to the ground. The cute family at the end of my row looks at me.

"Sorry," I whisper.

The little girl giggles at me. "Shush, Addy," her mother says. Her wispy blond hair bounces as she whirls her head straight, and then she looks back at me. I smile at her and reach for the strewn personal contents of my purse as Pastor Dean starts to speak.

"'The Pharisees came and began to argue with him, seeking from him a sign from heaven to test him. And he sighed deeply in his spirit and said, "Why does this generation seek a sign? Truly, I say to you, no sign will be given to this generation."' Mark chapter eight, verses eleven and twelve. We all know people like this. The ones who say, 'If there's a God, prove it. Tell Him to give me a sign.'"

A hum of agreement sounds through the church. "Go to John chapter twenty, verses thirty and thirty-one. 'Now Jesus did many other signs in the presence of the disciples, which are not written in this book; but these are written so that you may believe that Jesus is the Christ, the Son of God, and that by believing you may have life in his name.' God, Jesus, and faith have never been about the signs. As we know from Hebrews chapter eleven, verse one, 'Now faith is the assurance of things hoped for, the conviction of things not seen.' Faith is about the believing."

Pastor Dean's serious expression changes to a loving look as he glances at his wife. "As Carla knows, I despise step ladders. She teases me mercilessly, but I promise you, the one we have is a giant—even if it is only three steps."

A wave of laughter roars through the church.

"I'm not afraid of the ladder. We could in fact live peacefully with the ladder buried in the closet. What I'm really afraid of is falling off this ladder. Maybe it will collapse under me, and maybe it won't. A sign that the ladder will support me would be reassuring.... Or I can believe." He turns around and pulls a step ladder from behind the amplifier. "I may not be able to see if this ladder will support me from down here, but I can take my assurance, hope, and conviction and believe that it will hold me!" He opens the step ladder and takes the three steps to the top.

No one laughs now. Pastor Dean looks at the congregation, his face a mask of pure seriousness. "We all have a spiritual step ladder. We can stay at the bottom and demand signs from God, or we can take steps of faith up the ladder of belief. But you will never get anywhere without believing. And that starts with Jesus. Take the steps up your ladder by putting your trust in God. This is something we all need to do in our walks with God."

"In closing, I just want to challenge all of you to look at your walk with God. Ask Him if you trust Him, or if there is a step of faith you are refusing to take. Let's pray.

"Father, we come before you today, with humble hearts. There are things we are holding back from you. Areas where we refuse to trust you. Please show us where we need to take those steps of faith. Lord, we believe, but help our unbelief! Be with everyone here this week, and with those who couldn't make it. Bless them. Amen."

Kaylee comes bounding over. "I didn't see you when we got here. We sat over there." She waves her arm a few rows over. I see a flash of magenta. "What did you think of the sermon?"

I fidget. "I thought it was fine. Do you want to go anywhere for lunch?"

"It's so true, isn't it? How often do we refuse to trust God? I mean, He's the creator of the universe. He knows everything, what's best for us, how to lead us. Why don't we trust Him?"

"Stuff happens. It wounds us," I mumble, grabbing my purse.

"Yeah, but—"

"Kaylee, what do you want for lunch?"

She raises an eyebrow but doesn't pursue the topic or address my rudeness. "How about we go to that soup and sandwich shop on Main Street? It's perfect for this time of year."

"That's a good restaurant." My heart starts the jumping jacks, causing my breath to lodge itself somewhere in my chest like it's a solid mass.

"Good morning," James says.

Kaylee grins. "Good morning, James." She frowns. "Sorry. Miles. I'll work on that. Sorry. So, what did you think of our church?"

"I love it. Good message. Good worship. Good people." His eyes linger on me and then flicker back to Kaylee.

Kaylee apparently noticed, too, because her smile gets bigger. "I agree completely. Where were you sitting? I didn't see you, but I missed Izze, too."

"I was actually sitting two rows behind Izze." He looks at me again, his blue eyes light and beautiful, make my heart beat a little faster. "That woman's shushing was louder than you were, by the way."

I close my eyes briefly. He saw my graceful moment. Great.

"Miles"—Kaylee smiles, clearly proud of herself for remembering to call him the right name—"would you like to go to lunch with us?"

"I would love to, Kaylee, but I'm meeting a buddy of mine in about an hour for lunch. I appreciate the offer. I don't have a lot of friends here."

"Izze, dear," Mrs. Sherman calls. "Could I speak to you for a minute?"

"Of course." I smile awkwardly. "Excuse me, everyone."

Kaylee and James—urgh, Miles—continue talking. Mrs. Sherman stands there grimacing. She's probably realized her granddaughter's endowments are too much for a sweetheart neckline. I prepare myself for twenty more minutes of shop talk.

"Izze, dear." She very obviously looks around and leans closer. She widens her eyes, indicating that I should do the same. I lean closer, trying to keep the what-is-the-crazy-woman-doing look off my face. "Here." She stuffs a card in my hand. I look at it.

It's a business card.

For a doctor.

"You really should get that checked out, dear." She looks pointedly at my previously water-spewing hands and then scurries away.

Maybe I could use this to my advantage and get a few extra days off from work.

Chapter Four

It's the Thursday following the near miss with Miles at church. Yes, Miles. I have decided to start thinking of him as Miles. Maybe this way I will hate him less because the memory of James Rude Guy won't be quite so vivid. Anyway, I haven't seen him much this week, which has been good because it's allowed me to remain distraction free. God decided to give me a break. At last.

I'm standing at the desk, submitting an order for some glittery tiaras, when the phone rings.

"Thank you for calling Ever After Bridal Salon. This is Izze. How may I help you?" I answer the phone on autopilot. I could do this in my sleep. Which, according to Kaylee, I do.

"Hi!" an exuberant woman says. I'd bet twenty dollars that she's a bride. I can tell from the greeting alone. "My name is Kate O'Shany. I'd like to set up an appointment. I'm getting married!"

Somebody owes me a twenty.

No? Fine. I'll settle for the satisfaction of winning.

"Congratulations! I would be happy to set up an appointment for you. What days and times would be best for you?"

"I'll take any appointment you have available for your monthly, ten percent discount day."

"Okay, I'd be happy to set that up—wait, what did you say?" Ten percent discount day?

"Oh, no! Are you all filled up this month? Please, I have to get my dress ordered. My wedding is in seventeen months!"

"Miss O'Shany, we don't have a ten percent discount day."

"Yes, you do. I read about it in the paper." Panic laces her voice.

I have to think quickly, "Miss O'Shany, we are currently booked for the ten percent discount day. May I put you on a waiting list? If we have any cancellations, I will call you immediately. You are my first call on the waiting list."

"Okay, I will only be able to wait a couple of weeks. Oh, dear. I might need to change my wedding date." She continues muttering but hangs up before I can try to soothe her fears.

Dodged a bullet there.

Time to get to the bottom of this.

I stick my head into the offices. "Lilly?"

"Come on back."

I wander back to Lilly's corner to see her smashing the buttons on her computer faster than the Flash.

She looks up at me. "Is there a problem?" She doesn't even stop typing. I don't understand how some people can type that fast. Their fingers are just a skin-colored cloud hovering over the keyboard.

Which is a little gross if you think about it too long.

"Yes, a potential bride called and wanted to set up an appointment. However, she requested a time on our monthly, ten percent discount day."

"Well, I don't see a problem with that. Give her the appointment if we have an opening. The customer is always right." Her head snaps up at me. "What ten percent discount day?" She starts shifting paperwork on her immaculate desk. "I don't remember a ten percent discount day."

"That's what I said, but when she started to freak out, I put her on a 'waiting list.'" I use air quotes for waiting list. I use air quotes

whenever I can. Makes talking fun. "She said she read about it in the paper. Did you get your morning paper today?"

"Yes!" Lilly shouts. She digs around in her recycling bin for a second before she pulls it out and thrust it into the air like she's found treasure. I wish I had a camera. It is the perfect "caption this" photo.

I would have gone with, "Take Back What Recycling Doesn't Give Back."

"Oh, dear." Lilly has flipped open to the advertisement section. Taking up half the page is an advertisement for Ever After Bridal Boutique in big, fancy scroll. It says:

> *Introducing Ever After's Monthly Sale*
> *TEN Percent Off Selected Gowns!*
> *Come find The Dress of your dreams,*
> *for the price of your dreams.*

"Oh!" Lilly says as she drops the paper before I can finish reading the article.

"That catch phrase is ridiculous."

"I didn't realize he was going to do this so soon." Lilly gapes at the newspaper article.

"Who?" I don't know why I asked this. I already know who.

"Miles."

"Fire him."

Her brow furrows. "I am not terminating him. I asked him to do this."

"You just said you didn't know he was going to do this. Meaning that, ultimately, he went behind your back."

"Izze, be quiet."

"Fine, fine." I hold my hands up in surrender. "I'll just leave you in peace so that you can handle this."

I leave the office, but I hear Lilly punching the keypad of her cell phone before I've even left the cubicle.

"Thank you for your patience. I assure you, if there is a cancellation, I will call you immediately." I'm cut off by the twenty-third panicked bride that has called to make an appointment since Lilly and I discovered the advertisement, almost two hours ago. Ever since I came back to the front desk, it's been nonstop phone calls, along with fourteen brides who came in personally to make an appointment.

Any faint glimmer of attraction to Miles that I may have experience on Sunday disappeared after the seventh bride to stop by the store swore at me for ten minutes when I did not give her an appointment then and there.

I'm considering nominating her for *Bridezillas*. She would be absolutely perfect.

Lilly comes out of the office looking harried. I say harried because she has stray hairs flying out of her chestnut bun, her lipstick is not refreshed to an annoying shade of pink, and she has taken off her dress jacket. For a normal person, that's just a normal day. For Lilly, that's an awful day. I almost think her hair is grayer than normal.

Lilly walks over and picks up the list of brides who want in on the discount day. I try to discreetly study her temples.

"What are you looking at?" Lilly squints at me, trying to figure out what I'm doing.

So many people have tried to figure that out. Tried and failed.

"Nothing." She definitely has more gray hairs then she did two hours ago. I understand though. It has been a stressful two hours.

My eyes widen suddenly. My hand flies to the sides of my dark, curly hair. What if I've developed gray hair over the last two hours

as well? I yank on the ends of my shoulder length hair, pulling a few strands straight so I can see what color they are.

"Now what are you doing?"

"Checking for grays." I don't see anything, and I let go of the curls. A strand lands on my lips, and I peel the curl away from my lip gloss.

She rolls her eyes. "You're twenty-five. You've got about three more years before you need to start checking for grays."

"That's not always true." I hold up my left index finger. "In junior high school, there was a boy in my class who had a patch of gray hair on the top of his head, right in the middle."

She stares at me for a second. "What are you saying?"

"That you can get gray hair anytime."

Lilly ponders my revelation for a moment. "At any rate." She stretches the words out for a few seconds longer than necessary.

"What are you going to do about Miles?" I'd like to be rid of him. He makes things complicated. He makes me feel...things.

"He and I are going to discuss the article. He should be here any minute." She studies the list again. "This is quite the list."

"It is." I say this grudgingly. I don't want to give Miles any credit. Even if this sale works—which it won't—he still went about it the wrong way. "She might be more trouble than she's worth." I indicate the name of the rude, swearing bride and fill Lilly in on the details.

She nods. "We can't accommodate everyone. You can refuse service when the situation calls for it. I can handle bossy, rude, and just plain crazy. However, there is no reason for someone to call my associates obscenities over an appointment."

This isn't the first time I've been told to refuse service to those kinds of people. I've never done it though. I always feel too weird, too weak, and let's face it, too scared to do it.

My mind flashes back to this afternoon.

Then again, there's a first time for everything.

The bell on the door jingles, and Miles strolls into the store.

It always seems weird to have men in here. You can't get much more girly than wedding dresses. I can almost see the dresses swirling away from their hangers and kidnapping Miles with an intricate waltz of taffeta, tulle, lace, and satin.

"Good afternoon, ladies." He smiles his charming, confident smile. The dimples on both sides of his big, soft lips deepen.

I whirl around. A hot blush creeps up my neck. Breathing deep, I pretend to straighten the picture of a young woman, in the early nineteen-hundreds, wearing a lacey, sleek wedding dress. All the artwork in Ever After is Regency or Victorian themed. Very classy. There are even cloth-covered editions of Jane Austen's novels in addition to the standard bridal magazines. My idea. Thank you.

The bride in the painting looks excited, eager, and blissfully happy. This is one of my favorite pictures because the woman glows with love and life.

That's the way it should be.

"Miles, why don't we go into my office? I'd like to discuss the ad for the discount day." Lilly gracefully motions to the door.

"Of course," Miles says. The man is confident. Very confident. Arrogant. Prideful. Reminds me of a Bible verse in Proverbs about how pride goes before destruction, and a haughty spirit before a fall.

Or as Yoda would say, "His undoing, that will be."

A little over an hour later, Lilly comes out of the office looking... pleased.

Now I'm confused.

"Lilly?"

She gives me a smile that would melt the ten-foot snow banks in our parking lot. "Yes?"

"I'm sorry, but what happened?"

"What do you mean?"

I wave to the office door. "An hour ago, you were mad about the article being run. Now you seem happy? I'm not trying to step out of place, beyond my bounds. I'm just confused."

"I wasn't mad. I was surprised. I shouldn't have been. I told James to get an article running in the next paper."

I want to kick myself as I remember Lilly saying she had asked for this article. I didn't listen. I speak quietly, "Whose idea was it to do this sale?"

"Miles. He had some excellent research that supported the idea."

Do I ever listen? I've been so bound and determined to hate this guy that I've failed to notice that in the short amount of time he's been working with Lilly, he's executed all of her wishes immediately. He may actually be doing a good job.

"So not knowing the article was in the paper was a misunderstanding on your part?" Now I am incredulous. Such an error is not at all like Lilly.

Lilly shrugs. "It was. He even sent me an e-mail, but I hadn't added him to my contacts so it went straight to my spam box."

It was. Look at that.

Miles comes out of the office a moment later.

"Why don't you fill Izze in on the peculiarities of the sale?" Lilly smiles at Miles.

"I can definitely do that." When he turns that dimpled smile my direction, my heart flutters a little.

"So." He pushes up the sleeves of his long-sleeve polo. The light blue compliments his blue eyes, and the black frames of his glasses only make them pop even more. "The sale is not for the gowns only. It will actually bounce around from item to item."

"Okay, I'm with you so far."

"Basically, one month it might be all last year's gowns are on sale. Another mouth, jewelry will be discounted. Then, any dresses by a certain designer, which would be especially good for new designers. They will just be happy to have their gowns sold, and that would set your shop apart from the others. You would have some unique gowns that most boutiques don't."

I'm impressed. "It sounds like a good plan."

"Of course it is. I came up with it."

I roll my eyes. Mostly because he's not kidding.

"You don't think it's a good idea?" He raises his left eyebrow at me.

I match him, eyebrow for eyebrow. "I think the idea has merit, but we won't know if it will work until we test it."

"I've done an extraordinary amount of research."

"That doesn't mean it will apply to every situation." He's rather irritating when he thinks he's right. Even more so when he has the knowledge that he is probably right.

"That's very true. However, in this situation, it will." His voice has a tone, like why am I questioning him? An annoyed expression flickers across his face. His blue eyes are like ice, and he stands close enough that I can see brown flakes near his pupils. In the light, they look like gold and blue fireballs.

I just roll my eyes in response.

"You look like a child when you do that."

Oh, now the fight is on like Donkey Kong! I absolutely despise when people say I look like a child. My face burns from humiliation.

"You know what your problem is? You think because you worked on a few successful cases at your old company that you know it all. You went to college, earned a fancy degree, and have been telling other people what to do ever since. Corporations

come up with plans all the time, but they absolutely stink. By the time those plans get to the ground level, where they will actually be used, it is too late for the people implementing those stupid procedures to do anything! Then they are stuck trying to make the big bosses who don't know anything about the job happy. So, pardon me if it takes some time for me to believe that you won't run my aunt's business into the ground."

I'm breathing heavily, and somehow during my passionate argument, we both come to stand directly in front of each other. His husky, hulky build makes me feel very small. He is so tall that I feel like the weight of his words would crush me by the time they fell from his mouth to my head. His breathing comes in rapid, short puffs. Then, without another word, he turns and walks out the door.

Miles pushed opened the door and stalked through, letting the heavy weight of the door bring it to a thudding close.

That woman was absolutely ridiculous. Infuriating. Stubborn. Clueless. Frustrating. Annoying, and did he mention infuriating?

Miles yanked his car door open, got in, and turned the music up loud. He wanted to tear through the parking lot like a crazed maniac but controlled himself. Ten minutes later, he pulled into another parking lot.

The parking lot was connected to a large building where little office spaces could be leased. When he moved here, he had arranged for the office and started payments on that before arranging for an apartment. He lived out of that office for his first week in town. It was like home to him.

Striding through the revolving doors, Miles smashed the "Up" button on the elevator. Moments later, it dinged and the doors opened. He rode the elevator to the third floor, took a sharp left, and found his office door.

His company didn't have a name. He had settled on the James Miles Clayton Company. His name was printed on the door like an old Hollywood detective. Underneath his name it read: *Business Consultant. Specializing in Finances, Marketing, and Advertisement.*

He opened the door and walked through the maze of boxes in the waiting room/receptionist's office and into his office.

Miles settled into the plush leather chair behind his mahogany desk. Now this was a real chair! The desk and chair had been the only things he had splurged on when he started his business. They made him feel like he was an accomplished man, and not a ten-year-old boy doing his homework at his father's desk. They helped sell the image.

He pulled off his glasses and pinched the bridge of his nose. *This is not the way I thought things would be going.* At this point, Miles thought Izze would at least tolerate him. They had made some real progress when he visited her church the other day. Miles had been impressed with the description of the church that Izze had reluctantly given him. It made him want to attend. Of course, it helped that she was going to be there, too.

It had been one step in the right direction. However, today had resulted in seven steps backward.

"I wish she would just take the time to get to know me," Miles spoke to the empty office. The words formed a little white puff before dissipating. Maybe he should turn up the heat, but honestly, he was comfortable.

Miles reached over and pressed the button to bring his computer to life. He would work here for a few days until things fizzled out a little. It would be a pain, though. He had access to bank statements, files, and such when he worked on-site. Here, he had to wait for someone to take the time to send the information

over to him. And despite what Izze thought, that was how he accustomed himself to the environment. It helped him see what was working and what needed fixing. That's how he knew this plan was going to work.

But did she see that? No.

Suddenly, an idea sprang into his mind. At first Miles shoved it away as pure foolishness, but it came back again and again, determined to be heard.

Maybe, just maybe, this idea would work. Or maybe it would blow up in his face like everything else he had tried.

The end of my shift draws near. I haven't seen Miles since he stormed out the door after I yelled at him. For the rest of the day, I've been looking over my shoulder, watching the door, actually hoping he will come back.

Which is ridiculous because I don't care what he thinks, or if I offended him.

The doorbell chimes, and I look up from the computer. Candace comes strolling by me. "Hi, Izze. How are you doing today?" She smiles at me.

"I'm good. There is some promotion stuff that Lilly wanted to go over with you personally. She's in the office and instructed me to send you to her first thing."

"Okay. I'll be back soon." With a swish of her black hair, Candace disappears.

I don't have to wait too long.

"Do you have any big plans tonight?" Candace asks me.

"No, not really," I mumble. My immediate plan is go get an iced coffee from Whipped Cream.

She smiles at me. "Well, have a good night."

"Thanks."

I grab my purse and coat and walk down the sidewalk of the strip mall for my coffee.

What a lousy day.

I push open the doors, and the smell of coffee attacks my senses. It's a nice feeling. Grant waves at me from where he wipes down a table. Walking to the counter, I plop onto a bar stool, set my purse on the stool next to me, and drop my head on the counter.

I hear a sigh, footsteps, and then the sound of ceramic sliding against the countertop.

When I don't look up, I hear Grant sigh again. Then I hear the musical sound of whip cream flying from a can.

Raising my head, I can see that Grant has given me a large mocha chip frappe with whipped cream. I raise the cup to him and then take a sip.

"Bad day?" he asks.

Nodding, I suck the delicious drink down the straw so fast that I become completely oblivious to what happens next.

Someone walks in and takes the seat next to me.

I don't even notice for three full minutes. Then, like any normal person who realizes there is a presence next to them, I turn to offer a polite smile.

And lo and behold, there is Miles.

My mouth drops, and without even bothering to shut it, I say, "What are you doing here?"

"I came to offer you a proposal." His face is all business. I can't tell if he is still angry about what I said earlier. Maybe he has decided to go to war with me. He's keeping his enemy, me, close. What if he poisoned my drink? I glance at Grant suspiciously.

He ignores me.

That's normal though.

I put on my most neutral expression and fully face him. "What?"

"Since you think I'm just some stupid, corporate monkey—"

"I never called you a monkey!"

Grant glares at me. Apparently, I am yelling too loudly.

"Oh, yes you did!" Miles's voice is tight, and Grant glares at both of us now.

I feel my jaw locking like it always does when I'm angry. I growl at him. "No, I didn't. I said that as a fancy business man, you wouldn't know what it's like to implement stupid procedures on the ground floor and be expected to make them work."

"Read between the lines. You think I'm incompetent." Miles rolls his eyes.

"'You look like a child when you do that.'" I deepen my voice to mimic Miles.

His eyes flash blue fire.

"I want to make a deal with you."

I huff. "What?"

"We are going to see how the sale works this month. If there is minuscule to no profit, then you win. From that point on, you can decide how sales and their procedures run. I will do whatever you say. I will answer to Lilly, and then to you."

I'm intrigued by this proposition. The idea of bossing Miles around holds some allure.

What's the catch?

"And if you win?"

"If we turn a dramatic profit, then I win. In which case, you will spend the first Saturday of the first weekend after the monthly totals with me."

I blink. That sounds an awful lot like a date.

"A date. So you can get to know the monkey calling the shots."

I start to bristle like a tea pot boiling with molten hot water. I should say no to this idiotic plan. "This plan won't work, you know. One month does not prove I'm right."

"So you think two months will prove *I'm* right then?"

I want so badly to throw my head back and just scream as loud as I can. Instead, I remain silent.

"In this case, you are right. We will tally the numbers every month, and follow the same rules for the winner every month. Every month, there will be a victory and a loss. At the end of the year, twelve full months, we will tally the year's numbers and see if there is a profit or a deficit." Miles leans back a little, waiting for me to review the proposal in my mind, waiting for me to agree to or reject the terms.

"What happens if I win?"

He folds his hands on the counter in front of him. "Then I will leave Ever After to her own devices and take my services elsewhere, since they won't have worked."

My heart starts to beat faster. Miles gone? Just like that? I ignore the ping in my soul, and nod anyway. "And if you win?"

His eyes are intense. They hold mine, searching, scathing. I want to tear my gaze away, but I can't. I just can't.

"Well, then you will have to spend a whole evening celebrating with me. Pure torture, I know. Hopefully by then, you'll know me better."

I don't know what to say. Part of this terrifies me. Part of this appeals to my competitive, must-be-right, know-it-all nature.

Without thinking it through anymore, I stick my hand toward him.

"It's a deal, Miles." My eyes grow wide, and I don't miss the fact that he's sitting up straighter, looking at me in shock.

That is the first time I've actually used his "friends and family" name out loud. Apparently, I've accustomed myself to it so well that now it just rolls off the tongue.

Miles continues to stare at me in shock, his face pensive as he studies me and my weakening, outstretched hand.

"Deal," I say again.

"Deal." He shakes my hand then immediately gets up and leaves.

I stare at the door where that frustrating man disappeared behind, and Grant comes to stand by me, shaking his head.

"What?"

"I have never seen a guy work so hard to ask a girl out." He continues shaking his head and walks back into the kitchen.

But I can't shake his words, just like I apparently can't shake Miles.

Chapter Five

It's been two weeks since I made that fateful deal with Miles.
Two very long weeks.

The sale is scheduled two days before the end of this month.
Lilly decided to focus the sale on ten to twenty-five percent off
of last year's gowns. Both bridal rooms are booked for the entire
day, and Lilly lured Candace and me into working ten hour days
with the shiny glint of paid overtime.

Fortunately, we are a small business. With just Candace and
me working with the brides, and each bride slotted for a two-hour
appointment, we are only seeing ten brides, five apiece. However,
that could easily turn into a nightmare. I've been praying that
none of them are planning a big, Greek wedding.

After making our deal, Miles and I parted ways. He's been
working at his office at lot. When he does come by, he will
occasionally make eye contact, and I will say the bare minimum,
or I will ask how he is, and he will grunt.

I shouldn't be frustrated. This is exactly what I wanted. I wanted
him to leave me alone. But when a man flirts with you, and makes
a deal that could lead to some serious dating, and then doesn't
talk to you, hardly looks at you, and barely acknowledges that
you are a breathing life-form, it's a little frustrating.

The stress has been very distracting. Kaylee, Apryl, and

Courtney have been giving me lots of space. After spending all day being perky, it's nice to come home, lock myself in my room, and relax. And if you have to lock yourself in a room, this is the room to do it.

I love the sunroom, but my room is just so cozy. My walls are a lovely blue-gray. The two windows have ruby red curtains with pop-out, tan flowers sewn on to look like they are falling. Bookshelves line every free wall, overflowing with books and pictures. However, the best part is the picture above my bed. A printed copy of my vintage bride at Ever After hangs there in a gold, antique frame. When my aunt found out how much I loved that picture, she searched for a copy for me and gave it to me for my birthday the following year.

Tromp. Creak. Tromp. Squeak.

I can hear my roommates tromping outside my bedroom door. The past few days, they've been whispering out there too.

"Should one of us talk to her?" I can almost see Courtney's furrowed brow.

"What's been going on at work?" Apryl's probably flicking the palm of her hand over and over while she tries to figure out the problem.

"Shush!" I imagine Kaylee's holding up both hands, trying to see if I will come out and bust them. "I think we are good," she whisper-shouts.

I get up from my bed and turn the stereo on just enough to drown out the sound of their whispers. Grabbing a book, I flop back onto my bed. My bedspread matches my curtains and is covered with eight red pillows of differing sizes. Yes, I bought all the little throw pillows that came in the set.

They must have given up and walked away. Soon, I'm distracted with the story, and I don't hear the lone footsteps coming back toward my door until it's too late.

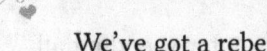

We've got a rebel.

The door cracks open.

Apryl sticks her head in the doorway. She's dyed her hair again. Instead of just black, there is now a slight blue tint to it. It looks really good on her.

She does the chin-up nod. "What's up?"

I close my book and sit up on the bed. "Not much."

"Oh, yeah?"

I shrug. "Yeah."

"I don't believe you. Spill it."

I don't want to spill it. "Really. Nothing is wrong."

Apryl doesn't wait for an invitation anymore. She comes completely into my room and shuts the door behind her.

Apparently it's girl talk time.

"You've come and locked yourself in this room every day for almost two weeks. Something is bothering you."

"It's stupid."

"Is it about Miles?"

I sigh. "What did Kaylee tell you?"

"How much was Kaylee supposed to tell me?"

"Nothing."

"She told me nothing."

I glare at her, but she grins cheekily at me. She comes over and sits on the bed beside me. "So what's going down with him? Is he still being a twit?"

I pick at a piece of lint off the red bedspread. "You could say that." Maybe I should lint roll this thing.

"What would *you* say?"

"He asked me out," I mumble. There is so much lint on the bedspread.

"He what?" Apryl's jaw goes slack. "Then why is he being so rude?"

I stand up and start rummaging through my junk drawer. I've got to have a lint brush in here somewhere. "It wasn't under the best of circumstances. We had just finished screaming at each other."

She rubs her forehead. "Wow. Kaylee is so behind on the details. What happened?"

Maybe I have one of those fabric shaver things. "I don't know. We got into an argument about the sale he came up with at work. I just said something about how corporate guys don't understand what it's like down on the working level. He got really mad and walked out. Then he cornered me at the coffee shop and struck a deal."

Apryl stands and puts both hands on my shoulders. "Hey. Stop for a second. He struck a date deal?"

I shrug. "I guess you could call it that."

"Explain please."

"Every month we will tally up the numbers to see if his sale caused an increase in revenue. If so, then I would go out on a date with him the following weekend. At the end of the year, we will total up the year's sale, and...I guess I don't know what will happen then."

"And you don't want to date another toad." Apryl points at me, her blue eyes flashing. "You stay right here. I'm going to take care of this." With that, she releases me, turns on both heels, and leaves.

I roll my eyes. Where am I going to go?

Maybe now I can find something to clean the lint off my bedspread.

Despite how much I don't want to talk about this with her, I love Apryl to pieces. She's like a fierce warrior, unafraid and determined. Perhaps if I had known her when I was dating "the toad," things might have gone differently.

Muffled voices come from the direction of the living room.

They are not bothering to whisper anymore, but I can't make out what they're saying.

Then it's quiet.

My door opens again.

Who's up for round two?

Courtney calmly walks into my room, holding out both hands with her palms down, like she is trying to calm a deranged lunatic.

I so don't appreciate what that says about me right now.

"Hey." She raises a neatly plucked eyebrow at me.

"Hey."

She takes a seat in my black and gray decoupage chair. "A lot of stuff has been happening to you lately."

"Yup."

"How does that make you feel?"

I shoot fire darts at her with my eyes. "Do not try the shrink thing again."

"Did you get it in writing?"

"What?"

"The date deal. Did you get it in writing? Was it written up in contract form?"

I stare at her for a full forty-eight seconds before answering. "Courtney, no!"

She nods. "Okay. Good. This means it's not a legal, binding agreement. Which means you don't need to go out with him."

"Problem solved!" Apryl's muffled voice comes through my ceiling. Apparently, she is listening from her room, directly above mine.

"This wasn't a legal business deal. In fact, I'm pretty sure this kind of thing would never be legal. This was just an agreement. I agreed to it. Backing out now would only make things worse."

"That's assuming his unpleasant attitude isn't his way of backing out of it himself." Courtney tilts her head, and her dark,

golden brown hair falls in waves over her shoulder to her waist. Apryl fixed her hair, in case you were wondering.

I throw my hands up and choke the air above me. "Argh! Courtney! Please! I don't know, and I don't want to think about it right know! If I guess and wonder every spare moment, then I'm going to be miserable."

Courtney reels back a little with my strong reaction, and I immediately feel awful. I shouldn't be freaking out at my friends for trying to help me. No matter how annoying that help might be.

"Courtney, I'm—"

She waves her hand, cutting me off. "It's fine. But listen to me. You *are* thinking about it every spare second because you *are* miserable." She gets up and leaves me with that same miserable feeling hovering in the room.

I fall backward onto my bed. Blowing the curls from my face, I grab a pillow to muffle my screams.

That's when Kaylee comes into the room.

"Your turn." I don't have to take the pillow off my face to know that she's there.

"Yup."

I lower the pillow and hug it to my chest. "What tactic are you going to try?"

"I was thinking of utilizing those water guns from the kitchen cupboard."

"That doesn't sound very appealing."

Kaylee smirks. "I didn't think so. How are you doing?"

I shrug for the zillionth time. "I'm fine."

She levels me with an I'm-the-big-sister-you-never-had look. "You know that's a big lie. We all know you're not fine. So let's cut to the case, avoid the same pointless conversation, and actually talk about this."

My mom's comments about looking like a pouting five-year-old with my round face and crossed arms runs through my head, so I refrain from crossing my arms. However, I'm sure the stormy look on my face is like a billboard advertising my displeasure.

"You like him." Not a question. A statement. A fact. A "let's face the truth" moment. Kaylee holds my eyes, waiting for me to acknowledge what I've been trying to burn, bury, and forget in my heart.

I don't speak. The tears in my eyes do.

"That's okay, you know. Maybe even a good thing. He's actually a good guy." She moves to sit on the bed next to me and gives me a side hug.

I can't even speak at first. Renegade tears rush from my eyes to comfort my face with their warm hugs. "I don't want to like him."

"Izze, not every guy is going to betray you."

"I won't know until I give him a chance."

"Exactly."

"But what if I always pick the wrong guy? He's not exactly inspiring a lot of confidence right now. He's been all over the place ever since we met. Up and down. Hot and cold."

Kaylee rubs her face. "You have to give this to God. Ask Him."

"Kaylee, I don't think I'm ready to trust someone like that again."

"You've always wanted to be married, to be in love, to have a husband. Don't think I haven't seen the wistful, envious looks at work, or the way you've stared at the gowns, fingering the fabric. The uncomfortable fidget every time someone announces their engagement at church. You want that. Are you really going to let one guy from your past wreck your future?" Her emerald eyes search mine for an answer.

I rub my face with the palm of my hand. "I am not letting what happened in the past destroy a future for me." But that's a lie, isn't it? Deep down I'm still afraid to trust again, despite the desires

of my heart. Which is most likely the reason that every date I've been on in the last five years always ended without any hugs or kisses, and no promise of phone calls or future dates.

"Well, what are you doing?"

"I am waiting for God." I say that phrase mechanically. I've been saying that phrase my whole life. It's my mantra. I've always said that I'm waiting for God to provide my desires. Fact is, I'm tired of waiting.

"That's a little contradicting, isn't it? You say you're waiting on God, but you won't trust anyone." She takes my hand in hers. "Or God Himself."

I don't know what to say to that.

"What if God sent you a note on beautiful, ivory stationary that had rosebuds trailing down the left side?" Kaylee asks, changing tactics.

"You mean what if God sent me a note on the stationary my mother gave me for my sixteenth birthday?"

"Yeah, because then you would know the note was especially for you."

I look at the fake white orchid on my nightstand. "Okay."

"What if God sent you a note saying you were His. Period. No questions asked. Could you accept that?"

Ah, a question I've asked myself many times in my singleness. What if the waiting never ended?

I don't trust that I won't be betrayed again, and even worse, I don't trust my God not to betray the desires of my heart.

"I don't know," I say quietly.

You can tell she's thinking really hard about what she's about to say. She opens and closes her mouth several times before standing up to leave. "Maybe you need to learn to trust God first."

An age-old saying kept coming to Miles's mind. Advice that Miles had heard his grandpa say jokingly, seriously, begrudgingly, even lovingly.

"Women. You can't live with them. You can't live without them."

It seemed especially fitting these days.

Miles watched the TV without really seeing anything. His mind was elsewhere. On someone. On her. Swinging his legs off the couch, he shuffled in his bare feet to the kitchenette for a drink.

He should really sweep his floor. Nah, it could wait. After downing some juice straight from the carton, Miles walked back into the living room and collapsed on the couch.

He didn't understand Izze. Whenever Miles went to Ever After, he caught her watching him. He could feel her eyes on him. But when he talked to her, nothing! She didn't even look him in the eye.

His cell phone rang. His brother. "Hey, Nate."

"Hey, man," Nate said. "How are things going with the new job?"

"Fine," he answered more gruffly than intended.

"Just fine?"

"I'm tired of feeling like a giant in a doll store." It was almost impossible for him to get his hulking frame around those mannequins. Heaven forbid he actually step on a dress hem. The real kicker came when he knocked over one, creating a domino effect. Lilly almost had a heart attack when she saw a dozen mannequins clad in expensive wedding gowns lying on the filthy floor. On the plus side, Izze had laughed.

Nate laughed, and Miles started to relax.

"So really," he said. "How are things going?"

Miles sighed. "All right, I guess. This store is an integral part of the community. They get a lot of business, but they are dangerously close to the red." Miles explained his plan to Nate. He would never

admit it to anyone, but the approval of his older brother was a big deal to him.

"Well, man, it sounds like you have a solid plan."

See? He had thought so, too. If only Izze would realize this.

"It seems like you are starting to turn the situation around. Why do you sound so frustrated?"

Miles hesitated. He didn't want to tell his brother about Izze. Not yet, given the chance that this relationship—if you could even call it that—could burst into flames at any moment.

"Uh...one of the employees basically said my corporate monkey ideas weren't going to work."

"I'm sorry, man. I know what it's like on the ground level of a corporation, so I understand his or her point. However, the reason your strategies are successful come from the fact that you spend time on the ground level figuring out what does and doesn't work."

"Yeah," he mumbled. If only Izze would understand that. He wanted to make things better.

"Miles," Nate said. "Don't let what this person said make you feel invalidated. You are a hard worker. You know what you're doing. But people don't always trust the new guy on the block with something so important to them."

Miles sat up, swinging his legs off the couch. That was it.

She didn't trust him with her aunt's store. Ever After was like a family heirloom to her. He needed to make her see that the success of Ever After was just as important to him as it was to her.

It's time.

Today is the day. Sale day.

Can you hear that? That is the sound of thirty anxious brides waiting outside our locked doors.

You might be wondering why there are thirty brides out there instead of the original ten brides. When Lilly saw the line of brides out there, she was moved with compassion. In ten minutes, she put together a system complete with waiting list. Presumably our ten scheduled brides are out there, but twenty other brides have called and put their names on the waiting list in case a bride breaks her appointment or finishes under an hour. Yes, if we finish in under an hour, we have to call for our next appointment or the next bride on the waiting list. Lilly threw that tidbit in there in the pre-sale staff meeting today. After said staff meeting, I went to stash my water and sodas in the mini-fridge in the office. I saw Candace guzzling one of those Starbuck iced coffees you can buy in packs at the supermarket. She downed it, popped open another one, threw her head back, and guzzled that one down, too.

Candace hates coffee.

Currently, Candace and I are standing behind the counter. We both exchange nervous looks. I know exactly what she is thinking right now.

These crazy girls are going to trample us into the floorboards.

Lilly stands in front of the glass double doors with the curtains drawn. I can almost picture all thirty brides with their noses pressed to the doors. Lilly paces back and forth, talking to herself, pointing at random things and checking them off on her fingers. Her hair swishes with all the rapid-fire movement.

"Okay, everyone!" Lilly claps her hands excitedly.

I don't think I had enough coffee to deal with this today.

"Remember what we've talked about. I will give you the gist; you pull the gowns and keep things moving." Lilly will be managing the floor and helping the brides who are next look through the racks, which will maybe speed up things in the dressing room.

Lilly unlocks the doors and lets in the tidal wave. They flood into the salon and fill every inch of the place.

No one falls on their faces when the doors swing open, which is a good thing. People being trampled and all that.

I look at the copy of my appointments that I am clutching in my hands. "Ciara Whiticker?"

"Here! Hello!" A cute, strawberry blond approaches me. She's about five foot nine, with shoulder-length, layered hair with those adorable bangs that I can never pull off because my hair is so curly. Two other strawberry blonds flank her. One roughly around her age, and the other twenty or so years older. "Hi," she says again.

"Hi, Ciara. I'm Izze. I'll be your consultant today."

"Wonderful!" She's beaming. "I've brought my mother and sister with me."

"The more the merrier. I'll lead you back to the dressing room. Is there any style of dress that you prefer?"

And so it begins.

"I just don't know if that gown suits her figure." The snotty woman cups her chin with her right hand and leans back on her left leg like she is the next fashion guru for *What Not to Wear.*

The day is only half over, and I've seen seven brides. Lilly wasn't kidding about moving things along. She's wearing many hats today, including acting bridal consultant. Candace and I tried to pull the gowns, but after our first appointments, Lilly took over that for us.

I use my right hand to rub my temple. I can feel the pressure building in my head. If I don't get some food and caffeine soon, bad things will happen. My family talks in hushed whispers about the Thanksgiving lunch that wasn't served until eight o'clock at night. My mother didn't want me to spoil my appetite, so she didn't even let me snack that day. I went all day without any food

until I just snapped. We ate immediately, and I was grounded for a week. After that, I stuck to a feeding schedule like clockwork.

I have not been able to stick to my feeding schedule today.

The woman, Cherrie, removes the sunglasses from the top of her head and runs her hand through the straight locks. She is the future mother-in-law.

"I just think it does nothing for her figure. She should try on a mermaid gown." Cherrie slides the sunglasses back onto her head like a headband.

The mousey, petite bride, Amy, looks anxious, and her eyes bug out of her head a little. In my personal opinion, she does not have the attitude to carry the body hugging gown her mother-in-law is trying to push on her. Cherrie spotted this gown on another bride and insisted Lilly get it. The satin gown hugs the figure like spandex. There are no embellishments, no sparkle, and no lace to add life to this gown.

That is, until you reach the bottom of the gown. Then there is life from another planet residing there. The gown hugs the body until the knees, and then it explodes into a swirl of feathers. Yes, feathers. Honestly, I avoid these gowns like the plague. They look good on one, maybe two women. And, no offense to Amy, but it does not look good on her. She has a good figure, but she doesn't have the charisma, the spirit to carry such a gown and make it fly.

You know, because of all the feathers on it.

However, I can't win every battle of the dress. In the end, Amy purchased the gown Cherrie picked.

In the dressing room, I tried to bolster Amy's courage, but she whispered to me, "I just want to have a happy marriage. Getting this woman off my back and on my side would certainly make things less stressful."

I watch Amy and Cherrie leave Ever After. Cherrie stops at the door, turns back to me, throws her head back, and waves. "Ta-ta."

Then she disappears.

"I need food." I look at my watch. Two o'clock in the afternoon is way past my lunchtime.

Lilly comes up to me. For all my grumpiness and for all the ways Lilly drives me crazy, I can tell she is really pleased with today's events. She has this sparkle in her smile that I have never seen on her. It's beautiful and completely lacking in the drill sergeant manner.

"Good, you finished a little early. Are you ready for your next appointment?" She's looking at the tablet she recently bought, and checks this off on her to-do list that she set up this morning.

"Lilly," I whisper, desperation clinging to my voice, "Candace and I need to eat. Is there a way we can rotate out for a few minutes and shove some food down our throats?"

Lilly frowns at the lovely picture I've painted for her. "I hope you don't actually eat like that. It's not very proper for a young woman. Regardless, Candace already rotated out for a snack. James, err, Miles brought a whole box of goodies for us to snack on throughout the day."

I raise an eyebrow. "Really?" Color me suspicious. After a month of awkwardness with the man, he's gone back to acting sweet just in time for the sale.

"He even brought some brownies."

"Really?" Color me impressed now. I don't turn down free brownies. Ever.

"You don't have long before your next appointment. I will get the process started in the lobby. Don't take too long." Lilly gives me a stern look and, using her index and middle finger, she points at her eyes, and then points to me. "Hurry. I will be watching for you."

So maybe the drill sergeant hasn't completely disappeared.

I look around and, when confident that a crisis isn't about to break out in the lobby, duck into the offices. Compared to the chaos out there, it is eerily quiet in here. I sniff. I can smell the warm scent of intensely concentrated, gooey chocolate baked to perfection. I start looking around for the brownies.

"Wow." Miles's makeshift desk no longer looks fit for business. Instead it looks like someone lifted a whole dessert case from a bakery, which is perhaps the greatest heist known to mankind. There is plate after plate of cupcakes, cookies, brownies, breads, and a bowl of mixed, mini candy. A little cooler sits on the desk to the left with water, soda, and energy drinks. A little handwritten note taped to the cooler completes the package. I read the note, my heart rate noticeably increasing and something within me flutters. *I thought you guys might need some extra sweets to get through today, so I stocked up for you. I know this sale will be a hit. Enjoy!*

I grab a brownie. My stupid bagged sandwich can wait.

That was really sweet of him, wasn't it? It's not just me, right? I don't understand this guy. He's up and then he's down. Something about that has awakened the smallest part of me that wants to get to know him and figure out what makes him tick. The rest of me is terrified of this notion. The impasse has resulted in me trying to ignore my growing feelings, and bury them deep inside of me, which has been working out so well. Not.

I grab two more brownies and a cupcake and go to set them on my desk. Ever since Miles and I did inventory, I haven't been able to shake him out of my heart.

I frown when I see my desk. There's a coffee thermos on it. It's a cute white one with two little owls sitting on a tree, but it's definitely not mine. I set my goodies next to it and see there is a Post-it note stuck to the lid.

My heart pounds and I can feel an immediate blush darken my cheeks when I realize that it's the same chicken scratch as Miles's note on the cooler.

Izze, I hate to say I told you so...actually, no. I love to say I told you

so. Mark your calendar for the Eleventh for my victory date. Miles.

I try really hard to be annoyed, but I just can't do it. This guy is good.

I can't feel my feet as I trudge up the porch steps at 11:00 that night. In the end, we saw twenty out of thirty brides. I ate more brownies and cupcakes than I care to admit to anyone outside of Weight Watchers. Lilly was bouncing as she locked up the doors. Bouncing. Properness and decorum has been thrown out the window for Lilly. In their place is a childlike giddiness and pure joy. Lilly loves being the owner of Ever After, and truthfully, it is a perfect fit for her.

I bang on the door, too tired and lazy to fish my key out of my purse. "Kaylee, come on and let me in, girl. There is a giant moth out here, and I don't like the way he's looking at me!" I bang louder. Honestly, I'm not sure where my key is at the moment. I am that tired.

The door creaks open, and Kaylee stands there with a very annoyed look on her sleepy face. "I have to get up early for practice tomorrow."

"Why are you practicing tomorrow?" Kaylee, in addition to all the other amazing things she can do, sings like an angel.

"A new guy joined the worship team. He's going to take over as head guitarist. He sings too. He's like a rock star." Kaylee mumbles and waves her hand. "How was the sale?" She yawns and doesn't even try to cover her mouth.

I yawn in response. Did you ever notice if someone yawns, it starts a chain reaction of yawns? This is especially fun to test in big groups. However, not so fun when someone yawns a question, and you yawn a response. Then it is just sad.

"I'll tell you all about it in the morning."

She smile-yawns at me. I bumble along to my room, rip my work clothes off, pull on some cozy pajamas, and fall into bed. I'm out before I make the landing.

Miles grins victoriously. The end of the month has come and gone. It is February 5, and Miles and Lilly have spent the morning closing out the month. The tally from the sale was more than the last month and the same month from the previous year combined.

I giggled at the look on Miles's face when Lilly yanked him into a hug, declaring him a superb genius.

"So." Miles leans next to me on the front desk. I had just finished with a bride and was entering the order into the computer when Miles and Lilly came to tell me the good news. "I just want to say that you can back out of our deal."

I try not to spin my head to look at him, instead opting for the nonchalant approach. "Do you want to back out of our deal?" Who am I kidding? Of course he doesn't want to go out with me. I've been mean and crazy to him. He should be running the opposite direction.

"No." I look at him then. He has good eyes. I can't help but think that every time I look at him. The glasses just seem to magnify the light blue hues. "No, I don't want to back out of our deal, but I don't want to force you either. I was actually hoping you may *want* to go out with me."

"I, uh...I." When did speaking become so hard? I try again. "I suppose I can go out with you."

An adorable cocky grin pulls at the corners of his full lips. "You do, do you?"

I lean forward, matching his pose. "I said I suppose. Now, are

we, or are we not going out on the eleventh?"

He studies me for just a moment and leans forward slightly. "We are." His voice is quiet, deep, and wonderful.

My breath catches as I realize his face is literally just inches from mine. It's moments like these when you pray your toothpaste and mouthwash really do help keep your breath fresh.

He leans away, breaking the spell. "I'll pick you up at noon. Dress warm." He heads back to the office.

Dress warm?

Suddenly, I am regretting this.

Miles stops at the door. "Oh, and get snow pants if you don't have any."

Uh oh.

Chapter Six

"I would make up a song to hold the boredom at bay, but all I can come up with is, 'La la. La la. La la la la.'" I give Candace a pitiful look.

"I'm surprised you could even come up with that," she says.

"It might as well be a symphony." Lilly sighs.

It's been a slow day. We had two cancellations and no surprise brides.

Candace glares at the front door. "I hate days like this."

I've dusted. I've polished the countertops and tables. I washed the windows. I took out the little fake vacuum thing and fake vacuumed the floors. Twice.

Ring. Ring.

Make that three cancellations.

Lilly glares at the phone. "That had better not be another cancellation."

Candace picks up the phone, greeting the unsuspecting person on the other end with an impressive mix of suspicion and sweetness. Based on her emerging frown, I'd bet my left foot it's another cancellation.

Candace hangs up the phone. "Well, Lilly..." She trails off, and Lilly groans.

I so called that.

"Brides are probably saving up for our next sale. It's only a week away."

Lilly nods slightly at my logic. "The sale day is already booked though."

I roll my eyes. "That didn't stop twenty other brides from showing up last time."

Candace points at me like I'm on to something. "That's true, Lilly."

Lilly nods again. "Candace, do you want to go for the day? I think Izze and I can handle the overwhelming rush of brides." Lilly snorts at her sorry attempt of a joke. I am in shock. I always assumed that snorting was not ladylike, and would result in yet another lecture.

Man, if I had known it was okay...

Candace glances at me. "Do you want to leave Izze?"

"I have an appointment in thirty minutes. A woman from church got engaged last week, and she made the appointment the next day. I don't think she would cancel on me at the last minute. She's not like that."

She shrugs. "Okay then. Thanks, Lilly."

After she leaves I try to pass the time by fluffing the gowns on the mannequins. I wish I could talk Lilly into buying new mannequins. I hate the headless ones.

But mannequins in general creep me out, so it probably wouldn't help any.

I stand directly behind one of my favorite dresses.

I glance over my shoulder really quick then turn the mannequin to face the wall, and stare at my reflection in the mirror running along the length of the wall behind the mannequins. I imagine the odd folds of my work clothes are not sticking out, that my hair is pinned up in an elegant, timeless hairstyle, with a bouquet of white roses in my hands. I close my eyes and imagine it all.

An image of Miles pops into my head, and I almost fall on my rear.

I wasn't going to go there. Not at all.

And definitely not with Miles. My stomach has been in knots all week thinking about our upcoming date this weekend. No need to add marriage to the mixture and make myself terminally ill. I like him and all, but despite how much I want marriage, I need to know that I can trust him.

I look up as the little bells on the door chime. In walks Amala Wilson and two other women.

"Hi, Amala. How are you doing?"

"I'm doing great! How are you?" Her eyes sparkle, and she has the glow that newly engaged women inherit once that sparkly ring is on their finger.

"Not too shabby." This is my routine answer. Along with, "Not bad," "I'm all right," and, "I'm good as long as the police don't find me."

I save the last one for people who have a warped sense of humor.

"I brought my mother and my maid of honor, Charlie." Amala motions to the women behind her. Amala's mother, Daya, is from India. Amala's grandparents fled the country when her mother was still a little girl. They wanted to live in a land that was free to worship Jesus. Daya married Tim Wilson, a simple farmer.

Daya, beaming with happiness, looks proud of her daughter. The maid of honor looks excited and sickeningly sweet. Her long blond hair is pulled into a high ponytail, her eyes sparkle, and not a hint of jealousy resides in those baby blues.

"Hello, ladies." I smile tightly. Maybe I should have given this appointment to Candace.

We continue to exchange pleasantries as I lead them back to Bridal Dream Room number one. We file into the room, and they

all take seats on the sofa.

And smile at me.

Oh brother. "So, Amala, do you have any pictures of gowns you like, or certain styles you want to try? Lace? Chiffon? Straps or no straps?"

"Yes, I brought some pictures of ball gowns I like. I want the sleek, satin look. And I want to follow an Indian tradition. I want a red dress."

Whoa!

"What?" Up until that point I had been nodding like an idiot as I took mental notes so I'd have an idea of what gowns to pull. But we've got a huge problem here.

We don't have any red bridal gowns.

We have a few, very limited number of red bridesmaid dresses. But there is no disguising the fact that it is not a bridal gown.

Amala laughs. "It's an Indian tradition. In India, red is the color used for weddings. White is actually used for funerals and times of mourning. So we want to buy a satin gown that can be dyed red."

Wow. "Uh, wow."

Charlie giggles. "I know, right!"

She is going to grate on my nerves. Really quickly.

"Think you are up to the task?" Daya asks with a raised eyebrow.

I slip out of my Stupid Face, and into my Accomplished Bridal Consultant Face. "I most definitely am. Would you ladies like anything to drink while I gather some gowns for Amala to try?"

"Just some water, please," Daya says.

"Oh, yes! Do you have bottled water?" Charlie squeals.

"Yes," I say. "Would you like any cupcakes, cookies, or carrot sticks to go with that?"

Charlie squeals again. "Oh, carrot sticks sound simply wonderful!"

Oh, for crying out loud! I plaster a smile on my face.

Amala smiles at me. "I would like a cupcake, please."

I knew there was a reason I liked her.

I grin at her. "I'll have your goodies and treats brought in to you, and I will be back in a few minutes with some gowns worthy of going red."

I exit Bridal Dream Room number one and run past Lilly shouting, "If you're still bored, they would like some cupcakes, bottled water, and some wonderful carrot sticks!"

Out of the corner of my eye I see Lilly shoot into action. This is the most excitement we've had all day.

I keep running into the storage room and flick on the lights while simultaneously trying to put the brakes on my mad dash.

I've fallen while running into this room before. I knocked over the rack of gowns and ripped my skirt.

Skidding to a stop, I let out a huff. Oh, dear. Where am I going to start?

An image of a Maggie Sottero gown pops into my head. Perfect place to start. Maggie Sottero is one of my personal favorites. She has a wide variety of styles to choose from. Something for everyone.

I grab a satin ball gown with a lot of pick-ups. Another slim, A-line gown with straps and a dramatic back. I'm tugging out another ball gown when I see *it*.

It's a satin, sweetheart neckline, full A-line dress with dramatic ruching from top to bottom. There is a beautiful lace motif starting from the top right, and it continues swirling down to the left hip.

This is The Dress.

I have the gift.

Convinced this is the dress, I rush back to Bridal Dream Room number one. Flinging the door open, I am about to proclaim my tidings of bridal dress joy when I hear Lilly utter something horrid.

"I'm sure Izze would love to dye your gown red! Only the best for our brides! We will assist you however we can."

I swear there is an evil gleam in her eyes.

But what can I do? Amala looks almost giddy. She apparently trusts the dyeing of her wedding gown to the girl voted, "Biggest Klutz," in high school.

Oh dear.

I will pretend I didn't hear that. Maybe if I don't know, it won't happen. Maybe.

Fake smile. "Hello again, ladies! I come bearing some gorgeous gowns!" Gag myself. There are days my perkiness sickens me.

"Izze, perfect timing!" Lilly grins at me. "Amala told me she was going to dye her dress red herself! That is awful, don't you think?"

I grimace at Amala. "I do think that will be really hard for you to do yourself."

"I'm so glad to hear you say that, Izze, because I told Amala that you would be happy to dye the gown for her."

Please no. I would get down on my knees, right here and now, if I thought God would stop this madness.

Frankly, I think He's enjoying it.

I was always told that honesty is the best policy. "Amala, Lilly, I am hardly a professional at dyeing gowns. I don't even dye my hair. I don't think I'm the best candidate for this task."

Amala looks slightly downtrodden. Lilly shoots me a glare that would kill a baby bunny. "You will dye the dress red." She says through clenched teeth. "We will make our bride happy."

Alas, it is fate.

"Nevertheless, Amala, I would be happy to do this for you."

"Really?" She raises her eyebrow at me just like her mother did. Lilly chimes in, "Absolutely. We love to make our brides happy."

"Anyways, I have some gowns for Amala to try." Forced smile here.

"Oh, fantastic!" Charlie squeals.

I need to get out of this room. Or I will be charged with attempted homicide.

"Yes, yes! Don't keep your future gown of glory waiting any longer!" Lilly says giddily.

Make that a double homicide.

"Come right this way, Amala." I lead her into the changing room within the appointment room. I hang the gowns up on the rack, take several deep breaths, and face Amala.

"Is your boss always like that?"

"Like what?" I feign innocence.

"Sickly sweet with a pinch of crazy?"

"Pretty much." So much for that plan.

"Oh."

"So do any of these gowns strike your fancy?"

"They all look beautiful." She gently fingers the first ball gown in the lineup.

"Well, why don't we work our way down the line."

Here's my secret: once I find The Dress, I stick it in the middle of all the gowns I've pulled. Pretty ones before it, and lackluster after it.

Never fails me.

"Okay."

I unzip the first gown for her. "Okay, so you can get in the gown, and once you're ready for me to zip you up, just crack the door."

I exit the changing room and smile at Daya and Charlie. It seems that Lilly has conveniently disappeared.

Lucky for her.

I hear the door creak behind me, and go back inside to zip up the back for Amala.

It's a good thing I know this is not The Dress, because she looks stunning!

The pick-ups are in all the right places, accenting her perfect figure. Her tan skin just pops against the simple white. I can see the wheels in her head turning. She can see herself as a bride.

I open the door. Walking out, I grin at Amala and motion for her to come out, too. I take a step toward the right wall, so that Amala can see herself better in the mirror covering the left wall. "This is the first gown."

Daya looks like the typical mother. Proud and happy with a little shock mixed into her expression. "You look beautiful, sweetie," she says.

Charlie jabbers away about how incredible Amala looks. She hasn't stopped since we came into the room. While I agree with her, I stopped paying attention after the first, "Oh, my goodness!"

Amala can't take her eyes off her refection in the mirror. "I look like a bride," she whispers.

Stepping up next to Amala, I place my hand on her shoulder. "You look stunning. Would you like to try on one of the other gowns?"

The next gown is a taffeta ball gown that I threw in there to be different. Then we have The Dress.

She gasps when she sees it. "Oh my," she mumbles as she fingers the shiny satin. "It's exquisite."

"Indeed it is." I unzip the taffeta gown she's wearing and unlace the corset back for The Dress.

I grin as I duck back into the room with Charlie and Daya. "I think you guys are really going to like this gown."

The door creaks and I pop back in with Amala. My heart is racing. You'd think it was *my* wedding dress! I can't wait to see what she says about the gown.

Amala is crying.

Not the reaction I was expecting. She didn't strike me as one of the criers.

"This is it," she chokes out between sobs.

I lace her up in record time. I'm anxious to see what her mother and Charlie think about the gown.

There are more tears.

Daya has a single tear rolling down each cheek. Mother and daughter hold gazes for a long time, each smiling through their tears.

Good ol' Charlie bawls like a baby desperate for a bottle.

She may be annoying, but I have to give credit where credit is due. She is genuinely happy for her friend.

That's the important thing.

"I don't even want to try on any other gowns! This is it!" Amala squeals, and Daya and Charlie jump up to hug her.

Now that's the reaction I like to see.

Once Amala decided on The Dress, the rest of the appointment went by in a blur. We picked out a veil, talked jewelry, shoes, and hair. Lilly helped me take Amala's measurements, and we decided on a style of bustle. Then we confirmed the date of the wedding, and the shipping dates for the dress. Now we are all standing in the lobby. I'm typing like a mad woman on the computer as I push the order through to the designer.

"The wedding is in four months, so there is definitely a time crunch. However, this is a priority gown, so I could get this particular style in three weeks if I needed it that quickly."

"Okay," Amala says.

"Four months from now, you will be a vision in red." I share a smile with her.

Daya and Charlie are looking at a necklace on one of the mannequins. Amala stands by the counter, sliding her credit card

back into her wallet. "Everything is happening so fast. It's like a dream." Her voice is soft, and her eyes hold that radiant look of a woman in love.

"I bet it is." Can anyone hear the wistfulness in my voice?

"I feel like a kid waiting for Christmas. Do you know what I mean?" Amala throws her wallet into her oversized purse and tucks a stray strand of dark hair behind her ear. "I don't think I'll get any sleep for the next four months. I'm so excited for that day. For marriage. For everything." She flashes a brilliant smile. "For the chance to be able to wear my wedding dress for more than the length of an appointment."

"Hey, you can always purchase a second dress. One for wearing whenever you want."

Amala laughs. "Seriously?"

"I wish I could say that hasn't happened."

She laughs even louder.

Daya and Charlie come back over. "So we will give you the information about how to dye a satin gown and the red dye when it arrives. When will that be again?" Daya pulls a notebook out of her red purse to record the date. Apparently red is a trend in their family.

"The order has been placed. I should receive an e-mail tomorrow confirming the order. With no rush placed on it, the gown should be here in two months, the halfway point. Two months before Amala's wedding date will be plenty of time to complete those alterations and, well, dye it red." Hopefully.

"That sounds perfect."

"It does." Mother and daughter exchange a look. Soon, the three of them are on their way.

I want that. I want that whole package.

I go about straightening things up for the next bride, when a thought hits me.

I might not be as far away from that as I thought. And I'm okay with that. Suddenly, I feel like a kid waiting for Christmas morning, too.

Only it's a handsome man and a mystery date.

We are driving.

I know not where.

Just that we have been driving for a while.

We passed the border for Keene about ten minutes ago. I'm not sure what town we are in now.

Miles takes a turn leading into a state park. I can see from the cozy comfort of the car that this is no restaurant. Just a hill. A big hill. A swarm of little children, in various states of action, slide down this hill.

"Why are we at Goliath's Hill?" I raise my eyebrows.

He turns off the car. "We are at Goliath's Hill so we can go sledding."

"But it's like, two degrees outside. Without the windshield."

"That's why you were supposed to dress warm."

I tug on my coat sleeves, trying to pull them down around my hands in order to add that extra smidgen of warmth. "I almost dressed warm."

"So by the time we're done, you'll be mostly frozen." He winks at me, and the action sends shivers of a different variety through my body.

"You're really going to make me brave this weather? On the first date? Isn't this the kind of torture you save for the fifth date? It's the kind of thing that screams, 'It's time to run!'"

"I prefer we just get that out of the way now."

I awkwardly reach into the backseat and grab my purse. Then

I turn to Miles's amused face and pat his shoulder. "Well, it was really nice getting to know you, but I just don't see 'us' going past this."

Miles grabs my hand from his shoulder and holds it in his. "I'm not letting you get away that easy." My heart starts pounding in a beat that's unfamiliar to my body. "We had a deal."

"Uh…"

His laugh is wonderful. As beautiful as a child's laugh, but attractive and alluring with the deepness of his baritone. It's the kind of sweet sound that I want to record, so that on a rainy day I can pull it out and listen to it over and over again.

I'm not a stalker.

I'm not sure what I am.

He drops my hand, interrupting the moment. I move my hand back to my lap, avoiding his gaze.

"Ready?"

"I'm going to freeze."

"We already determined that." He opens the car door, and gets out. I watch in the rearview mirror as he makes his way back to the trunk. The trunk pops up, blocking my view of him.

I take my time getting out of this car. Once I step out there, ice cold air will attack all my senses, rendering me helpless. I need these precious seconds to gather as much warm air as I can into my body. I pull a ski cap out of my purse and tug it onto my head.

I'm going to be a sledding ski bunny today.

"Hurry up." His voice sounds muffled though my cap.

I get out and walk back to the trunk. At least, that was the plan. I don't quite make it there. The parking lot has basically been transformed into an ice rink. Two steps toward Miles, and my feet slide out from underneath me. My butt hits the ground next, and I start sliding toward the trunk. My aching head makes up the end of the parade. The grand finale. I'm sure my face is priceless. "Ouch."

Miles tries not to laugh too hard. "Are you okay?"

"I'm peachy." I stick my hand in the general direction of his face. "Help me up. Please."

He seizes my gloved hand and effortlessly pulls me to my feet in one solid motion. "When I told you to hurry up, I didn't mean run."

"Someone didn't tell me there was ice."

"I didn't see the ice. There wasn't any on my side. There must have been a frozen puddle on your side of the car."

"Swell. When we leave, I'm getting in on your side of the car."

Miles chuckles as he reaches into the trunk and pulls out two pairs of ski pants and coats. "I brought these, just in case you didn't realize I really did mean dress warm." He winks again. "The light blue is for you. They'll probably be a little big on you. I borrowed them from my sister-in-law."

"Thanks." I pull the ski pants on over my dressy jeans. I remove my wool coat and tug the ski coat on over my sweater. I look down at my dress boots.

Next time Miles tells me to dress warm, I will.

"Eh-hem." Miles holds out a pair of brown winter boots with warm fuzziness spilling out of the mouth.

Aww.

He really did think of everything.

"Thanks again." Now that I'm in ski pants, I plop on the ground, tug off my boots, and pull the winter boots onto my feet. I grin and hold my nice shoes over my head. Miles takes them from my raised hand and lets them plop into the trunk. He has the sled—an old, ready-to-fall-apart sled—out on the ground, beside his feet.

"Going to get up?"

"I thought I could just roll onto the sled, and you could haul me up the hill."

"Get up." Miles starts walking toward the aptly-dubbed

Goliath's Hill.

I pretend to huff. "What a lousy date!"

"And quit your whining."

I carefully stand and jog toward Miles, slowing my pace to match his. It's a beautiful day. The sky is an icy blue. The air is crisp and freezing. Everything else is white, with little pops of color running up the hill and then flying down it.

We walk in silence. I wonder if this is normal. Miles has always seemed like an introverted man, so I know the silence isn't necessarily a bad sign.

However, the silence makes me nervous.

Someone once told me that when you are truly comfortable with a person, words become unnecessary; the silence is no longer awkward, and you no longer feel the need to fill in every lull with conversation.

News flash. This is the first date. I am not comfortable with the silence. At least, not yet.

"So what made you think of sledding?" We start trudging up the hill.

"It's crazy, simple, and fun."

"Do you go sledding in you spare time?" I'm already starting to pant. I need to exercise more often.

He throws me a funny look. "I haven't been sledding since I was thirteen."

"Why? Was there a reason?"

"I was trying to impress a girl. But she didn't pay attention to me at all. So I did something really stupid. I tried to ride down the hill like the sled was a snowboard. But it was one of those saucer sleds. And the hill was bigger than this one."

"It didn't end well?"

"Nope. Broke my leg." He makes a noise that sounds like a cross between a chuckle and a groan.

"Didn't get the girl?" Duh. He's here with me. I want to slap myself.

He laughs. "Didn't get the girl."

"So..."

"More questions?" He raises an eyebrow.

I can feel two circles of searing heat on my cheeks. It's nice to know that even in below freezing weather, I can still blush properly. "Just making conversation."

He reaches for my hand and gives it a squeeze. "I'm just teasing. Ask away."

A speeding bullet, roughly the size of a ten-year-old, speeds past us.

Miles's head whips around to watch the kid's flying landing. "That was close."

"I don't feel safe out here in the open."

"I think the only safe place is the top of the hill."

"Yikes!" a little voice screams.

"What was that?" Both our heads swing toward the sound.

Then, for the second time today, my feet are swept out from under me.

I am tumbling down the hill. A little voice screams into my ear. The owner of the voice is a little girl, maybe eight years old, and she is entangled in my arms. Her golden-brown curls are in her eyes and mouth.

Somehow, I know that Miles is unharmed. That he is probably still standing, staring at the cloud of smoke that is shaped like me. Hopefully, he realizes that we are *never* going sledding again.

The ice cold tentacles of the wind, that were whizzing and wrapping themselves around us, have loosened their grip. Our speed slows down, until finally we come to a stop.

Goldilocks peeks at me from around a curl. "Why did you get in the way?"

Miles comes to a skidding halt next to me. He grabs me into his arms, crushing my body into a jagged, lumpy version of its former self. "I should have brought you a helmet! Are you okay?"

"Oh great. Are you going to kiss her?" Goldilocks says. "I'm fine. Thanks for asking."

"I'm fine. Really." I mumble. My ego is just bruised with total humiliation. In my mind's eye, I am shaking a fist at the sky. Why does this have to happen to me? And on a date!

He releases the death grip on me and looks at Goldilocks. "Are you hurt?"

The little girl rolls her eyes. "I said I was fine."

"Oh yeah, she's fine." I grunt. "You got a name?"

"My mom told me to never tell strangers my name. You could be a stalker." Goldilocks bobs her head at me in an informative way.

Miles laughs harder than I've ever heard him. "This seems familiar somehow." He shoots me a knowing look.

I return it with a glare. "Listen, we will just call you Goldilocks. Where are you parents?"

"They are in the orange van over by the pine tree." GL raises her eyebrows at me. "Goldilocks? Why can't I be Cinderella?"

"You don't want to tell us your name because we could be bad people. And because you crashed into me. That means I get to pick your name." I raise my eyebrows back at her, challenging her.

Miles clears his throat. "Izze, let's not fight with the little girl. Let's go sledding."

"Yeah, don't fight with me." GL smirks in that way children do when they know they are annoying you. Know it and like it.

"I already went sledding." GL and I took a wild ride.

"Well, I want to go sledding with you." Miles pretends to pout. "Please."

"Yeah, yeah." I mumble.

"My mom says that mumbling can eventually lead to the lack in

proper speaking abilities due to the lack of muscle coordination," GL quotes.

I blink at her. No wonder she's like this. "Goldilocks"—the little girl raises her eyebrows at me—"my friend, Miles, and I are going sledding now. If you'd like to walk to the top of the hill with us, then let's get moving. Otherwise, go see your parents."

"I think I'll come with you."

Oh joy.

Sometimes I wonder why lightning doesn't strike me.

Miles holds out his hand toward Goldilocks. "I'll carry your sled up the hill." Her sled looks like a left-over inner tube from the pool, like it hopped in the car hoping it could pose as a sled's long lost twin. It seems like a test you had to do in first grade. *Can you name the item that doesn't belong?*

And together we, the next generation of musketeers, start climbing the hill.

"So..." Miles begins, and I angle my head to get a look at his handsome face.

"What?" Goldilocks and I say at the same time.

"Goldilocks, I think it's reasonable that we get a real name from you now. It could be your mom's name for all I care, but give me a name to call you. I, for one, am not calling you Goldilocks all day."

"But you just did. Twice." I point out.

He ignores me. Very sweet, that man. "Just tell me your name, please."

I cup my hand around my mouth and lean down to the little girl on my right side. "I wouldn't tell him my name when I first met him either. He's kind of weird." I wiggle my eyes from her to Miles, in a way that clearly says, "That man is *crazy!*" She giggles at my silly expression. "He could be a real stalker."

"Really?" The eyebrows furrow on her small face.

"No!" Miles bursts, his right hand flying up and choking the

air in its grasp.

Hehe. "Payback isn't pleasant, is it?" I grin unrepentantly at him.

His annoyed look melts into something tender and sickly sweet. Something that says he doesn't mind that I'm picking on him.

"Hello. I'm still here."

"We know," Miles and I both mumble. That funny little flutter in my chest takes flight again. I sneak a glance at Miles. He's looking back at me, with an intense expression. One I am not familiar with.

Man, I wish he would kiss me.

I gasp, which causes both Miles and Goldilocks to look at me like there are unicorns tap dancing on my head. Where did that come from?

I like him. I *really* like him!

I knew I was starting to like him. But this is serious. Like, I don't mind if you use my toothbrush, serious. I mean, I'm thinking about kissing him, for crying out loud!

This revelation sends a stampede of wild horses down my back.

I think I'm going to be sick.

"My name is Lilath," Goldilocks, ahem, Lilath says.

"That's a really pretty name." Miles smiles at her, and I swear the little girl looks at him like he's Sleeping Beauty's Prince Charming. It's sweet.

He's good with kids. That's a point in Miles's favor.

Finally, I can see the top of the hill in sight. Lilath waves at us and runs off to rejoin her friends. We walk a few feet away from the majority of the kids, and Miles plops the sled down.

"Ready?"

"Ready to die? Not really."

"Ready to slide down this hill so fast it will pull your eyelids away from your eyeballs like you're some kind of cartoon character?" He grins and wiggles his eyebrows at me.

I feign annoyance and roll my eyes. "You say that like it's a bonus."

He spreads his hands out in front of him. "Isn't it, though?"

"Yeah, I'm not sliding down on that thing by myself." I point at the sled. It's so old, it will probably fall apart underneath me as I'm going down the hill. Then I'll be left clutching a single board as I navigate the hill currently known as Goliath's.

I know you can see it, too.

"Then I suppose you will have to ride with me." A mischievous glint flickers in his eyes. A flutter runs through my body, and I attempt to look normal despite feeling like my heart is skipping every other beat.

"Okay," I squeak. Yeah, that sounded totally normal.

He plops down on the sleigh, and it slides a little like it's a wild horse trying to shake off whoever is on its back. Miles manages to regain control and smiles. "Get on behind me."

I take my turn plopping on the antique sled. It feels awkward sitting down so low.

"Now pull your knees up to your chin, while scooting as close to me as possible. Then wrap your arms around me, and whatever you do, don't let go."

I silently obey. It feels exhilarating to be basically hugging him, even if my knees are separating us. It's really only a little bit in the grand scheme of things.

"I'm going to push off on the count of three. Are you ready?" He awkwardly turns his head to look at me.

The date would be perfect if we could just sit here like this. Why ruin a good thing by moving down a hill at neck breaking speeds? "As ready as I'll ever be."

"One." He rocks the sleigh back and forth a little. "Two." The word hangs in the air for just a split second before he shouts, "Three!" He digs his legs in to push off strongly, and we fly down

the hill.

At first, I keep a death grip around Miles's stomach and keep my eyes closed tight. We hit a bump, and I shriek. Before I realize it, my eyes are open; I can see the world blur by us.

It's actually kind of fun.

We approach the bottom of the hill, and Miles holds us steady. Slowly, we come to a stop. A giggle of pure joy escapes me. More bubble up inside of me until I'm laughing so hard, I can't possibly keep myself upright any longer. I fall off the back of the sleigh and stare up into the icy blue sky.

A verse I memorized when I was in high school, Psalm 118:24, floats into my mind. "This is the day that the Lord has made, let us rejoice and be glad in it."

And man, oh man, it is a good day.

We probably spent two hours just climbing up and sliding down that hill. Only once did I forget to hang on tightly. We hit a bump just right, I lost my grip, and went flying off the back of the sled. Miles lay on his stomach a couple times and rode down the hill like that. He even convinced me to ride by myself. I chose to ride it like I was on the Olympic luge team. All in all, I had an awesome day.

Now we are sitting at Whipped Cream, relaxing and reminiscing about the day's funniest moments over warm drinks. I finger the little vase on the table, the scent of daisies and lilies mixing with the scent of coffee. Does it get any better than that?

"This is a great place," Miles says.

"Thanks, man," Grant calls out from his place behind the counter. He's been chatting with us. Mostly Miles.

"Yeah, it is," I say loudly enough for Grant to hear. "When Grant and Miranda opened this business, Miranda called every single aunt, uncle, and cousin in our family for opinions on décor. She claimed Grant didn't have a clue about how to decorate a piece of paper, let alone a restaurant. I was only too happy to offer my opinion."

"Shocking."

"I know." I grin.

Whipped Cream *is* a great place. It has a sunny beach theme to it. A taste of what we natives long for in the middle of a frozen tundra. The walls are painted a warm beige color. Tons of black-and-white photos, showing all sorts of things—dogs, people, landscapes, and random objects like beach balls and umbrellas—are scattered on the walls collage style. My favorite is one of a little girl looking out at the endless ocean.

Grant pops open the cash register and starts counting the money. I'm having such a déjà vu moment. The counter has gray barstools with black cushions, and the back wall is mostly shelf space. It looks remarkably similar to the back half of Luke's Diner in *Gilmore Girls*.

He yawns. Poor guy has been listening to our antics for an hour now, but I have to hand it to him, he's been pretending to pay attention.

Just then, Grant lets out a huge moan. His mouth opens so wide it would rival a lion preparing to attack his prey. "Sorry about that." He smiles sheepishly.

"Excuse me, guys. I'll be right back." Miles nods toward the rest room and takes off.

Grant walks over and flicks my arm.

"Ouch! That hurt." I glare at him and rub the life back into my arm.

"Quit your whining. Sounds like you guys had a successful first date."

"We did until the proprietor of this establishment decided to permanently injure me."

He rolls his eyes. Grant is more than just my cousin. He has been a good friend of mine for a long time. He is like the older brother I never had. "You'll live." He takes our empty mugs. I can't help but grin like a big old dope. I did have a good time.

Miles comes out a few minutes later. "Are you ready to go?"

Not really. That would mean this day is about to end. "Yeah." I hop off my stool and grab my purse. Miles holds the door open for me, and I hop into his car like I've been a fixture in that front seat for years instead of just hours.

The drive back to my house goes much too quickly. I chitchat nervously the entire time, and, bless his soul, he doesn't act like I'm being really weird.

The end of the date is and always will be the most classic moment for a first kiss. I am very nervous. I haven't kissed anybody since...

I blink harshly as the face of my past comes into my vision.

I am very nervous. The fact that I just polished off two coffees is not helping matters either.

Miles pulls into the driveway and turns off the engine. Silence fills the car.

What do I do now?

More importantly, do you think he'll notice if I check my breath?

"I'll walk you to your door." His breath forms a huge cloud in front of him. "I had a lot of fun tonight."

"Me too." I smile at him. Even though it's dark, I know he can see it.

"So she admits it? Give it up for Miles everybody. The victor!" He raises his arms like he's a rock star greeting his fan base of screaming teenage girls.

I don't say anything. Anything I could say would ruin all this day has been.

Hope.

The snow crunches underneath us. The porch light is still on, and that could mean my friends were thoughtful of me. Or, and most likely, they are watching from one of the windows and wanted to be able to see what was happening.

"I had a really fun time."

"Good."

I stand there unsure of what to do. How long do you wait before it becomes silly?

I've reached my limit. "Well"—I try to keep my voice light and breezy—"I should be heading inside. Good night."

"Good night."

I turn away from him very slowly, moving to go inside, knowing what I'm doing, but my eyes have never left his face.

"Wait." His voice stops me. In one smooth motion, he frames my face with his big, warm hands, and his lips meet mine in one sweet, sweet good night kiss. Brief, yet lingering and dizzying. Time stands still, yet his touch fades in an instant when he pulls away. His face is still close to mine, and I can feel his breath on my cheek. "Good night, Izze."

I nod. He lets go and, after flashing me one more smile, bounds down the walkway to his car. I give a little wave before heading inside.

Courtney, Kaylee, and Apryl are all sitting nonchalantly on the couches. Too nonchalantly. They saw, and they know that I know that they saw.

I know this because none of them can wipe the huge smiles off their faces.

"So." Apryl bats her eyes innocently. "Have fun?"

"Good night, guys." I make a run for my bedroom, but I'm

not quick enough. They start throwing the couch pillows at me, laughing and whistling their approval.

Oh, yeah. I had fun.

Chapter Seven

"Izze?"

I poke my head out from around a dress rack. That sounded like my aunt.

"Izze?" Aunt Jill comes into view.

I wave at her from behind the dress rack. "I'm back here."

Her shoes clap, clap, clap as she comes over to me. "Oh, is that a Melissa Sweet?"

"Yup." Beautiful gown with a vintage twist. Buttons down the back, illusion lace, and a blush colored sash. "What are you doing here?"

"I came to see if I could steal you for lunch. Spend some time together." She fingers the racks, looking at the new gowns. Despite the fact that she sold Ever After to Lilly, this business is in her blood. She's lived and breathed it for years.

"Let me go see if that's okay with Lilly." She nods, and after lingering on an elegant satin gown, moves to one of the couches.

I head to the offices and tap on Lilly's wall. She peeks up at me. "Is there a problem?"

"No, everything's fine. Aunt Jill is here. I was wondering if I could take my lunch break now."

She glances at the clock. "Yeah, that's fine. Have a good lunch. Tell Jill hello for me." She goes back to the paperwork on her desk.

I grab my purse from behind my desk and go out to meet Aunt Jill.

In the lobby, Aunt Jill is standing by one of the mannequins, attempting to fluff the rosettes on the dress.

I smile. "All set."

"Great. What are you in the mood to eat? My treat."

"Up to you." When someone tells you that your meal is on them, it creates all kinds of pressure. Don't pick something too expensive, but not so cheap that they know you are trying to go light on their pocket book.

"How does soup and sandwiches sound?"

"Sounds great."

"Okay, there's great little place just down the street. Wilma's Kitchen or something like that."

"I've heard about that place. It's supposed to be really good."

We head out to Aunt Jill's car, a modest green thing.

I have never claimed to know cars. It's four doors, and made by Chevrolet, and that's honestly all I can tell you.

Dropping my purse in first, I then lower myself into the car. "So, are you going to be at my parents' house for dinner this weekend?" I'm going to my parents' house every week now. I shouldn't have let life interfere. I've missed them a lot.

"No."

Now normally a simple "no" is not cause for suspicion; however, she's not acting comfortable with this line of questioning. She avoids my eyes while being uncharacteristically quiet. White spots form on her knuckles from gripping the steering wheel so hard, and the car jerks back and forth ever so slightly from her fidgeting.

"So how are things going with Miles?" Her voice squeaks at the rapid change of subject.

I raise my eyebrows, but she ignores me. Fine. I will work my powers of subtlety and find out another way. "Better."

"I heard rumors of a date."

I stare at her in shock. "How did you hear about that?" Who's the snitch?

"About that, eh? That means my sources are correct." She tosses an impish smile at me.

"Oh, look! We're here." I breathe a sigh of relief as I see the restaurant come into view. She pulls into the parking lot to Wilma's Kitchen. From the looks of things, they are pretty packed. We waste no time heading inside where we find a college age girl standing behind the hostess station.

"Good afternoon. How many today?" She smiles politely at us.

"Two, please," Aunt Jill says.

She marks something down on her chart and grabs two menus. "Right this way, please." We follow her through a maze of tables that are much too close together. It's in times like these that I offer up one of my most frequent prayers: *Please Father, don't let me fall into the laps of any strangers or stand uncomfortably close to them. Again.*

The hostess lays our menus down on opposite sides of the table. "Wendy, your waitress, will be right with you."

"Thank you."

"Thanks," I echo.

A mini earthquake rumbles from my stomach, and my mouth floods in anticipation of a delicious lunch. "Thanks for taking me out to lunch."

She smiles at me from over her menu. "I love doing stuff for my one and only niece. Plus, we haven't seen a lot of each other since Lilly took over sole ownership of the shop."

It's true, and it has totally stunk. Aunt Jill and I use to see each other almost every other day. Despite the thirty plus years separating us, my aunt is one of my best friends. Lunch dates like this were more of the norm back then, but everything changes.

Even my utter dismay hasn't seemed to stop the changes of late.

"Yeah, we haven't seen a lot of each other in the last two months." Suddenly, the memory of Aunt Jill running out of my parents' house during dinner comes to mind. An inquiry forms, and I run with it. "You won't be at dinner this weekend?" Even though we've gone over this already, I say it like a question again, not a statement.

She fiddles with her napkin and the little paper ring holding her silverware, but before she gets a chance to speak, the waitress shows up.

"Good afternoon, ladies. My name is Wendy, and I will be serving you today. Can I start you two off with something to drink?"

"Raspberry iced tea, please." Aunt Jill smiles at Wendy like she is a hero. That, however, only awakens my curiosity more.

"A peach smoothie, please." I smile at Wendy.

"Do you ladies need another minute to decide, or would you like to order now?"

I shrug across the table. Aunt Jill speaks for us. "I think we are ready to order." I nod my agreement.

Wendy scribbles down our soup and sandwich orders. Then she smiles widely at both of us. "I'll put that order right in for you guys." Then she disappears into the maze of tables and people.

I lean back into a disinterested interrogator pose I saw on some cop show. Cop shows are Apryl's kryptonite. The raven haired beauty owns about a hundred different seasons from many different cop and investigator shows. "So," I draw out the word like I'm drawing a blank at ideas for decent conversation. "Hey, since we haven't had a chance to touch base, is everything okay with you?"

She frowns at me. "Yes. Why do you ask?"

"Well, last time I had dinner with my parents, you ran out of there in a big hurry. I've been so tied up in the new changes at work, that I haven't had a chance to ask you about it." I am fishing for information here, and she knows it.

She starts fidgeting again. "Oh, that." She waves her hand and laughs nervously. "It was nothing. No big deal."

She's not ready to crack, but now I know that the reason she left in a hurry then is linked to why she will not be at my parents' house this weekend. I will find out what is going on with her. Mark my words.

"So what's going on with you and Miles?" Oh, boy. Now it's her turn to attack, and she looks giddy at the idea.

I should just get this over with now. I know what she's waiting for, and unlike my aunt, I crack much easier than most people. I could never be a spy.

"He's a nice guy."

"Is he now?" She quirks an eyebrow at me.

"Yes. I misjudged him."

She has a triumphant smile on her face. "Yeah, I know."

My know-it-all, lovable aunt. Doesn't help that she's always right.

"Yes. So now we are getting to know each other through the pre-agreed date deal."

"The what?"

"It's a long story."

She checks her watch. "We've still got another forty minutes. Is that enough time to fill me in on the details?"

"Should be."

She leans forward eagerly, elbows on the table, and rests her chin on her folded hands. "Okay, give it to me."

I match her position. "Well it all started when Lilly asked me to do inventory with Miles."

I pour out my story for her. I'll figure out the story she's hiding

another day.

There are days when you get up, and you just know something is going down today. Sometimes you even know in your gut if it's going to be good, or if it's going to be bad. Then there are other days when you wake up, and you don't have the slightest inkling that something is about to happen to make your life so much more complicated.

In case you were wondering, today is the latter.

Today started off perfectly normal. My ten-thirty appointment was right on time, and the girl was a peach. She brought four people with her, and we all crammed into Bridal Dream Room number one. It was an easy appointment. She was very straightforward and happy, and her friends and family were wonderfully supportive. At the end of the appointment, she walked out of here knowing that she would be wearing a vintage style, lace over tulle ball gown with off the shoulder cap sleeves, a sweetheart neckline, and so many fabulous lace appliqués, it looked like she was a walking cloud of dainty flowers. She looked gorgeous.

My following four appointments went just like that. Absolutely perfect with no problems, no drama, and no missed appointments.

See, that should have been my first clue that something was going to happen. I will not make that mistake again.

Now I am sitting in the offices with Candace. I know she has the same look on her face that I have on my own. "Are you crazy?" should be stamped on our foreheads. I think both of us have entered some sort of trance. We are too stunned for words. Stunned isn't even a strong enough word. I am truly and utterly flabbergasted.

Lilly snaps her fingers at us, causing me to jump. Candace

blinks her eyes furiously.

Lilly glowers at us. "I'm disappointed in you two. This is a wonderful opportunity for Ever After. As my two prized consultants—"

"Your only two consultants," I mumble under my breath.

"You should also be looking out for Ever After's best interests. Miles went to a lot of trouble arranging this. The least you two could do is act a little excited."

Miles arranged this. I'm not even surprised. The man is learning though. He made sure he was scarce for the big reveal. Probably so I wouldn't jump the desk and try to strangle him.

Hey, I like him a lot. Doesn't mean some of the things he's convinced Lilly to do don't drive me crazy. I feel like in a healthy relationship, you communicate that so that you don't end up exploding.

Candace is the first one to break the silence. "Lilly, I don't understand."

Let me catch you up to speed. We are going to be on television.

Yes, that's right. Television. TV. The ever popular box with the moving picture in it.

Take a moment and adjust to the news.

Lilly purses her lips at Candace. "What exactly do you not understand, Candace? We are going to be on television."

Candace starts stuttering like she's speaking an unknown language. Lilly looks at me like she's hoping I can interpret that mess. That's so not happening. I shrug helplessly. After a moment, Candace quits trying to speak and practices Lamaze breathing.

"I think we are both just a little stunned." I shoot Candace a comforting look, and she smiles weakly in reply.

Lilly harrumphs. She comes out from where she was sitting and leans on the front of her desk. "I asked Miles to do some research because I wanted to arrange for us to have a regularly

running television advertisement. It will run on Channel Seven, also known as The New Hampshire Archives."

"The New Hampshire Archives?" I ask. What on earth is that?

Candace beats me to the punch. "What is that?"

Lilly sighs again. "It's the name of Channel Seven. They do a lot of stories and commercials about locally owned and operated New Hampshire businesses."

"How did this happen?" Candace asks quietly while fanning herself. She looks even paler than usual, and she has always been pretty fair skinned. Almost translucent.

"Miles knows how to get these things done," Lilly says flippantly. "He created a storyboard, which is very much like TLC's *Say Yes to the Dress*. He's working on a base script now. He has hired a production company to film the commercial and has already purchased the broadcast time on the station."

"Are cameras going to follow us around all day?" I don't like this idea, as I'm rather klutzy and I tend to make silly faces.

"In a manner of speaking," Lilly says offhandedly, like it's no big deal. She pulls packets of paper off of her desk. "Release forms are necessary for you as well as for the brides in the commercial." She gives each of us a packet. She looks so pleased. It's kind of sick.

Wow. I finger the packet in my hands, completely unsure of what to do next.

"So it's a TLC's *Say Yes to the Dress* theme." Candace has gotten her second wind. I notice some of the color returning to her cheeks.

"Yes." Lily says. "Only our official campaign theme is going to be, 'We Believe in Love.'"

"So, we are really going to be on television." Candace states this with a dreamy look on her face. Gone is the panicking, apprehensive woman of only moments ago. Now she appears downright giddy at the idea. "We could be stars."

"I don't know about that," Lilly says. "It's just a local

commercial."

"Way to spoil the dream, Lilly." Candace sighs in disappointment.

"However," Lilly says. "We still need someone to narrate the commercial." She looks at me hopefully.

I hold up my hands, "Hey, no! No, no, no. I'll be on television, but I'm not the right person to handle that. My commentary is far too sarcastic."

Lilly sighs again as she moves back behind her desk. "You're right. I can't have anyone shadowing the gowns with such negativity. We want to portray an upbeat image."

I'm not going to lie. I didn't expect her to agree with me. Relief abounds.

An idea turns and churns in my head. It's so deliciously wonderful, yet devious, that I'm sure I look like a villain from a Disney movie.

"Lilly, what about Miles?"

Her brows furrow. "What about him?"

"What if you ask him to narrate the commercial?"

I can see the wheels in her head turning. I can tell by the slow smile working its way onto her face that she likes the idea. "Do you think I can ask him that?"

I offer my most convincing smile. "I don't see why not. I think the offer would make him feel like he's more a part of the team."

Lilly taps her index finger against her lips. "I think you're right."

"I think it's a good idea, too," Candace says.

See, it's not just me. Granted, my motives aren't completely innocent.

Pointing at me, Lilly says, "But what if he says no?"

I stand up and point right back at her. "Don't let him say no." I wiggle my eyebrows and smile.

"For goodness sake, don't do that. It looks like two caterpillars are wiggling around on your face."

I try to hold back my smirk by pretending to pout.

Candace grins. "I think that's a perfect idea, Izze."

One point for Izze. Approximately a million points for Miles. I'm catching up to him. I wish I could be there to see Miles's face when Lilly tells him the news. The very thought is totally worth all the ways I will probably embarrass myself in the making of this commercial.

I hold in my chuckle. Totally worth it.

After several minutes of quiet, Candace and I exchange a look and stand up.

"Where are you going?" Lilly holds out her hand, commanding us to stop. Her entire demeanor displays just how in control of this situation she is. Her dark hair is swished up into a tight bun which only adds to the commanding effect.

"We were going to get back to work." Don't bosses normally like that?

"We have more to discuss," Lilly states.

Candace and I answer at the same time. "We do?"

"Ever After will also be featured in an exclusive interview with *Bridal Biz Magazine* next week. There will be pictures, and in-depth interviews with all of us."

Stunned, we stand there. To go from light, general marketing to commercials and in-depth interviews is a lot.

Lilly picks up more paperwork from her desk. "The interview also requires release forms and paperwork."

Of course it does.

Miles came to an abrupt halt. "What are you doing?"

Izze dropped the paper she was looking at on his desk. She took an innocent step back, but she couldn't wipe the guilty look off of her face. "Nothing."

Yeah, he didn't buy that. "Oh, really? What's the matter? Did you get lost?"

"Yeah. I have a terrible sense of direction. I still have to hold my hands up in the shape of the letter L to determine left or right." She made a production of looking around. "Sorry. I guess this isn't my office."

Miles stepped in front of her, effectively blocking her into the corner between his desk and the wall. Bantering with Izze sounded like fun. He could use an afternoon pick-me-up, and no caffeinated drink worked quite as well as she did. "What did you expect to find?"

Izze shrugged. "A horrible sketch of you with the word *Wanted* underneath and a dollar estimate of how much you're worth."

"They always mess up my eyes in that picture. So flat and one-dimensional. I have soulful eyes."

"You wish."

Miles took a step closer, catching a waft of her shampoo. "Izze."

She sighed. "I was just curious about the script for the commercial."

"You think I would keep that here?"

"I had hoped," she said wistfully.

"I keep that in the safe behind my father's picture."

She rolled her eyes. "Funny guy."

"I'm glad you think so."

She fingered a piece of paper on his desk. "So you have a father?"

"It's kind of how God designed things."

"I've just never heard you mention him." She tried to glance at the paper again.

Miles felt his body stiffen. Why did that always happen when he spoke about his father? "He's not my favorite person."

Izze looked up, sensing the change in him. "I'm sorry."

"Not your fault. He shouldn't have driven his family away with his need for perfection and control. He was a master at emotional abuse." He let out a deep breath. "Sorry. My father is a touchy subject."

"Your parents are divorced?"

Miles felt the wounds of his past as if the blows were being delivered one by one right now. "Yes."

A light, tender touch warmed his arm. It took Miles a few seconds to realize that Izze had placed a comforting hand on his forearm. He stared at her little hand. He liked it there. A lot.

"Um." He swallowed in an attempt to clear his throat. "It's okay. Really. I've forgiven him, but sometimes those old scars reopen in an attempt to infect and kill me with their poison."

Izze gagged. "That's a little gross, but I'm still sorry. It must have been hard." She squeezed his arm before letting go.

Miles tried to focus on their conversation once again and not on her touch. Who knew such a small feat could be so difficult?

"Thanks." What else could he say? He had spent most of his life behind a false mask of perfection. It was nice to finally have someone offer their heartfelt sincerity.

It was even better knowing that person was Izze.

Chapter Eight

Dinner with my parents did not shed any light on the mystery surrounding Aunt Jill's disappearances. They were just as clueless as I was.

However, my brilliant plan that Miles narrate for our store commercial was underway. Candace was there when Lilly told Miles. She said it was quite the treat to watch. According to her, Miles tried to back out of the ploy by literally backing away from Lilly and out the front door. However, Lilly is nothing if not determined. She chased Miles down and made him agree. Not literally *chase* though, because, according to Lilly, proper ladies don't ever chase men. It looks wrong.

Just over a week ago, we completed another monthly sale. Such joy. This month Lilly decided the theme would be a twenty-five percent discount on accessories with the purchase of any gown. While this day was just as crazy, hectic, and exhausting as the last one, I feel like Candace, Lilly, and I are starting to develop a system. That in itself is a scary thought.

Once again the sale was a major success. I think these victories will be developing into a longstanding pattern. Miles hasn't let me know when our corresponding date is yet, but I politely requested that it be somewhere where the likelihood of getting snow down my pants equates with liver becoming a well-liked food in the

average American household. Yeah, about as likely as flying pigs.

Today, however, is a very special day. Today we have our *Bridal Biz Magazine* interviews.

Lilly has been fluttering around the boutique straightening, moving, and rearranging things for the last three days. She is very concerned about making a good impression since this article will be for all to see. This is a popular magazine in the wedding world.

Currently, Lilly runs from one end of the store to the other with a duster in hand. She is so frantic that she isn't acting like a normal person and dusting around the store in a circle. Nope. Instead she sees a spot across the room, and runs to dust that speck or straighten the slightly rumpled dress without finishing what she was doing. Then she will see something else, rush to fix it, and then realize that she never finished the original task.

Goodness, I think a strand of hair has escaped her bun. The world will now end.

I scrunch my eyes shut and then take a little peek. Nope. Guess it's not God's time.

Lilly starts beating the pale pink curtains in the display windows with the feather duster. Uh oh. Time to intervene.

"Come on," she says through clenched teeth.

I hold both palms up as I approach her. "What are you doing?"

"I am trying to get the dust out of the curtains." She smacks the curtain again, but now the curtain is fighting back. The entire left rod falls out of place, and the curtain catapults toward Lilly. It lands on top of her head, claiming the victory as she lets out a shriek of terror.

"They are going to be here any minute."

The door jingles as it opens. Fabulous. Lilly's breathing shifts into hyperventilation.

"Good morning." I smile when I see Miles. He gives me one of his cute grins, and then frowns. I instinctively run my tongue over my teeth to check for food remnants. Let's face it; it happens to all of us.

"What's up with your human curtain?" Miles nods toward Lilly, who continues to shriek. She finally throws the curtain off her head. Her hair is definitely a mess now, with strands pointing every which way. Honestly, it defies the laws of gravity.

"Oh, no," she moans pathetically. I awkwardly reach for the curtain rod, trying to smooth it. "Lilly, I'll take care of this. Why don't you go fix your hair?" The woman bolts to the backroom faster then I devour brownies.

Miles takes the curtain from me. "Here, let me. I'm taller."

I shrug. I stopped being offended when people called me short a long time ago. I actually get out of a lot of stuff because I'm too short to do it. That comes in handy.

I used to try to tell my mom I was too short to put the dishes in the top cupboard.

He stretches his muscular arms out, and places that rod into place with no effort at all. Turning from his task, he smiles at me. "So."

"So."

"It seems we have another date to plan."

I roll my eyes for his benefit. "I'm sure you've got it planned already. You were so sure you were going to win."

"I did win."

"Minor detail."

I love the sound of his laugh. It's loud, the kind of laugh that comes from the gut because the person is genuinely happy. It suits him, and I never tire of hearing it.

"Just no place with snow."

"You live in the north country. Every place has snow."

"Just no place where we partake in the snow."

He dons a pretend, concerned look. "I really hate that you let

the little kid inside of you die."

"That kid didn't die. That kid was just never fond of having snow down her pants."

He laughs again, and I swear, the dimples on his face look deeper. "Well, you are in luck because this next date is relatively by the book."

"Oh, are we going hang gliding? I should tell you, I'm not so big on things where my feet don't touch the ground either."

Miles shudders. "Hang gliding? What kind of a sick joke is that?"

Ah, it appears we've found something the chivalrous knight detests. "Not a fan?"

"My brother went hang gliding for his twenty-third birthday. He came back with two broken arms and an upper body cast. Then on this twenty-seventh birthday, he went sky diving and came home with two broken legs. Then on his big thirtieth birthday, he went bungee jumping." Miles doesn't continue, but he gives me a pained look.

My stomach starts churning. "What happened to your brother?"

"Broken tailbone. He couldn't sit the way God intended for five months. His wife told him that the rest of his birthdays will be planned by her."

I chuckle and play with the curtains, straightening wrinkles that are not there. "So, you have a brother, a father, and a mother. Any other siblings?" Despite our weird beginning, I am basically dating this guy. I should learn more about his family.

"Nope. Just the one brother. He's seven years older than me. He's been married for eight years, and they have a five-year-old boy and a two-year-old girl." Miles smiles like the proud uncle he must be. I bet he's great with his niece and nephew. "How about you?"

I shake my head. "I'm an only child. However, Kaylee and I

basically grew up together. We fight like sisters but are best friends. Basically, it's the best of both worlds."

"Is that how Kaylee and you ended up working here together?" He's got a curious glint in his eye. I can't quite read it.

"Yeah, I guess so. Aunt Jill knew I loved this business. Kaylee needed a job. It just sort of fit together." What is going on underneath that head of wavy brown hair?

"Izze." Lilly comes speed walking out of the backrooms. "Where is my duster? I need to finish dusting."

"Lilly, you've dusted everything ten times. The place looks amazing."

"It really does look very neat in here," Miles adds. At his reassurance, you can see Lilly calm down and the stress roll off her. "Okay. I guess it's time to wait then."

I sneak off to the bathroom so that I can check my appearance one more time. When I come out, Candace and Kaylee have arrived, but our interviewers have not.

I glance at the clock. They are half an hour late. This would not bode well with Lilly.

Miles entertains Lilly with some business talk. Hopefully that will keep her distracted until they arrive. Candace, Kaylee, and I talk quietly by the front desk as Candace and I catch up on paperwork and check the status of pending orders.

Forty-five minutes later, a woman and a man walk through the door. The woman has an air about her that reminds me of the reporter from *His Girl Friday*.

Sigh. Carry Grant.

Where was I? Oh, right. Got distracted for a second.

The man's arms are loaded with camera bags, tripods, camera reflectors, and other equipment that I couldn't name in a million years. The bead of sweat on his brow indicates he was a hair away from dropping it.

Lilly marches up to the woman and sticks her hand out. "I'm Lilly Marshall, owner of Ever After Bridal Boutique."

"Nice to meet you, ma'am. I'm Gina, your interviewer." Little crinkles form in the corners of her almond-shaped eyes. She points to the equipment-laden man. "That is Gerry. He's our photographer."

Lilly's head swivels back to us. She mouths, "Get up here, and introduce yourselves." Candace and I approach. "These are my consultants, Candace and Izze." Candace shakes Gina's hand first. Great, now I have to shake her hand, too, or it will be rude.

I hate shaking hands. I've been told I have a weak handshake.

I release Gina's hand as quickly as is socially acceptable, and step back so Lilly can finish making introductions.

She points to Kaylee. "This is Kaylee; she is our part-time seamstress. She does the minor touchups, repairs, and bustles." Kaylee just waves from where she's standing instead of shaking Gina's hand. Lucky.

I hold back a laugh at the look on Gerry's face when Lilly says *bustle*. He clearly doesn't have a clue what that is, but kudos to the man for nodding along anyway. How did he end up being a photographer for a wedding magazine?

Then her arms sweep to Miles. "This is James Miles Clayton. We call him Miles. He is our business advisor. He's become a real asset to Ever After."

"Good to meet you," Miles says, and they shake hands.

Gina lays out the plan. "Okay. Here is how this will work. We can interview you guys on that couch over there, and Gerry will be snapping some shots while we talk. We will interview you one by one. I'll ask you questions about your lives, how you came to work here, and things like that. We want it to sound more like you're telling your story than that someone is interviewing you. Makes it more personal."

Lilly nods. "Sounds like a plan."

Gerry walks in a little circle, both hands forming little L's as he talks. "Afterward, I am going to get some shots of the place. No room is off limits. We want the readers to feel like they have been invited into every area of this place." His tie and dress shirt look out of place with his faded jeans.

Lilly bobs her head again.

Gina walks over to the couch. "Just so there isn't any awkwardness about who gets interviewed when, I'll set the order now. Lilly, then Miles, Candace." She points at me waiting for me to supply my forgotten name.

"Izze," I say.

"Izze," she continues. "Then Kaylee. Okay, Lilly. You're up."

Lilly settles onto the couch, and the rest of us stand back out of the way, awaiting our turn. Gina smooths the skirt of her gray suit before sitting on the other end of the couch. "Lilly, how did you first come to work at Ever After?"

I lean forward, interested. Lilly has been here forever. I don't think I've ever heard how she ended up working here.

"Well, I was a troubled young woman. I went to finishing schools from kindergarten to twelfth grade. After graduation, I rebelled and acted out in inappropriate ways. Eventually, I hit rock bottom. Out of sheer desperation, I started going to church, and cried through the entire service. A woman, Jillian M'Lyde who was the previous owner of Ever After, came up to me, hugged me, and just sat with me. She gave me a place to sleep, a job at her bridal boutique, and I helped her with the teens in the youth group for a number of years. I've worked my way up, and Jillian sold me the business this year."

I blink furiously, trying to keep the water building in my eyes from spilling over and onto my face. What a story! All this time, I had no idea. I always thought she was prim and proper Lilly. I feel

guilty for having judged her without knowing her, for mocking her bizarre ways, for being cranky with her. I pray to God, asking His forgiveness for all the ways I could have been better to Lilly. From now on, I will try harder. Sure, she will continue to do uptight things that will drive me crazy, but I'll put the cap on my bottle of harsh judgement.

"That's quite a story." Gina continues asking Lilly questions in such a way that it rolls out of her like she's talking to her best friend, all the while taking notes for the article.

She wraps up with Lilly, and Lilly and Miles switch seats.

"So, how did you become involved with Ever After?"

"I moved into the area this past year. I was a business advisor to The Lemonade Stand at my former agency. I started my own agency when I moved here, and Lilly contacted me. After our initial meeting, she hired me. However, before I could meet the rest of the staff, I meet Izze at a bookstore coffee shop."

Oh, no. What is he doing? Oh, no.

Miles continues easily, clearly not caring about my panic attack. The others shoot me looks. I never did tell them that I met Miles first, or how I met him. "She gave me a taste of how fun this job was going to be, although I didn't yet know it. She accused me of being rude, even though she wouldn't share her table with me. When I walked into that meeting, and saw her sitting there, completely stunned, I knew without a shadow of a doubt that this was the job for me."

Miles just outed our relationship.

Gina gobbles this information down like it's a lobster dinner. "So, is there something special between you and Izze?" I close my eyes, and cover my face.

Miles grins. "She's a wonderful woman. I enjoy her company immensely."

What is that supposed to mean? Does he not want to admit

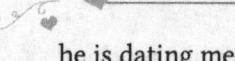

he is dating me?

"Unrelated question"—Gina leans forward—"do you believe in love at first sight?"

Oh, have mercy! Uncle Jesse from *Full House* is the voice in my head.

"Absolutely."

Gina gets some more background from Miles and thanks him. Then she calls for Candace. When she sits down, she asks her how she started at Ever After.

"Well, about four and a half years ago, my sister was getting married. She came here to try on gowns. While she was in the changing room, I was pursuing the racks, alongside another bride. She asked me what I thought of the gown she picked. I said it was hideous, and pulled out another gown for her to try, which she ended up buying. Jill M'Lyde saw the whole thing and offered me a job."

I smile at the memory. Candace started working here while I was still new. It made me feel like we were conquering the new world together.

"Are you married too?"

"Yes." Candace smiles. "I've been married for six years, and we have a two-year-old boy."

Gina smiles. "Kids. I bet the little one keeps you busy."

Candace laughs and moans at the same time, and points to the corner of her eye. "He keeps me busy, all right. Do you see these wrinkles around my eyes? I developed them while he was still in the womb."

They talk about her crazy life as a mom for a few minutes, and then she's done.

I gulp. The interviews went too quick. How can it be my turn already? My knees feel weak.

"Izze," Gina calls.

I try to gracefully walk to the couch and sit down. I'm sure I looked more like someone who was trying to walk and sit with some type of horrible rash. I hear the click of a camera, too. Great. Please don't laugh at my terrible pictures. I'm not photogenic.

"So, Izze. Tell me how you got started here."

I try not to stare at Gerry and his camera and focus on Gina instead. "Well, I fell in love with weddings when I was the flower girl at my cousin's wedding. Ever since then, I became obsessed. I recorded the wedding reality shows, and I was fascinated with wedding dresses. I loved how it could be the one thing to tie everything else together. I studied body types, fits, and designers like I should have studied my chemistry in high school. Seven years ago, Kaylee and I moved here because Jillian M'Lyde offered me a job. She's my aunt, and she had watched my fascination with weddings grow over the years. She says that God let her know that I was perfect for this job."

Gina gives me a coy smile. "You seem to be good friends with Miles."

"Uh, yes, uh. Well, we haven't known each other very long, but he's a good guy, albeit a little cocky sometimes." Now, who's in the spotlight, Miles?

Gina nods. However, she's not done sniffing around for that scoop. "So, Izze, do you have anyone special in your life?"

As an unmarried, Christian woman of twenty-five, I can't tell you how much I detest this question. At any rate, how do I answer it now? Miles's interview really made this complicated.

"I'm dating somebody right now."

"I thought so." Gina leans forward, and points her pen at me. "Izze, do you believe in love at first sight?"

Oh, no. I see what she's doing. She's going to publicize our blooming romance in *Bridal Biz Magazine*! She's going to make us into the forced, unexpected love story of Katniss and Peeta, only

the Ever After version. I do not want my dating life displayed for all the world to see! Been there, done that, and I despised it.

"I think that if it's two people God ordained for each other, then anything is possible." Seems like a safe answer.

Thankfully, that just about covers my interview. Gina calls Kaylee over after asking me about my family.

"Last, but not least," Gina says.

Kaylee sweetly explains how she moved here with me and took college classes. When she couldn't find a job after graduation, Aunt Jill offered Kaylee a position as a minor seamstress solely based on the curtains she made for Aunt Jill for Christmas the previous year. They talk easily, and even though Kaylee is also single, Gina doesn't pester her about the love at first sight question. This just proves my suspicions about Gina's motives.

Gina stands like she hasn't just spent the last two hours sitting perfectly still. However, I'm sitting here thinking about my poor old bones!

"You all did wonderful. Gerry is going to take those pictures now, and then we will be all set. It will be a couple months before the article is published, but currently it is slotted for April."

She sticks her hand out for all of us to shake again. "It was a pleasure meeting everyone and talking to you. I think readers are really going to like your stories in particular." Gina grins pointedly at Miles and me. I take a deep breath, and Kaylee gives me a look that says I will not escape the redhead's dreaded questions.

If today is any indication, then my love life is in for a crazy ride.

Chapter Nine

A week after the interview for *Bridal Biz Magazine*, I jump and whirl when Lilly taps me. My arms are stretched out like I'm a ninja and I'm about to do some really cool twirls, leaps, and kicks.

She raises an eyebrow at my odd stance.

"I didn't hear you. You startled me." I have never heard a person move as quietly as Lilly does. If she lived with me, then the elephants constantly parading around my house would disappear.

However, I thank God that Lilly doesn't live with me.

"We start filming for the commercial next week."

"Really?" I've been checking shipping dates and invoices on gowns. I spin back to the computer, save all the information, and close out of the program. I turn to face Lilly. "That was quick."

She nods, and you can't miss how excited she is about all of this. All traces of the frantic, dusting lady from the day of the magazine interviews are gone—for now. I'm sure they will be back for filming. There are some things in life that you can just count on happening.

"Well, that's great! If you need help with anything before then, let me know. I will do my best." I'm sticking to my resolution to be more helpful to Lilly. She deserves it.

A pleased expression replaces the look she had been giving my odd antics. "Thank you, Izze. I may just call upon you." She starts

back to her office, and then stops. "Izze?" She hesitates, opening and shutting her mouth like a little fish in her attempt to force out words, and I smile awkwardly.

"I just wanted to make sure you're not angry that your aunt sold the business to me, and not to, well, you."

I blink. I was so not expecting anything like this. Judging from her grimace, and the worry in her hazel eyes, this has been something she has wanted to talk to me about for a while.

What do I say?

I've always been ecstatic to do what I love, even if some people still think I'm a nutty airhead. Yes, it hurt a little that Aunt Jill didn't even approach me about buying the shop, but in reality, I'm not angry. In all honesty, God knew this wasn't my time to run a business.

It just took being rejected, and this unexpected moment for me to realize that.

I smile softly. "Can I speak honestly with you, Lilly?" She nods ever so slightly for me to continue. "I think a part of me was angry. I've always loved this business and hoped that one day I would be able to run it, but I've realized my favorite part of this job is the brides. It's dressing them, talking with them, and being the one person on their side when their families are being completely awful. Let's face it—I'm twenty-five, I still have a lot to learn before I can run a business. I want to learn from you, and maybe one day, if God wills it, it will be my turn."

"I would love nothing more than to teach you," Lilly chokes out. "I want to promote you to assistant manager, head of the sales floor."

My eyes fill with unexpected tears. *Wow, Lord!* In all these years, Lilly and I have never been even remotely close to friends, yet hearing her story, and this sweet conversation, has opened a door for us. I think that I can truly learn from her now, and I think

that I am truly *ready* to learn from her.

Lilly looks uncertain but pulls me into a hug. It's awkward at first, with years of unspoken tension still fighting for dominance, but slowly it's dying.

From here on out, it's just blossoms, rainbows, and chocolate.

I run up the porch steps of my house. I was at work later than usual due to my newfound camaraderie with Lilly. Shortly after our heart to heart, she took to showing me some of the things I will be in charge of.

I'm actually really excited for the changes that are going to be happening at work. Shocking, I know. It's refreshing after how things started a few months ago though.

I kick off my cute flats just inside the door and leave my purse on the little table. I have a date with Miles tonight. The clock in the entryway chimes, and I gulp. I am running fifteen minutes behind schedule.

My roomies are all sitting in their usual spots on the couches. Kaylee and Courtney say hey, and Apryl flashes me a peace signal. As I run for my room, I shout hey back to them. Throwing the door shut, I start digging through my closet.

Am I the only person in the world who has nice stuff one day, and then the next day, every single piece of clothing is absolutely disgusting? I rip off my work clothes as I think about what to wear tonight. The black lace dress with the pink, black, and gray leggings? A pair of skinny jeans, tall boots, and a long, cozy sweater? Go for a layered look with a red tank top, brown long sleeve top with the cowl neckline, and a white sweater vest trimmed with fake fur or something like that because I know I didn't pay for any real fur? I'm much too cheap.

I decide on the jeans, boots, and long sweater. It's casual and warm, but the boots and sweater have a classy look about them. I pull the sweater over my head. The sleeves are long and wide, and they go almost to my knuckles. It's a dark rose color that really compliments my hair and eyes. I tug on the brown boots next, and then refresh my makeup. My hair is a force to be reckoned with, but there's only so much I can do in... I glance at the birdcage clock in my room. Uh oh. There's not a lot I can do to fix it in three minutes, not if I want to get outside quietly without my housemates causing an embarrassing scene when Miles picks me up.

Annoying man wouldn't let me meet him anywhere. He had to insist on being a gentleman and picking me up at my house. He didn't understand that these girls would insist on meeting him, and then would grill him about all the personal details of his life.

Granted, I didn't come right out and say that. How does one say that? Should I have said, "Sorry, Miles. You can't pick me up at my house. You would be held hostage for forty minutes under the guise of 'making your acquaintance.' Really they just want to know if you're cute, if you love God, and about any information they can trick you into spilling regarding your past relationships."

No, I didn't say that. So now I must sneak out of the house. Hopefully, before they realize what is happening.

A knock sounds at my door.

Oh, they are getting good. They must have left the television running so I wouldn't hear their footsteps.

"Hey, open up in there." Apryl's voice is muffled by the door and the still-blaring sound system.

"Nope. I'm trying to change clothes. I have a meeting."

"No you don't," Kaylee chimes into the conversation.

This is hopeless. I open the door, and my three roommates are standing shoulder to shoulder, arms crossed, pursed lips.

Courtney does a little chin up motion, and the gesture looks

ridiculous on that preppy girl. "Where exactly do you think you're going?"

"I have a date."

"With Miles, I presume," Courtney fishes.

"Nope. Miles is old news. I met this guy named Clem. He was delivering the bridal gowns from Alfred Angelo. I was signing for the order. Our hands touched the pen at the same time. It was fate."

Kaylee rolls her eyes. "We want to meet him."

I point at her. "You have met him."

"I've met him in a working environment. Now we need to meet him as the guy who is dating our friend." Her green eyes blaze. I swear, no one has brighter, clearer eyes then Kaylee. Her red hair falls over her shoulder like a flaming torch. Her hair is not in its normal sloppy, at-home bun. Actually, Apryl and Courtney both look nice, too.

"You knew already," I breathe out. "How?"

"He called," Courtney states mater-of-factly.

I raise an eyebrow. "Why?"

"To let you know he was running a few minutes late. He should be here in ten minutes."

I narrow my eyes. "Why didn't he call my cell phone?"

"Said he left a message for you there, too, but wanted to make sure you knew."

I glare at them and point my finger in the air. "I will introduce you. Then you guys will disappear. Got it? I am a grown woman, and I don't answer to any of you. Now if you'll excuse me, ten minutes is long enough to try and fix my hair." I squeeze past them to the bathroom.

I emerge ten minutes later having achieved something close to a hairstyle. Curly bangs and tendrils hang around my face. I'm hoping they frame my face instead of looking like I don't own a hair straightener. The rest is pinned back into a low, curly, albeit a little messy, bun. However, I find that Miles arrived a few minutes early and has been cornered.

We have a hostage situation. I repeat, we have a hostage situation.

I charge into the living room, and grab Miles's arm. Touching him sends a jolt of heat into my hand that rushes into my heart. "Well, I see you've met Apryl and Courtney." I point at them. "They are twin sisters. You already know Kaylee from work, and that's everyone. So, see you later." I wave and yank on Miles's arm, tugging him in the direction of the door.

"Wait up a second." Apryl holds up both hands, stopping me from dragging Miles any farther. Well, all hope is lost now. Hopefully this won't scare him away for good. "What's your full name?"

Not a horrible question.

Miles smiles. "James Miles Clayton. I was named after my grandfather. My friends call me Miles." When he says that, he looks over at me and smiles. I smile back, remembering when I started calling him Miles instead of James. It was a turning point for us.

"Is that name going to be in the police database?" Courtney crosses her arms. Great, she's going into lawyer mode.

"I have no idea. There are probably hundreds of people with the same name."

"Sure. Likely story."

Apryl crosses her arms, too. "Spoken like a man who has something to hide."

Kaylee holds up her hands. "Guys, I'm sure you're overreacting." She turns to Miles. "Do you have your driver's license with you?"

"Guys," I growl through clenched teeth.

"It's okay." Miles winks at me, and then turns back to my certifiably insane friends. "I have never been arrested or charged with anything. I did get two speeding tickets; they were four years

apart. I have no excuse for them. Sometimes we do stupid things. I've never done drugs. I don't drink. I clean my bathroom twice a month. I can separate my lights from darks while doing laundry, but usually I just buy the same colors so I don't have to bother. I like spinach. Need anything else?"

"Are you currently married, or seeing somebody else?" This from Courtney.

"No, but do you think that I would answer that honestly if I was?"

Courtney harrumphs.

"How many romantic relationships have you had?" Apryl grins sinisterly. She loves to ask this question. I don't date around like some serial dater. I've had a date here and there in the last seven years, but no boyfriends since high school. The longest I've "dated" someone was for three weeks, a night or two a week. However, this interrogation became standard for any of us after the time Kaylee went out with her third cousin by accident.

"I went to dances and things in high school with the same girl, but we were never a couple. Four years ago I dated someone for seven months, only for us to simultaneously look at each other in the realization that there was nothing between us. Decided I wouldn't date anyone after that just to date. I gave it into God's hands and haven't looked back."

My heart flutters nervously. What does that even mean about us? Then I get worried. Could he look at me one day and decide that I'm not wife material? I chew on my lip while contemplating these thoughts.

I mentally slap myself. Get a grip, and relax. No one is getting married today.

"Where are you guys going tonight?" Kaylee asks with a smile.

"I thought I'd take Izze out to dinner. I hadn't decided on a place. Thought I'd see where she wanted to eat."

Kaylee continues to smile suspiciously. "Izze loves Chinese food. You should take her to The Chow Man."

"That sounds great." I grab Miles's arm, and tug on it again. "We should get going."

Miles looks relieved. "Okay. It was nice meeting you two and seeing you, Kaylee."

They all echo his good-byes, and we head outside. We walk to his burnt orange car in silence. He opens the door for me and then goes around to get in on his side. He starts the car and pulls out of the driveway. We go a few minutes down the road before he speaks.

"That was interesting. Will they do that every time I pick you up at your house?"

"Just the first dozen or so times."

"Something to look forward to." He looks over at me, and even though it's dark, I just know he is giving me that gorgeous smile of his. I don't even have to see it to experience its power on my nerves.

We chat normally the rest of the ride and pull into the parking lot for The Chow Man. We head inside the restaurant and wait to be seated.

The Chow Man never seems to have more than seven people eating at any given time, although tons of people come for some takeout. It's not filthy or anything like that, it's just so far out of town that nobody really knows it's there. The only reason we know about it is because Kaylee and I got lost trying to find our way to the apartment we were sharing when we moved here.

The hostess who doubles as the waitress comes out of the kitchen. "How many?"

"Two," Miles says.

The place is empty, as usual. Well, almost empty. There is a small group of people in the back of the restaurant next to the

restrooms. She places our menus on either side of the table and says she will be back to take our order.

"This place is quiet."

I wiggle my eyebrows. "It has atmosphere."

He smirks and looks down at his menu. "What do you want?"

"I love egg rolls, Peking ravioli, and lo mien."

"Let's get some orange chicken and beef teriyaki with that, and we've got a meal."

"A man with a plan."

"I always am." He gives me one of his cocky winks, and I pretend to roll my eyes.

Just then I see a menu flash up to cover someone's face.

A face I know all too well.

"I can't believe this."

"What?" Miles looks at me with a frown. "We can get a different kind of meat if you don't like orange chicken."

"No, not the food. Look at the table behind us and directly in front of the rest rooms." I nod my head toward the table.

"I see a group of people holding their menus over their faces." As he says the words, I can see it dawn on him. "It's them, isn't it?" he asks, sounding incredulous.

"Yup."

"How did they beat us here?"

I scrunch my nose. "You took the highway. The back roads are actually quicker when you come this way."

"So they are going to spy on us all night?"

"Yup."

He looks slightly annoyed but then forces a smile. "Well, on the bright side, I've always wanted to know what it would be like to be a famous person. Guess we'll find out tonight."

"What kind of famous person?"

"When I was growing up, I wanted what every kid wants—to

be president of the world."

"And now?"

He gives me a very serious look. "I still want to be president of the world."

I laugh, and he reaches for my hand across the table. I can see Kaylee hit Apryl with her menu, and Courtney strains in her seat to get a better look at us. I should glare at them, let them know I see them, but I don't care anymore. Miles is holding my hand, and that may seem very middle school, but the way my stomach flip-flops says this is a big deal. And hey, we might as well give them something to spy on while we're here, and I think holding his big, warm hand is the perfect place to start.

"Did we lose them?" Miles glanced in the rearview mirror. "I don't see them anymore."

Izze twisted her head left and right, trying to see behind them. "I don't either." Her signature scent of vanilla shampoo wafted toward him. Oh, that was distracting while driving! He needed to focus.

"It's about time."

"Getting on the highway helped." She smiled at him.

He didn't want tonight to end.

Currently, the car was on course to take Izze home. However, an idea had popped into his mind. He glanced in the mirror before changing lanes and taking the next exit.

"Uh, where are you taking me?"

"It's a surprise."

"I hate surprises."

He smirked. "Tough."

"Is this the part where you kill me?"

"Will you be quiet?"

"No." Her voice held a note of laughter. A sound he found quite appealing.

He pulled into a large parking lot. Izze glanced around, confused. "You wanted to come to work? That's a weird way to end a date."

"Are we parked in front of work?"

She narrowed those gorgeous, chocolate-colored eyes. "Are you capable of answering a question with anything other than a question?"

"Are you capable of waiting patiently?"

Izze threw her hands up. "You are infuriating."

Funny. He thought the same thing about her.

Infuriating in a good way, though.

Miles parked in front of the bookstore, cut the engine, and turned to face his date.

Taking her in.

Wow, Miles thought. This beautiful woman had stolen his heart. She was a breath away from his every thought. The image of her face made him smile before he fell asleep. Miles hated the days he didn't see her, so he found himself checking the schedule to see which days she worked. All his masculinity and bravado melted into a pile of sniveling goo in her presence.

He brushed a wayward curl from her. He hadn't planned to do that, but his hand had a mind of its own. Cupping her cheek, a bolt of pure pleasure shot through him when Izze leaned her face against his hand. Slowly, he drew her head closer to his, noting the softness of her curls, her cheek, her lips....

He pulled back. His heart beat furiously underneath her hands on his chest, but he had to come up from the fog that claimed him whenever he kissed her.

"We need to change the subject," he said hoarsely.

"We weren't talking."

"Just change the subject, Izze," he growled.

"Okay." Understanding dawn on her face in the form of a blush. "Why are we at the bookstore?"

Miles chuckled. "Well done." He got out and walked around the car to open her door. "Let's go."

Izze hopped out of the car, and he took her hand as they walked inside the bookstore. The scents of paper and ink mixed with coffee greeted them. Miles smiled as Izze inhaled, obviously loving this smell. He squeezed her hand and tugged her in the direction of the in-store coffee shop.

He motioned for Izze to order first and pulled out his debit card so that she would know that he was paying.

Miles then ordered a smoothie. And noticed her raised eyebrow. "What?"

"What's with the girly drink? I would have expected you to drink black coffee."

"It's banana and ice that have been pulverized to smithereens. Any drink that's pulverized is manly."

"It's the drink mothers buy for their children because they don't want them getting addicted to caffeine yet."

The barista chuckled but tried to cover it with a laugh.

Izze pointed to the barista. "See? She knows that I'm right."

The barista handed them their drinks. They walked to the tables, but before she could sit down, he held up his hand.

He set their drinks on the table. "Izze," he said, taking her hands in his. "Will you share a table with me?"

Izze smiled. "I think you're too charming for your own good."

He pulled her chair out for her. "Afterward, you can peruse the books to your heart's content."

"Yup. Too charming."

"I didn't think there was such a thing."

Izze sipped her coffee. "You defy normal standards."

"Why Miss Isabel Vez, I do believe that was a compliment."

"There's a first time for everything."

He took her free hand and squeezed it. "Well, hopefully it's not the last."

Chapter Ten

If I thought the day we did interviews was a crazy day, then I was just kidding myself. Today is the very definition of a crazy day.

Lilly had Ever After's lawyer draw up some paperwork for the brides to sign. Basically, it stated that they wouldn't try to sue us if they ended up on television. Most of them heard the word television, and they started screaming so loud, you suddenly had a vivid picture of what the proposal must have been like for the poor, now-deaf fiancé.

The lawyer advised Lilly that we should contact the brides beforehand, and have them and whoever is accompanying them sign the release forms the day of their appointments. If any brides refused to sign, they were rescheduled to a later date to avoid any accidental filming.

Lilly has been twittering in excitement ever since the production company gave her the dates. We have spent the last week preparing. I have never wasted so much time dusting the same thing a million times, but I didn't want to rock the new friendship boat I have been paddling with Lilly.

Tony, the director, and roughly a thousand other guys working on lights, microphones, cameras, and set up run around the store. Tony works with Miles, trying to help him unleash his inner Vanna White.

It's going really well. I wish I had popcorn.

I stifle another giggle as I watch Tony take a couple of steps and pretend to motion to the busy bridal shop behind him. He gives Miles a pointed look, clearly expecting him to mimic his sage instructions. Judging from the look on Miles's face and the words forming on his lips, he's saying that a whole fleet of pigs would have to take to the skies before he did that.

"How's it going?" Kaylee suddenly appears at my side.

I grin unrepentantly at her. "It's going great. This would rock as a sitcom."

"Still having none of it, is he?" Kaylee tilts her head to the side and grimaces as Miles finally attempts the step-and-gesture motion. "It takes a special kind of person to gesture so casually that it becomes famous. Miles is not that kind of person."

I snort. Yes, I can snort in unashamed wonder now. One of the major blessings of my new partnership with Lilly is that she doesn't lecture me as much anymore. It's great.

Tony shakes his head at Miles, and I presume that he declares him hopeless. "All right everybody. I want everyone to get to the designated starting positions that we talked about earlier. Miles, on my cue, start your attempt at walking and say your lines. Just like we practiced, but don't dally. I don't think those brides will be patient forever."

Everyone scurries to their places. Candace joins Kaylee and me as we stand next to the office door. Miles takes his place just to the right of the front desk, and four different camera guys focus on him. Tony holds his right hand up, loudly counting down to the start.

Oh my gosh.

"Five. Four. Three. Two. And one. Action."

Miles starts walking toward the center of the room, and the men with the cameras for faces walk with him. "Here at Ever After, we

make your dreams come true. Why? Because we believe in love."

I snort again. Come on, that was cheesy. Oh, I hope that wasn't caught on my microphone.

We all join Miles in the center of the room. Congratulate, me. I didn't trip!

"And cut!" Tony shouts. "That was good, but let's get that take again. Really enunciate, everybody."

We do it two more times because one of the camera batteries dies during the second take. Why that matters when there are ten cameras on us, I don't know. I swear I hear the glass doors cracking as the brides and their respective parties push against them.

Tony starts shouting to the cameramen covering the front door to get into position. "Okay, Lilly. Let those ladies in, and greet your customers."

Lilly opens up the doors. "Thanks for coming to Ever After. Let's find your happily ever after look." Oh, goodness. Who is coming up with all this corny stuff today?

"Okay," Tony yells. The cameramen stop filming, and Tony gives them a run down on how to act before resuming his position off to the side. "Okay, ready? Action."

Lilly walks awkwardly in front of the ladies as she leads them over to us. "Right this way, ladies. Your bridal consultants will be with you momentarily." Lilly checks her clipboard. She was planning to call my appointment first. "Rozlyn, party of five? I will take you to meet your consultant, Izze. Jade, if you and your guests will take a seat, your consultant will be with you shortly."

Rozlyn is a tall, willowy woman with straight, auburn hair and a miniature sun on her left hand. Every movement she makes sends a blinding flash of light from her huge diamond.

Oh, Lord, please don't let her be snobby.

"Hello, I'm Izze." I stick out my hand, and Rozlyn takes it without hesitation.

"I'm Roz. These are my bridesmaids, and this is Nadia, my mother."

Nadia sticks out her wrinkling hand. Her hair is almost completely gray, but it's cut stylishly.

"Okay. If you'll follow me right this way." I lead them to the first room, and they all sit down. One of the unknown men follows us in, and two others stand just outside of the door, filming from slightly different angles.

This is going to be awkward. I try to focus on my bride, and not on the fact that someone is currently recording every odd little thing we do. "So what kind of gown do you have in mind? Silhouettes, fabric, designers, and that sort of thing."

"Wait," the camera guy in our room says. "My battery just died. Dave can you get me another one?" One of the guys runs for another battery.

And we're waiting. This is awkward.

"Okay," the guy finally says once he's switched batteries. "I need you," he points at me. "To repeat your question."

"So what kind of gown do you have in mind? What silhouettes, fabric, designers, and that sort of thing?" I ask for the second time.

Roz, Nadia, and the bridesmaids seem completely at ease. "I want tons and tons of embroidery and beading. Preferably in a contrasting color, like black, brown, gold, or rose." She hands me several pictures. Every photo has a gown drowning in bead work. Okay, then. I know what I'll be pulling.

I help Roz into the little changing room and excuse myself to go look for gowns. Two cameramen race behind me and almost trip over me in the storeroom as I wait for the light to flicker on and warm up to a non-threatening glow. "You have to wait for the light to warm up, just so you know," I call over my shoulder. I start running through the racks, grabbing all the gowns that even sort of fit her description.

The light flickers a little, and a halo of dust shines down onto a gown several feet away from me.

Ah, the gift.

I pull the signaled gown out a little. The entire dress is covered with embroidery, and the embroidery at the hem and top of the bodice are done in gold thread. The bodice has just as much beading as embroidery, but the skirt only has clusters of beads. The beads are in light gold and pale rose. It's a lovely, fitted A-line style, which pulls in a little more than normal at the waist. It is going to emphasis her tiny waist perfectly.

I giggle much like I imagine Rumpelstiltskin would. The tiny zoom of a camera lens comes from my left. Uh, oh. I forgot I wasn't alone. That guy just got all the proof my parents will ever need that I am insane. I'm not sure I like this anymore.

I speed walk away from him. No, I'm not running. Geesh. I have a bride waiting for me.

If I happen to lose them in the process, then so be it.

I bring in the gowns with the Camera Twins at my heels. Roz's group makes the appropriate squeals as they catch glimpses of the gowns. I knock on the door and wait for Roz's okay to enter before leaving camera guys in the dust.

"So I've got several gowns for you to try." I grin and wiggle my eyebrows, and she bounces up and down excitedly. I hang them up, one by one, and according to my system, the gown she will be purchasing today is in the middle.

How do I know?

I've told you. I have the gift.

Roz slips into a ball gown with embroidery covering the bodice, and touches of it at the hem. Everyone loved it, but I could tell that it was a little too much poof for Roz.

She doesn't immediately change out of the gown because one of the camera guys needed to change tapes. He comes back with

a fourth scrawny guy who's holding a light reflector. They finally start filming again, and Roz and I head back into the changing room. Then she sees it. Another dusty beam of light shines on the chosen gown.

"Oh my," she breathes while tracing the pattern of the delicate embroidery. "This is it."

"Do you want to try on any others?'

"Nope, this is it."

I help her into the gown, and the entire time I'm working on her corset, she keeps saying, "This is the dress." She walks out of the dressing room saying, "This is the dress." When one of her snooty bridesmaids says she should keep looking, Roz rebukes her. "Nope. This is the gown. Either get on board or go home, Kate."

Priceless.

Nadia looks at me with wide eyes. "How did you find that dress?" They all look at me expectantly, including three cameras.

Should I tell them about the dusty beam of light? "Oh, it was nothing. I'm just good at listening to what a bride wants."

"You are a genius!" Nadia pronounces. Then she looks directly into one of the cameras. "This girl can find the perfect dress for anyone." Camera Boy devours every word as Nadia continues to sing my praises. I feel my cheeks turn redder than a jar of maraschino cherries.

Soon thereafter, I usher them into the lobby where I start processing their order. Miles starts talking with them, asking them all kinds of goofy things like, "Did you find the gown of your dreams?" and "How does it feel to truly be a bride now?"

Seriously, who wrote this stuff?

I finish working with Roz, and she saunters out the door like a woman on a mission. I make eye contact with Lilly.

And give her my best withering stare.

It's going to be a long day, folks.

I've invented a new phobia. It's the fear of having your feet fall off at work. It's a very real problem, and I want to make everyone aware. As soon as I wake up, that is.

I'm approximately three seconds away from passing out on the front desk.

Somebody jabs my shoulder with a miniature sword.

"Ouch," I gripe. The front desk completely supports my body weight, and my arms are folded on top of the counter. They broke my fall when my head crashed into the top just moments ago. I don't bother to look at whoever stabbed me.

My enemy stabs me again, and this time I flop my head to the right to see my offender. Miles grins at me.

"I hate you."

"Good job today."

"Mm hmm."

"Get up or I'll call one of the camera guys over here to get a close up of the paperclip stuck to your forehead."

I touch my forehead. Sure enough, there is a paperclip stuck to it. I pick it off and toss it into Miles's face. "I thought the camera crew went home."

"Tony and a few of the guys are still here. They're looking for some hidden, artistic angles," Miles says in a matter-of-fact manner.

"Oh."

"It's closing time, you know. You can go home now." He pokes me in the shoulder again.

"Dude, you need to stop that." I glare at him.

He ignores my threating look. "So I think we should go out and celebrate."

"Can't celebrate tonight. My feet are going to fall off, and I

need to get to a foot doctor before that happens."

"Tomorrow night is good for me," he continues.

"My feet will be dead tomorrow."

"Izze."

"Oh, all right." I pretend to sputter. "So we're going out before the next sale. Does this count for next month's date, or is this an 'off the record' date?" I use my fingers to make little air quotations.

"This is a date for a special and beautiful woman I know. We're celebrating the recent and coming changes."

"Are we allowed to go on more dates than just those agreed upon for the competition?" I smile as playfully as my exhausted muscles will allow. Even my face hurts from all the smiling and enunciating I did today. I bet I come across looking more like a hungry zombie now, but to each their own. "Wait, did you say there are more changes coming?"

"That was kind of the whole point all along." He shoots me one of his heart pumping winks. "And God always has more changes for us. Helps to keep us on our toes."

"That sounds nice. The date. Not the changes."

"I'm sure it will all be nice," Miles says but there's a catch in his voice. Something flashes in his eyes, briefly, fleetingly, but then it's gone. He's not looking me directly in the eye now, and a sense of panic and dread settles onto my shoulders.

But then he looks into my eyes.

The world stops as he holds my gaze. I have no idea where everyone else is. For all I know, they are enjoying this romantic scene right in Ever After's lobby. I know Miles said a few of the camera guys are roaming the premises. Despite all that, right now, it's just me and Miles, our gazes locked. Slowly, he moves a little closer to me.

"I'm going to kiss you now, unless you have any objections," he murmurs next to my ear. I lift my face to his, and his soft lips claim mine. He caresses my face with his hands, and his mouth moves against mine in a slow rhythm that makes me think of a waltz. It's like our kiss is dancing. It's just a few fleeting moments before he pulls away from me, leaving me dizzy. Why does the kiss always seem to be over just as quick as it started?

"Good night, Izze. I look forward to seeing you tomorrow." He strokes my cheeks with his thumbs and then releases me completely. I stare after him as he heads out the door, but instead of closing the door with his back to me, he turns to face me as he shuts it. His soft, smoldering look has determined that I will be up until the wee hours of the morning thinking about this over and over again.

It's then that I hear that familiar little zooming sound. Looking around, I spot the smug looking camera guy. He lowers his camera and flicks the switch so that the little red dot indicating it's filming fades away. "You guys really do believe in love here, don't you?"

"That was private! Do not put that in the commercial!" I hiss.

"I'm not the one who will be doing the editing," Smug Guy says. "However, it's fair game."

"Is this payback for accidentally stabbing you with a coat hanger?"

He feigns astonishment. "I would never do that." Except he's walking away laughing, so I don't really believe him. Big baby. His hand only bled for like a minute.

Awesome. My parents are never going to let me live this down.

I help Lilly and Candace finish closing. Kaylee left much earlier in the day. There wasn't really much for her to do. Tony made sure there was some footage of the brides being fitted for alterations, but he wasn't overly interested in that part.

Soon, I'm heading home. The lights are out when I pull into the driveway, and I limp into the house. I go into my room and come out with my Bible. After that kiss, I am wide awake.

Tiptoeing to the sunroom while limping is no easy task, let me tell you. Somehow I make it and flick the light switch. Everything is quiet except for the snoring coming from Apryl's room, and the ticking of the hallway clock.

This peaceful time is perfect for stealing a few minutes with God.

One of the first Bible verses I ever memorized pops into my mind. I flip there and read the verse. It's highlighted, underlined, and circled. I've come here many times over the years.

"For I know the plans I have for you, declares the Lord, plans for welfare and not for evil, to give you a future and a hope." Jeremiah twenty-nine, verse eleven.

I go back to the beginning of the chapter to read the full letter Jeremiah wrote to the Israelites going into captivity. They were undergoing a huge change.

I smile ruefully to myself. I know a thing or two about huge changes.

Anyway, I go back to reading about how they were going into captivity for seventy years because of their sins against God. Jeremiah wrote that God wanted them to build homes, plant gardens, and get married—to basically settle into the land because they would be staying. The people should ignore the words of anyone who said otherwise because it wasn't the word of the Lord. My eyes scan over verses ten through fourteen again.

For thus says the Lord: when seventy years are completed for Babylon, I will visit you, and I will fulfill to you my promise and bring you back to this place. For I know the plans I have for you, declares the Lord, plans for welfare and not for evil, to give you a future and a hope. Then you will call upon me and come and pray to me, and I will hear you. You will seek me and find me, when you seek me with all your heart. I will be found by you, declares the Lord, and I will restore your fortunes and gather you from all the nations

*and all the places where I have driven you, declares the lord, and
I will bring you back to the place from which I sent you into exile.*

The words jump off the page at me, like someone grabbing me
by the shoulders, desperately trying to communicate a message.
I just don't know what the message is.

Chapter Eleven

Miles pulls into my driveway the following night fifteen minutes earlier then the time I told the girls he would be arriving.

I live and learn from my mistakes.

I bound down the porch steps two at a time. Since this is a celebration dinner, I decided to dress up a little. My dark gray sweater dress, light gray leggings, black boots, and a pink, lace scarf are the epitome of classy. I managed to work the whole smoky eyeshadow thing, and I think I look pretty good. Decent at least.

I slide into the car, and I can smell the spicy scent of his usual cologne. Miles wears a black, button down short sleeved shirt, and a black T-shirt underneath that says, "Expressions of a Wookie." Then it shows Chewbacca from Star Wars over and over again with the same expression, just different emotions written under each picture.

I am dating a Star Wars nerd. I'm not sure how I feel about this.

Yeah, I've decided I'm cool with it.

I grin and nod to his chest. "Nice shirt." I pull the seatbelt over and click it into place.

"Thanks, I got it online." He backs the car up and looks at me briefly before changing gears. "Do you like Star Wars?"

"They are pretty good movies. I'm not a die-hard fan that would

wear T-shirts and other paraphernalia."

"Other paraphernalia?"

"Hats, buttons, full costumes. I've heard about Comic-Con and the full costumes. I think it's best that you know this about me now. I don't wear costumes."

"I appreciate your honesty," Miles says in a serious voice. "I hope we can work on that in the future."

"Not a chance." I watch as we whiz by a nice, warm restaurant. Suddenly I have visions of a candlelit dinner in the park surrounded by the snow. Sounds beautiful, right? Well, it's also cold. "Where are we going?" Please say, *warm restaurant.*

"Just this cool little place I found just outside of town."

Oh, dear. "Is it warm?"

He gives me an odd look like I've just asked the same question five times fast. "It's a building. Why wouldn't it be warm in the middle of winter?"

I smile sweetly. "Cool." As long as it's warm, I don't care.

"No, warm. Not cool. Goodness gracious, Izze."

He pulls into a packed parking lot. I see a warehouse looking building, which normally would cause me alarm, but I can see families, couples, and teenagers walking into the building like there will be a tomorrow.

Miles and I get out, and he comes around to my side of the car and immediately places my arm through his. "I don't want you to fall again." He winks and squeezes my arm tight.

We walk toward the building, and there is a large sign that says, "Troy's Timeless Theater." Once inside, a huge blast of warm air smacks me in the face. I giggle at the warmth flooding my body. I can even feel my nose again.

Straight ahead there's a huge concession stand. To the right are men and women's restrooms, and to the left is a huge double door with a sign above it that says, THEATER.

"Want a snack?"

I nod but don't look at him. I'm busy craning my neck trying to peek inside the theater. We move up the line slowly but steadily.

"Next!" A tired-looking teenager with a vacant expression on his face stares into the abysses of people swarming around the lobby.

Miles smiles politely. "Hi. Can we get a large popcorn, a box of Skittles, and a large Coke?" He looks at me.

"Hey. Could I please have the bag of Starbursts, a box of cookie dough bites, and a medium lime Icee? Thanks."

The boy types our order into the computer while yawning. "That will be...." He pauses for another yawn. "That will be fifteen dollars even, please."

Miles hands him the cash. "Thank you."

"Thank you," I echo.

Gathering our supplies, we walk into the theater.

What I see makes my heart stop. Truly it was an act of God that I did not drop my Icee in amazement.

This huge room is ten times warmer than the lobby. So warm in fact, that actual green grass covers the ground. Covering the entire far wall is the kind of screen you would see in a drive-in theater. In neatly organized rows all the way to the projection booth directly behind us are...cars. Yes, cars. Trucks, VW bugs and buses, Cadillacs, and every car imaginable. Most of them are old, vintage inspired cars, but there are a few station wagons and sports cars dotting the room.

"Wow."

"You can say that again."

"I have no words."

He snorts. "Other than the words you are already saying."

"Be quiet. Give this magnificent place the respect it deserves."

He rolls his eyes as I stand there and take in the scene before

me. I turn to look at him. "How did you find this place?"

He motions for me to follow him. "In the paper, actually. I've driven by here a million times, but I never knew what it was. Then I saw an advertisement for it in the newspaper. So I came, looked around, and thought to myself, what person would get a kick out of this, but not quote car models to me all night?"

"Aww, and you thought of me? That's so sweet." I say this sarcastically, even though it is totally true.

We stop about five rows from the projection booth. "How about this one?" Miles motions to an old, rust-colored truck.

My nose wrinkles. I just know I'll be worried that rust is going to get on my clothes all night, even if it is paint. "No." I look around the dimly lit room. "What about that fancy motorcar?"

He doesn't look impressed at my choice. "That thing is so girly."

"No, it's ladylike. There's a difference." I'm already leading the way to the midnight blue beauty. I hop into the backseat and pat the seat next to me.

Miles winces as he lowers his bulky, six foot six frame into the tiny car. "This was built for midgets."

"No, just the prim and proper people of society."

"I bet the front has more leg room."

"No," I yelp. "We can't sit up front. It ruins the illusion."

He growls under his breath, and I pat him on the arm. "There, there. It will be okay."

I put my drink into the cup holder the owners must have had installed, and the credits for Cary Grant's *I Was a Male War Bride* start rolling across the screen.

"Oh, I love this movie!" I look at him excitedly, only to see that he is watching me. I feel something squeeze in my chest, first with happiness, but then with something else. Something sinister that robs me of this perfect moment.

And replaces it with a broken memory.

I am no longer at the theater with Miles. I am in the park one terrible, rainy afternoon. I can almost feel the rain pouring down onto my face, and burning my broken heart like acid. I can feel the physical and emotional pain again. I can almost see his back growing smaller and dimmer. The memory is like a poison, and slowly, it breaks me. It is my arsenic memory.

"I need some air," I squeak. "I'll be right back." With that, I jump up and run toward the door, leaving a very confused man behind me.

I push open the double doors, gasping for air. It's like someone has taken my windpipe and crumpled it into a little ball. I stand just inside the lobby, with my head between my legs, and both hands on my knees in order to balance myself. After a few minutes like that, I stand upright.

And completely freeze.

Right before my eyes is Aunt Jill, and she is not alone. A tall man, roughly around my aunt's age, frames her face with his hands while staring sweetly into her eyes.

"You want some popcorn?" Miles whispered.

"Um, no," Izze said in a monotone. Then she seemed to remember she was on a date, and offered a slight smile.

Was he mistaken, or did she just scoot even closer to the edge? Was she even sitting on the bench seat anymore, or was she positioning herself to bolt?

Miles casually glanced at Izze again. The theater was dark, and Cary Grant was bickering about the American Army. She was focused on the movie, almost smiling, but the way she practically hugged the opposite edge of the bench seat they shared was a good indicator that something had gone amiss. Again.

What did I do wrong now?

She seemed so happy at first. Their teasing affection had padded a hole in his heart he hadn't realized was even there.

Maybe it was his fault. As a kid, he had heard the expression, "The eyes betray you." Maybe his eyes had betrayed him. Maybe they showed just what he felt about her.

That he loved her.

They hadn't been dating for long, but whenever he prayed about their future, he just felt a reassurance that this was right.

If his eyes had indeed betrayed him and screamed the "I love you" that hadn't escaped his lips, maybe it had simply scared her.

Then again, as he looked at the space separating them and her rigid posture, Miles couldn't help but wonder if it was something more.

"Izze," he whispered again.

"Shush." She smiled again, and the light in her eyes shone a little brighter this time. "You shouldn't talk during movies."

"Izze."

"You're going to get us kicked out of here."

He reached for her hand, trying to pull her back to him. "I'm glad you're here."

She smiled, but the sadness in her eyes snuffed the light again.

I wave to Mr. Peabody as I walk into Ever After. He is our vendor for the few suits we carry. "Good morning. How are the wife and kids, Mr. Peabody?" He's one of those men who goes by mister, no matter who is talking.

He's standing next to Lilly behind the front desk, but Lilly is focused on the paperwork before her and doesn't hear me. "They are doing well. Susie feels much better, and Stacy has a ballet

recital next week. Dylan is still having a lot of trouble with his math homework, though. His teacher thinks he might need a tutor."

"Tutors aren't so bad." I stop next to him. "Just find an older guy who he can look up to and think, 'Dude, he's cool.' It will plant a seed of initiative in him."

"Susie is already looking up tutors on the Internet. I think she had a sophomore girl picked out for him."

I wince. "I'm sure you're trying to dissuade her of that."

He makes a face at me. "Sure am. Last thing we need with him is a case of puppy love."

I chat with Mr. Peabody for a few more minutes and, when he leaves, head to the offices. Lilly follows me, so I look back at her with a smile. "Good morning, Lilly."

She glances up from where she has taken a seat behind her desk. "Good morning, Izze. Amala's dress came in last night."

"Fantastic," I say sarcastically as I walk over to my cubicle and stow my stuff underneath my desk, hanging my coat on the back of my chair.

"Oh, that's right. You have to dye the gown red. It's a shame we didn't get that on camera for the commercial. Maybe—"

I leap out of my cubicle and into the doorway of Lilly's cubicle, cutting her off. "Lilly Marshall, I cannot do that here. If you have any affection for me at all, you will not arrange for this to be filmed." I drop to my knees, and grip both of my hands together.

"Stop acting ridiculous." She says this sternly, but I can see the smile pulling at the corners of her mouth. We are making progress, people.

I get up and rub my sore knees. "Seriously, though. Please. I don't think I can handle dyeing my first gown red and then reliving the experience day after day on television."

She waves her hand at me. "Consider it forgotten. I think it will take longer for you to dye the gown red than to finish up the alterations. All she needs is the bustle made, right?"

"Right. I will call her today, and touch base so we can get this thing going."

She nods absently. "Good."

I head out to the desk and wave to Candace and her client. I like to do the delicate queen wave, as I walk to the front desk all slow and proper like. Too bad Lilly can't see me now.

After making a quick call to Amala to set up an appointment, Miles appears.

"Hey." He looks at me tentatively. For the first time since I met Miles, he looks unsure of himself. Probably has something to do with the way I avoided him all weekend.

After spotting Aunt Jill, I ran back into the theater and awkwardly watched the movie with Miles. I knew that he could tell something was wrong, and after the flashback and the sight I saw, several things were very wrong. *I Was a Male War Bride* is one of my favorite movies, but I felt like I hardly enjoyed it due to the way my mind raced. Unfortunately, Cary Grant's charm and charisma could not erase what I was feeling inside. After the movie, Miles asked if I wanted to get some ice cream. I said I didn't feel good and bowed out of the date early. I knew my acting skills weren't up to snuff, but I just didn't have it me that night. I've avoided him for the last few days.

"Hey," I say back. "How are you doing?" I wince at the stiffness in my voice. It isn't Miles's fault that I was traumatized. I need to get over this. I give myself a little pep talk.

"I'm good. How are you?" He looks at me pointedly.

"Oh, you know. I'm good. It's been busy, but you know that because you've been here." In the words of Chandler Bing from *Friends*: Could this *be* any more awkward?

"Yeah," he says quietly. He looks so confused and sad. It's killing me. I just don't think I can take it.

"I'm so sorry about the other night, Miles. I know I acted really weird. I can't get into it right now.... It's a long story."

"You know you can tell me anything. You can trust me, Izze."

I've heard that before.

Oy. I mentally slap myself. I heard that with someone else. Not Miles. He's different. I can trust him.

Can't I?

I nod and smile at him, but I can tell that yet another strained smile doesn't convince him.

And it doesn't convince me.

"Hey, Kaylee." I nod to my bestie as I attempt to open the door. My hands are very, very full. On the top of the pile is Amala's wedding dress, completely protected by not one, but two, plastic garment bags. A huge bag of red dye is slung over my right elbow. There is a bag of instructions labeled, "How to permanently dye your own clothes," slung over my left elbow, cushioned between my purse and another bag from the bookstore.

The word "permanently" keeps flopping around in my brain. I will be dyeing something permanently. There are no re-dos. If it's ruined, then that's it.

A particularly comforting thought when you are preparing to dye said garment for one of the most important days of someone's life. No pressure.

I am having visions of bags of money being flushed down the toilet.

I kick the door shut with my right foot, careful not to catch the dress in the doorframe.

I'm going to be a shriveled up, shaking woman by the time I deliver this dress to Amala.

Kaylee watches me from the couch, but you can tell she is only half watching me. I spy the notepad sitting on her lap. She must be working on a new song. Kaylee writes music. She doesn't share her songs with anyone, not even the church worship team. Despite this, she seems to pop a new one out almost every week.

I hold the dress over my head like it is baby Simba. "Behold," I bellow. "The gown soon to be the color of crimson. The gown that will make history. Truly this is an important moment. People will call and reporters will flock just begging for a description of this glorious moment."

"The moment before everything went horribly, horror movie kind of wrong," Kaylee says sarcastically.

I nod while walking to my room. "Yup, that about sums up the situation." After using a shoulder slam that would make any cop proud to open my bedroom door, I gently lay everything down on my bed. This isn't my wedding dress. If it were, I would be calling every three hours on the dot to make sure it was okay.

My cell phone starts to sing *Wedding Bell Blues*—an adorable old song about some woman complaining that she wanted to be married to her boyfriend, Bill. Humming the lyrics, I look at the caller ID.

Right on time.

"Hey, Amala."

"Izze, are you home yet?" She sounds slightly frantic. I shoot up a quick prayer. *Lord, when I get married, please don't let me act all nutty and obsessive. Even if it's the most important day of my life.*

"Yes, I just walked in the door. The gown is absolutely safe."

"Okay." She breathes out a relieved sigh. "When will you start the first treatment?"

"Tomorrow afternoon."

"Good. What's your mailing address?"

Curious. "It's twenty-one Other End Lane. Why?"

"I'm inviting you to my wedding, and before you say no, hear me out. You're doing so much for me. You are dyeing my wedding dress red for me in your own home, for crying out loud! How could I not invite you to my wedding? It would be my honor. And you can't say no because I'm the bride."

I snicker into my phone. "Well, I suppose I can't argue with any of that. I would be honored to be there."

We chat about the wedding for a few more minutes, and I promise to send her a picture of the gown tomorrow after the first treatment. Tugging open my dresser drawer, I grab my favorite pair of coffee cup pajamas. I need to get some sleep. I have a long day ahead of me tomorrow.

I stare at the wedding gown in the upstairs bathtub.

After I brought it home last night, I hung it from the shower rod with the skirt flowing into the bathtub. The white satin looks a little out of place next to the black shower curtain spotted with pink flamingos.

How do I do this?

I've never dyed anything, not even my hair, and now I'm staring at the wedding dress I will most likely butcher.

Think positive thoughts. I breathe deep. All those exercising, yoga-like people tell you to breathe deep.

Really it's just hurting my gut.

I have had a reoccurring nightmare of this experience ever since Lilly roped me into it. In my dream, I'm trying to scoop the wedding dress out of the red vat of dye and instead, I fall into it. I'm flailing around, trying to breathe through the burning, red water, but the gown has wrapped itself around me, pulling me farther into the red depths.

Then I wake up. I swear, when I looked in the mirror first thing this morning, I looked redder.

Kaylee said I was crazy and should see a therapist. Apryl said I should wear a full body suit when I do this. Courtney said if this does happen, she would file a substantial lawsuit with the intention of receiving a huge, legal settlement from the manufactures to compensate for my untimely demise. My friends are so helpful.

I sigh. It's now or never. I spent hours reading instructions online on how to dye a satin gown, and that's in addition to all the material Amala sent me.

I turn the shower on as hot as I possibly can and take out two of the six bottles of red dye that Amala dropped off at Ever After earlier this week.

"That's a lot of red dye," I'd gasped to her.

"Yes." She beamed at me. "I've been reading up on how to dye satin. I've printed some examples for you. Most of the results were lighter than expected. So I got one of the darkest reds, and enough bottles to repeat the process three times."

Words could not describe how happy I was when she told me that.

Next, I put the stopper in the tub, and water swirls around, collecting and building. I jury-rig the shower so the water is spraying from the shower head as well as the tub faucet.

Time to pop open the dye. I gag. Oh, that's nasty smelling! Holding my nose with my left hand, I dump the bottles into the tub with my right hand.

The smell penetrates my hand barrier. I toss the second, empty bottle into the garbage and open a window. Ah, nothing like an eight degree, deep freeze in March to rush your nose and kill any sense of smell you have. However, I would rather deal with that than have the smell build up and burn my eyeballs out of their sockets.

Then I do it.

I take off the heavy, plastic garment bag.

I feel like I'm about to commit a sin.

I put the dress in the tub. The dark water soaks into the gown. I shoot up a quick prayer. *Please let this work!*

Once the tub is full and the dress is thoroughly soaked, I pull on some heavy duty dishwashing gloves that Amala sent along with the red dye. I carefully swirl the gown through the water, avoiding any splashing. I'm wearing some old jeans I had unearthed from the back of my closet, and a pajama shirt, but I still don't want any accidental damage.

The directions told me to use some kind of stick to stir, but I didn't want to risk stabbing holes into the gown on top of destroying it.

Why didn't she just get a professional to do this?

Steam rises off the water, giving the surface of the tub an unearthly look. The water is hot. Thankfully, I had the gloves in the freezer before this, and I have a bucket of ice water standing by for temporary relief.

Okay, this isn't so bad. I swirl the red water with my left hand while slowly jiggling the watery gown up and down with my right hand.

I do this for a while. I focus on the music playing in the hall. I didn't want to bring the MP3 player and portable dock into the bathroom.

Electrocution and all that. I'm terribly paranoid about that. It's one of my pet peeves.

How long has it been?

"Apryl!"

"What?" Her voice is muffled. Sounds like she's downstairs.

Yep. The walls are that thin.

"How long have I been in here?"

"What?"

"How long have I been in the bathroom?"

"Hold on. I'm coming up there." I hear some tromping. "Hey." She sticks her head in the bathroom. "What's up?" She does that chin up gesture to me. Her feathery black hair flies with each movement and then slowly settles back down.

"Oh, you know. Not much." I jerk my head toward the tub. "Just dyeing a wedding dress red. Nothing out of the ordinary."

She nods. "Cool."

"What time is it?"

"It's six-thirty."

So, I've been in here for thirty minutes. "Great, time to let her dry. Round two will commence in one week."

She smirks and ducks back into the hallway. Apryl watches from the safety of the hallway, where the air must be crisp and delicious.

Standing up, I pull the dripping dress out of the water and hang it back onto the shower rod. Now, that water is so dark, you'd almost think it was black. Amala's vision is crimson. The dress is a pastel pink.

"Oh, that's not good," Apryl mutters.

Don't panic. Take deep breaths. There are still two more treatments.

"I'm not panicking," Apryl says.

I must have chanted out loud. "Sorry. I was talking to myself."

Apryl nods. This is not an unusual habit for me. "What are you going to do?"

I shake my head. "The bride purchased enough dye for me to repeat the process two more times. Next time, I will probably let it soak longer than the twenty-five minutes that the directions said." I pull the plug on the drain and dump the ice water into the tub. It will take at least twenty minutes of scrubbing, so I get started

on that process. Ah, the price you pay to give reassurance that no one was murdered in your bathtub.

"Okay. Holler if you need anything else." With her hair swishing like a black cape, Apryl turns and tromps back downstairs.

The dress is still dripping dry, and I plan to leave it there overnight. Everyone has been instructed not to go into this bathroom. Not even under the pains of death.

I yank the gloves off my sweaty hands and wash them in the sink. There is a lot of red in the sink. At first I think it's actually the sink, but I never put any dye in there. Then, as I dry my hands, I realize what's happened.

The sink is red because of my hands.

My hands are red. Red, red, red. They look like a five-year-old who stuck his hands into the paint while his brush lies forgotten on the floor.

I've dyed my hands red.

What am I going to do?

"Apryl!" I scream at the top of my lungs.

Chapter Twelve

I tried running my hands under nearly-boiling water.

Didn't help at all.

I called my doctor.

She just laughed at me.

I called the manufacturer number listed on the bottle.

All they could tell me was that *eventually* it would wash out, and no, I wasn't going to die from it.

Swell.

My hands are not the only thing that remained red. The upstairs tub is covered in cherry red splotches. I dumped five gallons of bleach into the tub—promptly threw up—and left it to sit for a couple days. So far no luck with that.

So now I am walking into work with red hands.

"Hey Izze, how are you?" Candace asks from behind her desk, and I can tell the exact second she sees my hands. Her eyes form the shape of two very large dinner plates. "What happened to your hands?"

Miles is on the phone but pokes his head out from his cubicle to see me, a concerned look on his face. He raises an eyebrow at me, and I mouth *I'll tell you later* to him. He nods and keeps talking into his cell phone about numbers and profit margins.

"Nothing." I dump my purse on my desk, walk out of the offices

to the front desk, and wordlessly log into the computer. Candace follows me though.

"Izze," Candace says again, completely incredulous.

"I'm making homemade tomato sauce, and I apparently squeezed too many tomatoes."

"Really?"

"Yup. End of story." I purse my lips at Candace and flicker my eyes to the women who are browsing the flower girl dresses. Please take the hint.

"Okay," she says slowly.

The door jingles open, and an older woman with two brunette teenage girls come inside. "Hello," the older woman says. "I have an appointment with Izze? My name is Claire Bronxer."

"Hello, Claire," I stick my hand out there before I think about what I'm doing. She looks at it like I've just offered her frog intestines on a silver platter. She looks back up at me completely horrified, and I swear her hair just got a little grayer.

"Yeah, my hands are red. Little mishap with some clothing dye. No worries. It won't transfer onto you." I rub both hands on the white sweater covering my upper arms. "See? No red marks."

Claire still looks terrified, but carefully takes the tips of my fingers, gives them a quick squeeze, and then immediately pulls them back to inspect.

Now that she seems satisfied, I lead her and the two girls who she introduces as her daughters, Emme and Jayda, back to the second consultant room.

"So Claire, what kind of gown do you think you would like to wear?" I pull the cap off my pen with my teeth and poise it above the paper, ready to take notes.

"Well, my husband and I are renewing our vows," Claire starts.

Here's the thing: I don't have any problem with renewing your vows—except with the word "renewing." It's kind of like implying that the first time you said your vows was only good for a few years, and now it's time to renew them so that they will last for the next few years. Here's my opinion: If you want to have another, fancier party with the gorgeous dress, then have at it. Your vows don't run out, though.

I'm just saying.

Claire has this short, honey-colored hair. Her daughters must get their hair coloring from their father. "I'd like something very elegant and understated. Very little to no extra detail."

Emme, the older looking of the two girls, leans forward. "But we think that she needs a lot of sparkle. The ceremony and reception are being held at a yacht club at sunset. She needs to pop." She leans back with a coy smile on her face.

"That's right," Jayda says and points at Claire. "Our dad is in the military, and he is going to be wearing his dress whites for the ceremony. He's been gone for the last two years, so she needs to look like a million bucks."

Aww. See, that's a good reason to renew your vows. I'm all into this appointment now.

"Okay." I slap my notebook close. "I'm going to go pull some gowns for you, Claire. You guys wait here. I'll be right back." In the storeroom, I'm picking some simple gowns like the ones Claire described, some sparkly ones like her girls wanted, and some that are a meld of the two styles.

"Okay," I singsong once I'm back in the changing room, hanging up the gowns. "Claire, why don't you come in here and get into one of these gowns. Crack the door open when you're ready for me to button the back."

Claire goes in and cracks the door just moments later. She is wearing one of the simple ones. It is a slim A-line fit with no train and made out of heavy satin. The color is diamond white, which means it hurts your eyes because it is so bright, and it has thick

straps that plunge into a deep V-neck. However, it still looks classy because the only detail on the dress is the lace coming out of the V-neck, completely covering the plunging neckline.

She swishes in the skirt a little bit. "I like this one." She smiles and gathers her hair into a makeshift twist on the top of her head. "I can see me in this."

"Mom," Jayda whines. "This is supposed to be something completely out of the ordinary for you. It needs to dazzle."

Claire rolls her eyes. "I'll try on one of the sparkly ones."

The next dress Claire comes out in is an instant winner with her daughters. It is also an A-line fit with no train, but it is much more body-hugging. It is also a diamond white, but it is covered from head to toe with pearls and clear beads.

"Oh, this is the one." Emme claps her hands and squeals. "You look so beautiful."

Clare tries on all the gowns I brought for her before they officially narrow it down to the first one and the second one.

Claire studies herself in the full length mirror once again. "I don't hate it. It's actually really pretty. I just think the other gown is better for someone my age."

"Oh, age, smage." Jayda waves her hand. "What do you think, Izze?" Six eyes swing to me, waiting to hear my opinion.

"Oh," I stutter. "It's not my decision."

"You must think she looks better in this one, right?" Jayda's silver-blue eyes narrow at me.

I nervously start to twirl the ends of my hair. "I honestly think she looks beautiful in all of them, but really, it's what your mom wants. It is her day, after all."

In the end, Claire decides on the sparkly, dramatically beaded gown for her daughters. "They love this one so much, I just couldn't tell them no," she said to me at the front desk.

Honestly, they all looked good on her. As long as she's happy, then I'm happy. That, and I won't remember this appointment in three months anyway.

At the end of the day, only six more people have freaked out at the sight of my hands, and only one of them threw a two-year-old temper tantrum and insisted someone else work with them instead.

I'm ringing up the last customer when Lilly sticks her head out of the office.

"Have a good day!" I smile at the bride and her mother who just purchased a two-thousand-dollar gown.

Lilly waits for them to leave before speaking. "Can you come back here for a second?"

"Sure."

"Somebody's in trouble," Candace singsongs.

"Oh, hush now." All the same, I don't dally and make Lilly wait for me.

"Hey Lilly." I walk into her cubicle and sit down. "What's up?"

I see her cringe at a greeting so cavalier, but to her ever-growing credit, she doesn't say anything. "I wanted to talk with you about two things."

"Su—" I start to say sure, but opt for a more professional sounding answer. "Yes, ma'am."

See? Much better.

"Well first, I wanted to see what you thought about hiring another consultant."

I am all ears now. "I think that would be an awesome idea." Seriously, the way things are going, if we don't get some more help soon we are all going to burn out.

"Really?" Her brow furrows like she just doesn't see it.

"Yes. Lilly, it's crazy here, and business is only going to get steadier." She nods along with my logic, so I continue. "Some help would be great. We'd be able to see more brides, cover breaks, handle the special sales better. It's a perfect idea!"

"Miles approached me about it. He thought it might help productivity."

Why am I not surprised? Instead of being filled with annoyance like I would have been before, I'm actually proud of him and happy he thought of this idea.

Lilly motions to the paperwork on her desk. "The only problem is that the money just isn't there, but Miles is going to look into the problem."

I nod like I'm down with the program, but really the budget is outside of my area of expertise. This is a great road stop for learning, though. "Okay."

"The other thing is that I think Amala should try on her gown here during the next sale day once the treatments are finished.

"Lilly!"

"The world isn't watching you dye the gown and stain your hands redder than they are. They are just watching a bride try on a unique gown. Plus, the fact that we—"

I cut her off. "Not we. I."

"Plus the fact that *you*"—she *enunciates* this—"dyed this gown is a huge bonus point for us."

"What if more brides come expecting us to dye their gowns funky colors?"

She blinks, apparently just seeing the image of a bride in a tie-dyed gown walking out of our shop, spreading our reputation everywhere. We would be the COLOR to Vera Wang's WHITE collection. "I didn't think about that. I guess we will cross that bridge when we get to it. How many more treatments do you have left on Amala's gown?"

I control myself from growling. She is my boss. I need to respect that. "Two more treatments."

"Okay, how long apart?"

"It really just needs a couple days to dry, so I can clear it with

Amala, and have her in for her first fitting in about ten days." I sigh. I have resigned myself to this fate.

If anyone starts critiquing how terrible the color looks, I might attack them with a hoop skirt. I said approximately three hundred and seventy-two times that I am not a professional at this.

Oh, why a hoop skirt? Those things can cause bodily harm. I was unpacking a shipment of the hoop underskirts once, and then basically launched ten of the thirty at myself. How was I supposed to know that the only thing holding them inside was the tape on the box? They hurt a lot.

◦◦◦ ♥ ◦◦◦

My phone rings the second I get home. I kick off my shoes, rip off my coat, and drop my stuff while hitting TALK with my right hand. "Hello?"

"So when are you going to tell me what happened to your hands?"

I smile at the sound of Miles's voice. He had to leave right after finishing his phone call, so I never got a chance to tell him what happened.

"Well," I start. "Once upon a time, in a galaxy far, far away."

"Izze."

"Shush. Don't interrupt."

He sighs dramatically into my ear, and I settle into my cozy chair. "Once upon a time, in a galaxy far, far away there lived a talented and beautiful bridal consultant. One day a fair maiden from a neighboring planet—"

"Planet?"

"Yes, planet. Anyways, this maiden requested a red gown to wear to her wedding feast. An evil force coerced the hearts of many people until the talented and beautiful bridal consultant

was forced to dye the gorgeous white gown red all by herself."

"Lilly?" Miles interrupts again.

"No," I whisper. "An evil force." I let those words hang in the air menacingly.

"Izze."

"Miles."

"The abridged version, please."

Some people just can't appreciate the spice of life. "I was dyeing the gown red and the gloves I wore weren't very good."

"Well, I like your red hands."

I snort. "Sure you do."

"I do. I think you should keep them red. They suit your personality better."

Now I'm shaking my head. "Sure they do."

"So when can I see you again? Outside of Ever After."

Whew. It seems he's decided to shake off the other night at the theater. That's a good thing. I'm not sure I'm ready to get into all of that stuff.

"I don't know. When is the next monthly sale?" I tease. Even though we started dating due to the sale, I think that deal has pretty much flown out the window. I like seeing this guy way too much to only stick to one date a month. I just need to ignore all those old memories, and then everything will be fine. Right?

"Soon, please. I miss you." His voice gets all soft and tender, and my pulse quickens.

I like hearing Miles say that.

Miles grinned as he walked into Whipped Cream. "Well, well. Who do we have here?"

"Yeah. Yeah. It's not that shocking. My cousins own a coffee

shop. Of course I'm here before work. I get free coffee."

"Think again," Grant says from behind the cash register, counting the drawer.

Izze ignored him. "The real question is what are *you* doing here?"

"Well, I heard about the free coffee."

Grant looked up from his counting. "Are you telling people that, Izze? No one is getting free coffee."

She continued to ignore Grant. "But you don't like coffee."

"I like coffee sometimes."

"Mm hmm. I think you should admit that you were hoping to see me."

"Izze," Miles said in a low voice. "I was hoping to see you."

"Why?" She tossed her curls over her shoulder and tilted her head back to look him in the eye.

"The red hands. I'm a sucker for a girl with red hands."

Izze rolled her eyes. "Hilarious."

They both ordered and paid for their coffee, then walked over to a table next to a picture of a sailboat. Miles thought it was a little weird to have such a beach themed restaurant in the middle of a state that had three months of beach weather a year, but Izze insisted people wanted to be reminded that the snow and ice eventually melted.

"So I hear that you've convinced Lilly to hire another consultant," Izze said. She looked at Miles over the top of her coffee cup.

"Uh oh. Are you going to berate me for making yet another change?"

"No. I actually think this is a good change."

"I'm sorry. For a second I actually thought you said this was a good change. I must have wax in my ear."

Izze gagged. "Dude, that's gross. Especially before I've had

my first cup of coffee." She held up her paper coffee cup to prove her point.

He leaned forward. "Say it again."

"Fine." She glared. "It's a good change. Good job. Magnificent. Wonderful job. Let's have a round of applause for Mr. Bigshot." She stood up and clapped. The three other customers who happened to be there gave her blank, bleary-eyed looks. Apparently they hadn't drunk enough coffee this morning either.

"Thank you. Thank you. The cheers are not quite loud enough though."

"Oh, be quiet." She sat and took another sip.

"Seriously, though, thank you. It means a lot to me."

She shrugged and bit her lip. "Ever After means a lot to me. It's home. I love it there, so I'm protective of my territory. Like a momma bear."

"Izze," Miles said, taking both of her hands in his. "I know how important Ever After is to you. All the changes I've made are to help it flourish. All the changes I will make, will be for the good of the store. I promise."

"Really?"

He squeezed her hands. "I said I promise, and I mean it."

Izze pursed her lips and took a deep breath, and Miles could tell that she was deciding to trust him, just a little. Finally, she squeezed his hands back. "Okay."

Chapter Thirteen

Well, it is finished. I stand back and admire the luscious red gown hanging off the mannequin at Ever After.

Amala had no problem with rushing the treatments. In fact, I think the idea made her happy. I mean, who wants to wait three weeks after their gown comes in before trying it on again?

It is a stunning crimson color. I did that. I want to do a little happy dance for the world to see. This gown looks that good. I can't wait for Amala to see it.

The gown is set up in the middle of the room toward the back wall. Brides are milling around the room, looking at the different veils and headwear that are on sale today, but each one of them stops and stares at Amala's dress. Some, to my utter horror, say they want a gown just like that.

The guest of honor arrives a few agonizingly slow minutes later. She runs up the sidewalk and through the doors, but the minute her eyes locate her dress, she freezes perfectly still.

"I can't believe it," she says finally. Her face is completely expressionless, and her mouth hangs slightly agape.

What do you think? Does that mean she likes it?

Amala must have hit the pavement running, because Daya and Charlie are just pushing the door open. They see it, and Daya immediately starts blubbering while Charlie hops up and down.

"Try it on! Try it on!" she squeals.

Amala's gaze swings to me, and I give a little nod. Her face splits into the biggest grin I have ever seen on her. She follows me as I wheel the mannequin into one of the consultant rooms.

She looks thrilled.

I undo the gown from the mannequin's form and hang it up for Amala. "I'll be right outside."

She slips into the gown quickly and cracks the door open, signaling me to come in. "Do you see this?" She stares at herself in the mirror. The lace motif, the way it hugs her shape and then flows out in exactly the right spots make the dress look truly perfect on her. If I weren't already positive this was The Dress, I would be convinced now. The red looks perfect against her natural tan.

I did good.

"It looks incredible, Izze!"

I start tugging and pulling the gown to fit around her exactly right. I can see that it is a little long on her, and the bustle needs to be made, but that's why we have Kaylee. She's waiting in the lobby, pins and measuring tape poised and ready.

"Izze, how am I ever going to repay you?"

I pretend to think about it for a minute. "Don't make me participate when you throw the bouquet." I hate that ritual. It may be funny for the bride and all the happily married ladies to watch girls clawing one another's eyes out, but speaking as someone who survived such an incident, it's really not that fun.

My second cousin's wedding was rough. I had the bouquet, but some snotty girl yanked it out of my hands and took off running. Not a happy memory for me or my mother. She wants grandchildren.

Amala straightens the smooth fabric on her stomach. "It just feels so soft. I love how it looks on me." She catches my eye in the mirror. "Anything else I can do for you? I owe you big time."

"What kind of cake are you having at your reception?"

"Mocha truffle with a raspberry filling and butter cream icing."

I nod, salivating like a dog. "I want two big slices of cake. One for the reception and one to take home."

"Done."

I finish tugging the dress to a close around her perfect frame. "Well, my friend, your public awaits you. You look like an old Hollywood star."

"Perfect!"

I open the door and go out first, immediately moving to the left and dramatically presenting the empty doorframe with a sweeping gesture. "Ladies and gentlemen, it's the moment you've all patiently awaited. I give you Amala Wilson." With that I dramatically bow and back away, and Amala fills the doorframe.

Everyone showers Amala in praise, and I grin. Kaylee directs Amala to stand on a small pedestal so she can begin measuring and adjusting the hem.

Thank you, Lord, for having Lilly force me into doing this. Otherwise, I never would have been a part of this, and it was worth every second spent on it. Red hands and all.

❤

"Well, another satisfied customer." Miles says as I open the door to greet him for our impromptu celebration date.

"I'll say."

"She seemed really happy with it today."

I nod, and we wave good-bye to Apryl, Courtney, and Kaylee. They have stopped following us on our dates and barely acknowledge us anymore. "Thankfully, because there is no way to fix a white dress once it's been dyed red. I looked it up on the Internet just to be sure."

"I don't think that needed Internet validation." He opens the car door for me.

I shrug once seated. "It's comforting to know. So what are we doing tonight?"

"I thought we would go out for a nice dinner at that seafood place and then walk down the street to the bookstore."

I nod along, but as soon as he mentions a bookstore, I sit up straight. "The Christian bookstore that is down the street?"

Miles looks over at me briefly before redirecting his eyes to the road. "Yup. After that I thought we'd get ice cream."

"That sounds perfect."

"I know."

"Cocky."

"I prefer that it be looked at as an excellent way of anticipating your needs."

"I need ice cream to add to the pounds on my hips?" I fake an attitude.

"Your hips are perfect just the way God made them." He winks at me. "What about the books?"

"What about them?"

"Well, do you need more books?"

"Miles," I say completely aghast. "I always need more books."

"Well then, you just proved my point."

Miles and I were having a perfectly lovely evening until right about now.

We ate a delicious dinner of fried scallops and French fries, browsed the bookstore for over an hour, before he sweetly bought two books for me and dragged me out before I could find more. We delivered my new treasures to the car and walked to Ginnie's,

the ice cream shop which is renowned for their homemade ice cream and fudge brownies.

He was talking about his childhood and high school years while I nodded occasionally and ate my ice cream out of the little Styrofoam bowl. My mother started telling me from a young age not to eat ice cream cones on a date. The slurping, licking, and general pigging out is not attractive to a perspective mate. That little rule has always worked out well for me because I don't like ice cream cones that much.

All of a sudden he says, "What about you?"

I lick another scoop of ice cream off my spoon to buy some time. We are just kind of walking down the sidewalk. It's warmed up considerably this month. It's about fifty-seven degrees right now. And after having a winter averaging negative twenty degrees, fifty-seven is like summertime in New Hampshire. There are even people walking around in shorts and T-shirts.

"What do you mean?"

He gives me a funny look. "I thought it was self-explanatory. Tell me about your childhood, your family, and your most embarrassing high school moments. I want to know more about you."

I quickly scoop another bite of peach ice cream into my mouth. My most embarrassing high school moment? How do I tell Miles that my most embarrassing high school moment consists of my old boyfriend dumping me for someone else?

I don't know what to say. My ballet flats are slapping loudly against the sidewalk. When several minutes pass and I still don't answer, Miles tries another approach.

"Did you go to college?"

Ah, an elemental question you would have thought we would have covered much earlier in the relationship. However, anytime my past has come up, I've expertly changed the subject.

Tonight I am having no such luck.

Tell me, how do I tell my current boyfriend that I didn't go to college because my former boyfriend talked me out of going to college so that we could save up and get married the year after I graduated high school?

"No." Hopefully that will suffice.

"Why not?"

"Because." My answer is quick and sharp, and he looks at me surprised. "Look at that sunset, will you?" I point at the sunset in front of us. The sky goes from bright pink and muted purple to pastel blue at the top. Very pretty.

He doesn't even glance at it.

"Izze." He takes my hand, gently pulling me to a stop. "What's wrong?"

"Nothing." I know I sound annoyed, but I just don't want to talk about this. Why can't he just drop it? "Is it a crime that I didn't go to college?"

He answers my question with one of his own. "Why don't you want to talk about it?"

"There's nothing to talk about." My hands inadvertently ball into little fists.

"You act like you don't want to tell me about yourself. Why?"

"There is nothing to talk about." I say each word slowly and with enough poison to stop a mammoth in its tracks.

"Look, I'm not asking for a chart about your family's medical history. I'm not asking for a list of past boyfriends. I'm not asking to meet the parents. I'm just asking my girlfriend about her life before I met her because I'm interested in getting to know her better." He's waving his left hand around like I've noticed he does when he's upset.

"We are still getting to know each other. You don't need to know everything about me immediately." I know that as soon as I say it that it was the wrong thing to say. The worst possible thing to say.

I can literally see my words smack him in the face.

His nostrils flare up, and his blue eyes darken with anger. He doesn't say anything; he just throws his half-eaten ice cream cone into the nearest trash can. He continues walking toward the car, and I mutely follow behind him.

When we get there, I throw my melted cup of ice cream into the trash right before getting inside. He starts the car, puts it in reverse, and backs out of the parking space without a word. He drives me home in silence and doesn't even turn on the radio or pop a CD into the player. He just drives with this angry glower on his face.

Finally, after the longest car ride known to man, we pull into my driveway. Miles turns the key and yanks it out of the ignition. Neither one of us moves. We both just sit there fuming.

"I'm sorry," I finally say.

He doesn't respond at first. He looks out the dark window, at the lights glowing from his dashboard, and at the steering wheel before he finally looks at me. All I can see on his face is the hurt. The hurt that says I won't let him completely into my heart, and he knows it.

"Look, I know everyone's past isn't all sugar, spice, and *Powerpuff Girls*, but Izze, you've got to decide if you're going to trust me. No, forget me. Trust God."

Say it. Say it. Come on and say it. Say, *I trust you. And God.*

I open and close my mouth seven times, but nothing ever comes out of it. "I'm sorry," I say again while massaging my temple. I'm getting a headache from all this stress.

He sighs, recognizing that we are not getting anywhere with this tonight. "Look. I'll call you later. It's late. We should both get some sleep."

I nod because my throat closes, preventing me from speaking. I open the door and climb out, and Miles says, "Good night, Izze." Then he disappears down the street. I stare after his car for a long time before I go inside to cry a river that will take me to dreamland.

Four hours after he had dropped Izze off, Miles found himself at his office. He had gone home first and, in a vain attempt to distract himself from his relationship problems, played a video game for a while. Despite the fact that he had set a new record which would have his older brother crying in an outrage, he didn't feel any better.

When that failed, Miles decided he might as well be doing something productive, so he went to his folding table at Ever After to work. Lilly had given him a key shortly after he had started, but not without reminding him that there were security cameras.

Right. Like he was going to steal wedding dresses. But as Miles had come to learn, that was just Lilly being Lilly.

Determined and focused—well, sort of focused—he went through file after file, trying to figure out why there wasn't room in the budget for a third consultant.

How had Ever After survived for so long?

"How are they even affording this?" Miles asked himself. He compared the numbers on his spreadsheet to those on the computer. Sighing, he stood up. He needed to stop staring at the computer screen before the white light permanently burned his corneas.

Sitting back down, Miles looked into the older records. The more Miles looked, the more he realized that Izze's aunt Jill had taken a huge pay cut to help everyone else stay afloat. However, the store was dwindling because of it. They had limited resources, limited time, and limited revenue.

Thanks to the monthly sales, they were turning a profit again, but would that trend continue? Miles thought about his promise to Izze. He had promised he would do everything in his power to help Ever After.

And he meant it.

In order to keep his promise, and make Ever After the family legacy Izze envisioned it to be, there was only one solution.

Miles took a sip of his water, the wheels in his head churning. There may be only one solution, but he was brilliantly creative—not to be arrogant. He could make this work. Yes, he could. He would be able to keep his promise to Izze, while at the same time making a profit for Ever After.

Chapter Fourteen

Mrs. Sherman eyeballs my red-stained hands like she's worried some of the color will transfer onto the sample gown her granddaughter picked.

"Be careful with those, dear," she calls out after me. I throw a forced smile over my shoulder and knock on the door before entering the changing room.

Her granddaughter, Minnie Sherman, waits not so patiently for me. "There you are." Exasperation drips from her words. She is a younger, snottier version of her grandmother.

Sorry, Lord. Help me be nice.

"The red on your hands isn't going to get on my dress, is it?" She looks pointedly at them.

"Nope," I say while hanging the dresses up, one by one. "We made sure of that before I started working. Rest assured that they have been scrubbed raw, which I personally think happens to make up most of the color on them at this point."

"Whatever."

This ought to be fun.

She points at the rack. "These are all the gowns I picked out, right?"

I smile, closed mouthed, and nod twice.

She sighs again. "Okay. I'd like to try this one on first."

I slip out of the room while she shimmies into the gown. Mrs. Sherman sits across from me, with her thin, penciled-in eyebrows raised at me.

"So," I say lightly. I might as well make small talk. "Minnie's parents must be thrilled that she's engaged."

Mrs. Sherman shrugs. "They are. I flew Minnie out here special so that I could buy her wedding gown."

I frown. Why fly out here when they could have gone somewhere like New York City?

"Her mother was going to make Minnie's gown." Mrs. Sherman says this like it was suggested that Minnie wear a white sheet down the aisle. "I told my son that was simply unacceptable and flew Minnie out here. She should really go shopping with me, anyway."

"I'm ready." Minnie's muffled voice comes from the changing room. I briefly look at the door, and then back at Mrs. Sherman. I imagine I look like a deer caught in the headlights. I'm not sure who is worse.

I duck back into the room with Minnie. She models a vintage style mermaid. It's so clingy my mother would have deemed it completely inappropriate, and the sweetheart neckline leaves little to the imagination.

I never understand how some people are comfortable dressing like that. I wouldn't even feel comfortable modeling that gown in front of a bunch of old women, and there's no way I'd bend over for anything without having one hand firmly planted over my chest.

Mrs. Sherman and Minnie coo over that gown and the four other bead-and-lace-covered mermaid gowns she tries today. Minnie ends up purchasing a six-thousand-dollar dress, one of the priciest that we keep in stock.

I do a little happy dance when I see their car drive out of the lot. Just because a person goes to church doesn't mean they are easy to get along with, and they are the frosting on top of that

metaphorical cupcake theory.

We've been busy today. There is no doubt that the monthly sales are drawing in extra business. A few months ago, I was making up show tunes to keep entertained. Now I'm so busy, I can't even eat those carrot sticks I brought with me for breakfast.

Okay, it was actually a muffin. I should pick up some carrot sticks if the increasing numbers shown on the bathroom scale this morning are any indication.

There are no less than twenty gowns that need to be brought back to the stockroom. They are all hanging on a rack. Candace is on her lunch break still, but I might as well put these back.

Wheeling the rack in while humming a song by Brit Nicole, I set to work. Soon, I'm not paying attention to anything around me, just completely belting out the song in my heart. I raise my hands up, not even bothering to set down the empty hangers in my hands. God is so cool; He even hangs out in a stockroom.

Something touches my shoulder, and I scream. I whirl around with the coat hangers still in my hands, prepared to valiantly face my attacker.

Which happens to be Miles, and he is smiling sweetly at me with a to-go bag from Dunkin' Donuts in his tanned hand. I hope it has a blueberry donut in it.

"What's that?" I point at the bag.

"Hello to you, too."

"Is that for me?" I give him my best puppy dog eyes.

"Really, it's so good to see you."

"Maybe a blueberry glazed donut?'

"Izze."

"Fine. Good morning, my dear friend. Perchance, is there a blueberry donut in the bag for me?"

"Yes, my dear Izze. There is."

My dear Izze. My entire face breaks out into a common rash

known as a blush.

Miles winks at me, the action sending yet another flutter from my heart all the way down to my toes.

Sometimes I really think attraction and falling in love are not healthy for the human body.

I take the bag from his outstretched hand and open it. Taking just a moment, I inhale the sweet scent of blueberry.

"Ah. That's right."

He raises an eyebrow at me but wisely doesn't comment. Things have been so much better between us. It's been good. He's seemed to bounce back to his old self after our terrible fight last week. He called me the day after, but he didn't bring up the fight, so I didn't either. There have been a lot of awkward phone conversations and clumsy waves to each other at work.

"What are you doing here?"

"Oh, I just came to work with Lilly on something." He glances away quickly, but then makes a grab for my donut. "Can I have a bite?"

"No."

He frowns.

I grin, and hold it out to him. "Go ahead." He proceeds to take a mammoth size bite. "Thanks," he says after he swallows.

I finish the donut and give him a quick hug, relishing the feel of his strong arms around me. We just stand there for a minute.

"Well." He holds me back slightly and smiles. "I should get in to help Lilly."

"Don't tell her that we had food in here!"

"I won't." He hesitates. "Izze?"

"Yeah?"

"You are so special to me. I'm so glad that God has brought you and your crazy little antics into my life."

"Thanks," I say dryly, but I flash him a sappy smile. "I'll see

you later?"

"Yeah." Once he's gone, I finish up in the stockroom and head back to the front desk. Candace stands there, looking happily fed.

We tend to get cranky when we don't eat.

"Your turn," her singsong voice announces.

"Sweet. I'll see you soon." I walk into the offices and grab my purse from under my desk. Instead of leaving, I stop in front of Lilly's cubicle. She and Miles are quietly discussing something, but abruptly stop the moment they see me. Miles smiles uncomfortably at me, but Lilly's curt question catches me off guard. "What is it, Izze?"

I blink in surprise. "Nothing. I just wanted to let you know that Candace is back, and I'm heading to lunch now."

"Okay," she says, softening her tone. "Have a good lunch."

"Thanks." I send Miles a what-is-with-her look, but he's got a weird, uncomfortable look, too. I shut the door behind me and wave to Candace. Once in my car, I catch a glimpse of Kaylee walking into Ever After. Weird. I didn't think we had any alterations scheduled for today.

I drive to the nearest Wendy's and park my car. Inside the warm fast food restaurant, I will eat my burger and fries while reading the book that I tucked into my purse this morning.

My father once told me it was bad to eat and read at the same time because both required a lot of mental focus, and if I was doing both at the same time, then neither would be done to the best of my ability.

The lesson to take away from his little fun fact was that I could choke to death if I was reading instead of focusing on properly chewing my food.

Dear old Dad.

My hour ends much too quickly, and I begrudgingly put my book away, dump my trash, and dash to my car. I drive five miles over the speed limit the entire time, but I make it back to Ever After with three minutes to spare.

Looking around, I don't see Kaylee's car. Bummer. It is really nice working with your best friend, you know? It opens the door to a lot of girl talk.

Pulling the glass door open, I immediately freeze. If ever I have felt tense air, it's now. It's so thick, it's like looking through Jell-O.

Tentatively stepping into the empty lobby, I search for someone nice who will shed some light on this.

"Candace?" I whisper while crouching behind a mannequin. I hope Mrs. Sherman and Minnie didn't come back to wreak more havoc.

"Izze?"

"Yeah. Where are you?"

Candace appears out of the first appointment room looking upset. "I was just trying to call you from back there. I didn't want anyone to hear me."

"What's going on here?" I wave my arms around to indicate the Jell-O like tension.

"Kaylee came in, literally just seconds after you left. Lilly had a meeting with her, and Miles was there, too. I was just minding my own business, but I got a phone call from your last client, Mrs. Sherman and her granddaughter."

"Oh, I knew it! They are going to be more trouble than they are worth. They kept saying that we should order the newest Vera Wang for her to try on, but at the last minute they decided on a different gown. They had me put a rush order on it. If they cancel that, there's going to be a huge fee and one angry designer." I drop my purse on the counter, and make a grab for the phone while looking up the number for the designer in the computer.

Candace grabs my arm with one hand and sets the phone down with the other. "Izze, that's not it."

"What is it then?" There is a sinking feeling in my stomach. I already know that whatever it is, it is much worse than Mrs. Sherman. My left eye starts twitching.

"They fired Kaylee."

I stare at her for a full minute, and then laugh. "Nice job. Did Miles put you up to that? It's not funny, but you pulled that off beautifully."

"I'm serious." Candace's eyes are not sparkling with humor. Her expression is tight like she's clenching her jaw. "I went back into the office so that I could have Lilly speak with Mrs. Sherman personally. I heard Lilly say that unfortunately, she needed to let her go. Then Miles spoke up and said that he had been over the budget, and that there was no way for them to hire a third consultant while keeping her on part time."

"They are going to reallocate her salary to pay for another consultant?"

"Yes."

"What about alterations? Are we just supposed to tell our customers to figure that out themselves?" My anger gets stronger with every word. I trusted them. I trusted Lilly, and I trusted another man who betrayed me.

Candace continues her saga. She sure eavesdropped a lot of information. "Apparently Miles has arranged a contract with Sew Magical down the street. They will do alterations for our brides at a ten percent discount for them, and we will be advertising them. They will be on our business cards, brochures, the website, the works."

My head feels like it has been spun in a hundred circles and then plopped back onto my shoulders. I can't seem to focus on any one facet or person. Kaylee? Miles? Lilly? Their faces just spin in my head. My vision is filled with spinning heads, which is disturbing on so many levels.

"They fired Kaylee?" I choke.

"Yes." The anguish in Candace's voice is heavy and real. "I ran out of the room before they realized I was there and told Mrs. Sherman that Lilly would have to call her back. Then I pretended the line was being disconnected and hung up on her."

I would laugh at the thought of Candace hanging up on someone, but I think my laughing muscles are permanently broken.

"She left ten minutes later. She was crying. Right after that, Lilly left in a hurry. She didn't even bother to find me. Just yelled out that she wasn't feeling well and was heading home for the day."

I take a wobbly step away from Candace and drop my head between my knees. It's too much to take in at once. Taking several deep breaths, I try to focus my thoughts.

But only one thought comes into focus.

Miles. Miles was the one who reviewed the budget. Miles was the one who suggested to Lilly that she hire a third consultant. Miles was at the meeting.

It all comes back to him.

It is only by the grace of God that there is nothing in my hands. Otherwise, I would throw it at him.

I storm through the boutique, leaving Candace gaping after me at the front desk. The only thing I care about is the fact that he is ultimately responsible for the dismissal of my best friend. He just destroyed anything we could ever hope to have.

I slam the door open and march to the tiny cubicle in the corner. Miles looks up with the start of a smile, but it freezes on his face with a confused, worried look climbing its way up to take over instead. "What's—"

"Don't you dare ask me what's wrong!"

"Babe, what's wrong?"

"And don't you dare call me *babe*, you selfish, terrible,

manipulative, lying—"

He grabs me by the shoulders and gives me a little shake. "Izze, tell me what's wrong."

The genuine worry in his voice breaks me. Tears cascade down my face, and my throat clogs up. I don't want to fight. I don't want to scream. I just want to know why. Unfortunately, there is no way I could talk, not even to continue my rant.

He uses my silence as a chance to get me seated. He almost shoves me into the chair.

Not the best thing to do to a woman on the verge of hysteria.

Miles props himself on the back of the desk, right in front of me, and he takes my hands in his. He tries to get me to look in his eyes, but I know if I look in his eyes, I will lose everything.

But I've already lost everything.

"Please. Tell me what's wrong."

I finally look up into his eyes. I study his handsome face. "Why?" It's the only word that would squeak from my constricted throat.

"Why what?" He squeezes my hands, trying to urge me on.

Anger bubbles back up like a volcano on the brick of decimating an entire village. Like thunder striking a tree. Like a tsunami pummeling the earth. "Why would you fire Kaylee?"

I'm pretty sure I showered him in spit. He drops one of my hands to mop his face off before answering me. "It was like I told Lilly—"

"I don't care what you told Lilly! She's worked here like a loyal servant for years. She's a hard worker. She needs this job."

"Izze, you need to stop cutting me off if I'm going to explain." His voice booms this command like a spell. I shut up. My eyes, however, are flashing the rest of my message.

He drops my hand and turns away from me.

This man had better hurry up and answer me. His chance is

almost up.

Miles turns back toward me, runs a hand through his wavy, dark hair. "The numbers are not there. There's no profit. From a business standpoint, it makes no sense to keep her on as a seamstress."

The numbers are not there. Oh, give me a break.

"You're telling me that Lilly wants another consultant—that she wants to hire another person in addition to our existing crew— but the numbers are not there in order to justify keeping one of the people already employed here?" I'm flabbergasted. I am truly flabbergasted. My eyes narrow. "Are you firing Kaylee in order to get the profit margin that makes hiring another consultant possible?" Please say no. Candace must have made a mistake. Don't tell me that you would do this to my friend. That you would do this to me. My very soul reaches out to him, pleading with him to say anything other than that.

His eyes drop.

Oh no.

"There is more to it than that. Listen, just let me explain!"

My hand slashes through the air, silencing him. "I think you've explained enough."

"I haven't even begun to explain this to you! There is more to it than you think."

"No, I really don't think there is anything to add. I got my answer, and now I see you for what you are. You are a smooth-talker with only your best interests at heart. I can't believe I trusted you." I watch as the blazing hateful words settle on his spirit. The spirit I was so growing to love.

I turn to leave when his angry voice stops me. "You are a self-righteous coward. You have already made up your mind about the situation. And you didn't trust me. You never did. Probably never would." I've never heard Miles like this. His words are like acid

eroding away the thin shield that covers my heart.

I turn back to face him. Prepared to defend myself until the stars fall from heaven.

But then I see his face.

Nothing could prepare me for what I see there. It's an awful mix of anger and the pain of a person who has been deeply wounded by someone they love. It's unforgiving.

"Did you even think about the fact that Lilly approved my plan? I didn't just go fire her. I took it to Lilly, and together we talked to Kaylee. Did you think about that?"

I feel sick now, and I clench my stomach with both hands.

His eyes are blazing angry fire, and he takes a step toward me. "No. You didn't think about that. You just came in here, ready to crucify me when I wasn't the one who made the final decision." His eyes are cold darts, and his hands wave some unseen message in the air. "You never trusted me. You took the first excuse you could find to get rid of me."

I need to leave. I need to get out of here. Otherwise, I will vomit all over the place. The nausea is awful.

But what's even worse is the fact that in my heart of hearts, I know he's right.

So I say the only thing I can say to protect myself before he says it first. "We're over, Miles."

Chapter Fifteen

I storm out of Ever After like someone possessed. I am so angry. I could actually punch someone.

If I was brave enough to punch someone.

I climb into my car, and an instant replay of everything hits me. We just broke up. He fired Kaylee. Lilly won't fire Miles. So I'm stuck dealing with him.

What am I going to do?

I bang my head into the steering wheel. Tears cascade down my cheeks now. I look up into the rearview mirror—the waterfall has combined with the mascara I applied this morning to form several muddy rivers running down my face. Two black orbs stare out of the murky waters at me.

I just sit and cry.

Tap. Tap. Tap.

My heart lurches. What if it's him? I can't talk to him. I won't talk to him.

"Ma'am?"

A stranger's voice. The coast is clear.

I look up, and there is Monica Nolan and her father. Great. She had another appointment to try on gowns today. If anyone was going to find me right now, why couldn't it at least have been a perfect stranger?

I roll down the window. "Hi, Monica, Mr. Nolan. How are you guys today?" I can be fake happy. Watch me.

Monica narrows her eyes at me. "Are you all right?"

"I'm peachy."

"You don't look too good," Mr. Nolan says.

Should I? "I don't feel very good." Liar. Liar. Pants on fire.

I really don't feel good. I feel like I will be physically ill at any moment. God, remember this, and please don't be too angry with me!

"Oh, that's awful!"

"Yeah, it feels awful." I mumble while rubbing my temple.

"Oh, Izze, you should just go home. Please! I want you to feel your very best when we are working on my wedding dress, and honestly honey, you do not seem to be at your best today."

Glad to know the gown is your top priority in this situation.

"She sure doesn't look her best today," Mr. Nolan pipes up again. Swell.

"I would hate to leave you in the lurch. I don't want to cancel on you." I don't, but I do. Conflicting emotions. Duty verses tragedy.

"Go home, honey. How about I come back tomorrow?" Monica suggests.

"I think that will be perfect. There was a cancellation at four o'clock tomorrow, if that works for you?"

"That sounds great!" She flashes me a beauty queen smile.

I am *so* not in the mood for perky brides right now.

Somehow, I ended up at The Chow Man. I couldn't go home. I couldn't face Kaylee. She's never been fired before. She's probably so hurt. In my head, I know I should be with her. I'm her friend, but she doesn't know that I know. The one thing keeping me away

is that I can't be there when she realizes that my boyfriend—uh, ex-boyfriend—wouldn't listen to me. I went to bat for her, and I let her down. So here I sit, crying into my Lo Mein.

It seems to be date night here. The one night this restaurant is actually busy, and I'm here. There are couples everywhere. Smiles, heads bent together, hand holding while passing the soy sauce. Just another cruel reminder. *You're alone. No one loves you. You've been betrayed once again.* Those thoughts echo inside my soul.

"Would you like some more water?" Lou, the waitress, holds a pitcher of water up.

"Sure," I mumble. I go back to spinning the noodles on my fork.

I hear Lou slide onto the bench across from me. I don't bother to look up.

"What's wrong?"

"What isn't wrong?"

"Don't give me cryptic answers. Tell me what's going on." Lou's raspy voice is firm. I look up, surprised.

"I've been a waitress a long time. I'm sixty-three years old, and I've done this since I was twenty-four. Let me tell you, there is no bigger ministry. The people God will bring to you, the ways He can use you here.... So tell me, what's wrong?"

I consider just leaving, but hey, what could it hurt to unleash my sob story on this unsuspecting woman? She asked for it. "I've been dating the consultant my boss hired at the bridal boutique where I work. I got to work today, and the other consultant told me he fired my best friend, Kaylee, so that he could hire another full time consultant."

Lou's eyebrows rise. "He has the authority to just fire anyone he wants? What about your boss?"

"Well, he said that he and Lilly, my boss, talked to her together and explained the situation." I stab a piece of shrimp.

"So is there more to the situation?"

"What?"

Lou gives me a look much too similar to an expression in Aunt Jill's arsenal of them. "What is his side of the story? Why did your boss agree with him? Is it possible that Kaylee agrees with them, too?"

I stare at her for a minute. "What?" I finally gasp.

"You didn't give that poor boy a chance to explain, did you? Have you even talked to Kaylee? This seems like a personal vendetta." She points her index finger at me.

"I didn't need to hear his explanation. And yes, it is personal because he fired my best friend to hire a perfect stranger!" I can't believe this. This is why I don't talk to people.

"There has to be a reason."

"He's insensitive." Why am I talking to this strange, nosy lady? I *should* just get up and leave. Yet there is something within compelling me to keep talking. Keep listening.

"This is business, Izze."

"If he can snap his fingers and kick Kaylee to the curb, then what's to stop him from getting rid of me? Clearly, Lilly is on his side!" My stomach lurches. "I have to find a new job." I know it seems stupid, but I always thought I'd work at Ever After forever. The bridal business has always been what I wanted to do.

Lou reaches out and takes my hand. Her grip feels comforting, like warm apple pie, mashed potatoes, and fuzzy blankets. I feel myself breaking, really breaking like a glass shattering, and from that broken pile my story spills out of the cracks.

"Have you ever had your heart broken?"

Lou nods slowly. "I have."

"Well, this is my second time having my heart broken." I shake my head. Tears burn my eyes like acid. "His name was Wyatt. I was eighteen, and he was twenty. I was in love, and I thought that we would eventually get married." My voice breaks. "Stupid, I know, but I really loved him. Anyway, two weeks before graduation I found out that he was cheating on me. She was pregnant...eight months pregnant, and they were going to get married."

"Oh, hon," Lou murmurs softly.

"Anyways, he took me to a park near my house to tell me. We were sitting on a bench, and then it started raining. He clearly wanted to be done with me because he rushed on, not bothering to stop despite the pouring rain. I remember hearing what he was saying, but feeling like I was watching it happen to someone else. I snapped. I went into hysterics, and I started calling him awful things. I called him a liar, a cheat, and a coward, among other things. Wyatt grabbed me by the shoulders in a stupid attempt to calm me down. Suddenly, I just couldn't stand the idea of him touching me, and I starting hitting him so he would let me go."

My throat clogs up, and I can almost feel the pain on my face again. Lou touches me gently, encouraging me to continue. "He had had enough at that point. He squeezed my arms so tight they were bruised for a month. Then he slapped me, pushed me onto the ground. My last memory of Wyatt is watching him walk away in the pouring rain as I lay sobbing on the ground."

I snort. "It just worked out for them to get married on my graduation day. So instead of my boyfriend filling the seat next to my proud parents, there was an empty chair holding purses and coats. Anyways, they seem happy, in love even. It's just...that whole year he told me he loved me, and on the sidelines he was... with her." Another hot tear rolls down my face. "I was so stupid."

"Oh, honey, you weren't stupid. You trusted someone with your heart, and he was unworthy. That's on him, not you."

"Yeah, meanwhile he lives out his happily ever after," I say sarcastically. "What do I get? Another winner. Go me." I give myself two thumbs up.

"Sweetheart, you don't know what their lives are really like,

but if indeed it's really as good as it appears, then you just need to trust God and accept the fact that He forgives them. You need to do the same."

"I have," I mumble.

Lou raises an eyebrow at me. "Then letting go is the next step. Letting go of those hurts, fears, and lies. 'To grant to those who mourn in Zion—to give them a beautiful headdress instead of ashes, the oil of gladness instead of mourning, the garment of praise instead of a faint spirit; that they may be called oaks of righteousness, the planting of the Lord, that he may be glorified.' Isaiah sixty-one, verse three. Allow God to turn your ashes into beauty."

"How?" I hiccup.

She smiles warmly at me. "By letting go and trusting Him, sweetie. When you give Him the things that controlled and defined who you were, His plans of beauty and goodness for you can blossom. Only God can take the truly worst of situations and use it for good. 'For I know the plans I have for you, declares the Lord, plans for peace and not for evil, to give you a hope and a future.'"

"Jeremiah twenty-nine, verse eleven." That verse has been on my heart a lot lately.

"Yes."

I stare across the restaurant at a couple eating. A future and hope and beauty always seem so elusive. Some people just had it, and others didn't. After Wyatt broke my heart, I decided to stop planning for my Happily Ever After and guard my heart. Build walls with barbed wire and grenades, so any blunders would blow the faulty out of my life forever. Miles is the faulty, and any reason is a good enough reason.

"Be that as it may, Lou, I won't be casting my pearls before swine ever again."

Headlights blinded him for a moment. Miles sat on the porch steps to Izze's house. If Izze's roommates had noticed he was here, they clearly didn't want to talk to him.

He didn't care, though. He and Izze were going to talk.

Now.

Period.

The engine groaned as it turned off, and the driver's door opened. Izze stepped out. Miles guessed that Izze had seen him the second she drove into the yard based on her expression.

Fire and ice coexisted like peanut butter and jelly, dominating her every movement, her delicate face, her wounded heart. Miles took a deep breath.

This wasn't going to be good.

"Get out of here, Miles." Izze stomped toward the house.

"We need to finish talking." He stood straight, using his hulking presence to block her escape.

"I heard everything that I needed to hear." She stood only a few feet away from him, but every foot felt like a country and an ocean in between them.

"Far from it." *Please just listen to me*, he pleaded silently.

"Nothing you could say would make this better, so don't waste your breath."

He reached for her, but she slashed her arms in a gesture that Miles could only assume was a karate chop to keep him away from her. He sighed. "Kaylee still has a job."

She blinked away the mocha colored curls that had fallen into her face. Her arms fell to her sides. "You fired her."

"Lilly and I laid her off, but I arranged a deal with Sew Magical. All Kaylee has to do is go there and apply."

"Apply for the job?" Her brown eyes narrowed. "Doesn't sound like she has a job."

"It's just a formality," Miles said.

Her eyes hardened again. She spoke through clenched teeth. "I don't care." She turned and inched away from him, probably debating whether she could make it to the car before he caught her.

"Why have you never trusted me?"

The question stopped her cold. Slowly, she turned around to face him, tears streaming down her lovely face.

"Why have I never trusted you? I'll tell you why. Because all men are the same. They make big promises and grand gestures, but then they betray you and break your heart. They lie to your face. They don't care about all the damage they've left in the wake of their devastation. They just do what they want."

"I am not like that, and you know it," Miles roared.

"Sure you are." She threw her purse past him and onto the old porch, and then marched up to him, pointing her finger into his chest. "You promised me the changes would be good. You promised."

"I know it doesn't seem good, but I was just trying to help you."

"By laying off my best friend? Wow. I'd hate to see what you do when you're not helping."

"Izze, I made a logical decision. The only logical decision that could be made. It was the only way to keep Ever After profitable and functioning. I did this for you."

"You did this for the money. Ever After's profit and your own profit. I had nothing to do with this decision. You don't care about me." She brushed past him, making it onto the porch.

"I love you!" He bellowed. "You were the driving focus behind every decision I made."

She whirled around, hair fanning out like the skirt of a grand ball gown. He'd obviously spent too much time around dresses it

he compared her hair to a ball gown in a time like this.

"Do not lie to me."

"How do you not understand this? Ever After was drowning. The profit we've been making is not enough, because when your aunt worked there, she was taking home practically nothing. There is no surplus!"

"We managed just fine all those years."

"By the grace of God alone, woman!"

"You are an idiot." Her words were like a jagged knife to the chest.

"Real nice, Izze. Real nice."

She laughed in bitter, cold anger. "I'm not really concerned with being nice right now. You are an inconsiderate liar. I could never trust you after what you did, and I'm glad I never did."

"Well, I guess there's nothing else to say then."

"No."

One last try. He was desperate. "Except that you're wrong, Izze."

"Get off of my property, Miles." Her command twisted the knife, piercing his heart.

Before Miles could leave, the front door opened. He blinked away the blinding light to see Apryl's head sticking out of the doorway. Miles could see Kaylee behind her, but she stood back where it was safe. Miles heard a window screech and looked over to see Courtney leaning out of the living room window.

"Guys," Apryl said, her eyes wide. "Maybe we should cool it down."

"I will call the authorities if necessary," Courtney threatened, oh-so-helpfully.

"Get him out of here." His ex-girlfriend and the woman he loved spoke through clenched teeth.

"Izze," Kaylee said softly.

Izze turned around and locked eyes with Kaylee. Neither of

them spoke, but both of them were whiter than the first snowfall of the year.

Kaylee opened her mouth, but Izze whirled back to face him. She fixed Miles with a look so hot that it could wilt a cactus. Without another word, she grabbed her purse and charged to her car. He didn't try to stop her this time.

"If you won't leave, Miles," she yelled, "I will."

Apryl and Courtney yelled, begging her to come back and talk to them. Kaylee jogged outside trying to catch her, but it was too late. Miles didn't move. It was pointless to move.

It was over.

Chapter Sixteen

Iknock on the old, red door.

It occurs to me that this might not be the best place to go, but I just don't know where else to run. Going home again is not an option, and I can't go to my parents' house. That's the first place they would look for me, and I can't face Miles or Kaylee again.

Or ever.

I knock again. "Aunt Jill, it's me. Please open up."

There's a rustle of feet, and no less than seven seconds later, the door opens to reveal my aunt.

"Izze, it is twelve o'clock at night. What's wrong? Are you okay? Are your parents okay? Are you bleeding anywhere? For goodness sake, girl, tell me what's happening!" She yanks me into the house. "Why are you out this late? Only creeps and weirdos roam the town at this time of night."

Tears and snot start flowing again. The confrontation plays through my mind on a never-ending loop. Despite the voice in my head that tells me to go home to see Kaylee, or call Miles and talk this out, I know that is not an option. I need to hide. Fortunately, no one has ever been to my aunt's house. "I need someplace to stay for a few days."

She studies my face for a few minutes, studies the tear stains and dried snot on my face, and the way I've heaving to breathe

through the sobs. It probably reminds her of the only other time I showed up at her doorstep unannounced. When Wyatt dumped me and left me in the park by myself. I walked my drowned rat looking self all the way to her apartment.

"Izze, what happened?"

That's when the sobs overtake me, and I collapse into her open arms.

The ceiling is pink. My ceiling is not pink. In fact, I hate this ceiling. It looks like Pepto-Bismol. Where am I?

I sit up slowly—my head feels like someone is tapping it with a sledgehammer. Looking around, I see the pink ceiling, the bookshelf on the wall across from me, and desk and chair against a backdrop of family and youth group pictures.

Aunt Jill's spare room. That's right. I ran to her last night.

Once I started sobbing, all Aunt Jill did was hold me. She led me into the house, sat me on the couch, and hugged me. The only time she ever left my side was to get me some water.

"You're going to get dehydrated from all the crying. Drink the water," she had said as she shoved the tall glass at me. Once I had drunk the water, she had instructed that at two in the morning, it was now time to go to bed, and we would talk after I got some sleep.

Knowing my aunt, we will be talking soon.

I lay on my back, staring at the pink ceiling. Actually, I wish I had some Pepto-Bismol now. It might help.

"This has got to be a nightmare."

Not only am I hurt, I'm mad at myself for trusting them. I want to go there and give them a piece of my mind. On top of that, there is a part of me that hates myself. I feel like a fool, and I am not very proud of myself right now.

"Lord, what do I do?"

Yet again, there is no answer from Him. It would appear He's going to leave me hanging, too.

"Sorry, God," I say. "That's how I feel."

A knock sounds from the door. "How long are you going to hide in there?"

I stay silent for a moment, hoping she will think I'm still asleep.

"Izze, I heard you talking to yourself."

I sigh. "No, you didn't."

"Get up and shower."

"Fine," I huff.

I get up and open the door. She's standing there with a pile of clothes in her hand. She holds them out to me. "Here. Put these on for now. They don't fit me anymore. Leave your clothes outside the bathroom door, and I'll wash them for you."

"Thanks." I take the offered pile and turn down the hall to go to the bathroom. A hot shower sounds nice.

Once in the bathroom, I crank the hot water handle to high and deposit my crinkled clothes outside the door. I get in and stand there for a long time. Maybe the heat will purge me, and the running water will wash everything down the drain.

Finally, once my skin is lobster red and I can't see more than two inches in front of me because of the steam, I get out and get dressed. Aunt Jill's old jeans, T-shirt, and sweatshirt are a little big on me, but they are the perfect wallowing clothes.

A rush of cool air greets me once I open the door to the sauna-like bathroom. I hear pots and pans banging in the small kitchenette, and the smell of coffee finds my nose. I follow the scent and find Aunt Jill making blueberry muffins, coffee, maple sausage, and instant mashed potatoes from those little tubs in the supermarket.

Comfort food.

This is the same exact meal she made for me the morning after the Wyatt breakup.

"Why are you making all this weird stuff for breakfast?" I had asked confused.

"This is comfort food. My own special mixture. I've been making this concoction since my first year in youth ministry," she had said. So we ate the breakfast food with a side of mashed potatoes and gravy, as I poured out my heart to her.

I walk into the kitchen, my sock-clad feet sliding a little bit. "I thought instant potatoes were cheating."

"Do you want to make mashed potatoes first thing in the morning?" Just then the microwave beeps. "Gravy's done," she says with a wink.

I smile a little at her and start helping her. Pulling the plastic plates from the cupboard, I start spooning the mashed potatoes high onto the plates. I make little craters in the tops and pour the gravy into them. Then I dig the tub of butter out of the refrigerator and start on the muffins.

Soon we have two huge plates of the weirdest looking meal ever.

We take them into the living room, and I settle back onto the couch carefully. After tucking my feet under me, I set my plate on my lap. "Mmm." The gravy and potato is always my favorite part.

We eat in silence for a few minutes, and then Aunt Jill sets her plate on the coffee table to her right. "So I think it's time you told me what's going on." She readjusts herself so that her back rests against the arm of the couch. The look on her face is non-negotiable.

"Miles fired Kaylee."

She chokes and spits out the bite of muffin she took.

Gross.

Grabbing a tissue from the coffee table, she picks up her

half-chewed food. "What? How? Wait a second, Miles can't fire anybody."

"I'm sorry. Lilly was actually the one to fire Kaylee. It was just Miles's idea." The snootiness just oozes from me.

"Go back to the beginning, and explain everything to me please."

"Well, you know about the monthly sales we've been having, right?" She nods. "They've been so busy, and have really brought in a lot of general business. Miles apparently said that we could increase the number of brides we see by hiring a third consultant. When we are finished with a client, and one of us is working with the girl at the front desk, the changing room is sitting empty. A third consultant means that when one of us is not using the room, another girl can be seen."

"Sounds smart." Aunt Jill takes a sip of her coffee. "It all sounds wise to me."

"Except the part where Kaylee got fired." I roll my eyes. "Apparently this increase in business hasn't meant an increase in the budget."

"Why let go of Kaylee?"

"There's no room in the budget," I say again.

"Izze, that doesn't make sense. There's always been room in the budget for a part-time seamstress." She stops abruptly, just staring at me. I can see it dawn on her what they've done. "There's not room in the budget because they are disposing of the seamstress position and using those funds for another consultant."

"Yes."

She's silent for several minutes. I can see the war on her face. On one hand, there is no denying that this makes good business sense. On the other hand, this is Kaylee we are talking about here. She has been a part of the Ever After team for a long time.

"What are they doing for a seamstress now?"

I shrug. "I don't really know. Candace said that Miles worked a symbiotic deal with the alterations shop in town, Sew Magical. Sounds like all Ever After's alterations will be referred to them, and they will give a ten percent discount for them. Basically Lilly agreed to free advertising for Sew Magical in the store. Supposedly Kaylee has a job waiting for her there."

She rubs her face. "Well, I understand why you are upset. It certainly stinks, but you didn't get fired. Kaylee wasn't even fired. She was laid off, but she has another job already lined up! While I feel awful for Kaylee, these things happen in business."

I just stare at her. "How can you say that like it's no big deal?"

"It was a business decision, not a personal one."

"If they can make a 'business decision'"—I use air quotes around the words—"to let Kaylee go, then they could make a business decision to let me go, too. Everything is about money now. When you ran the place, and even when you owned it, everything was about love and fun."

"That's how it should be, especially for the customers. But there's a business side of things that needs to be kept running. Sometimes that means making difficult decisions and sacrifices."

"Miles said that based on the old ledgers, your pay was insignificant. You did that for all of us. To help us. So I don't understand how you can say that so cavalierly."

Aunt Jill reaches for my hand. "Honey, I did what God told me to do, and He took care of me. Don't you think it might be possible that Miles did what he thought was best for everyone involved? That God even has a hand on this situation?"

"How would you feel if your ex-boyfriend had come up with the idea to fire a competent member of staff, and your very best friend?" I dare her with my eyes to disagree with me.

"Your ex-boyfriend?"

"I broke up with Miles when I found out what happened. I

can't date someone who would do that to my friend." I pick up my own coffee cup, just to hold the comforting warmth in my hands.

Aunt Jill abruptly stands up and starts walking back and forth in the little living room for several minutes. Finally, she comes to sit on the coffee table in front of me. "Why is the answer to hide?"

Not what I was expecting. "I..." I struggle to answer the question. "Because I can't trust someone who would do that?"

"You can't trust him, or you're not willing to trust him?"

"It's not just him I can't trust. I can't trust Lilly anymore either. She made the final decision."

"That's not what I asked."

"I can't trust him," I say through clenched teeth. I look away from her, not wanting to meet her piercing eyes any longer.

"I need to tell you a story." She looks down at the floor, and when she looks up, there are tears in her eyes.

Whoa. I don't think I've ever seen Aunt Jill cry.

"I think you know about your mother's and my childhood."

I solemnly dip my head, a silent *yes*. "Mom told me that your dad was abusive."

"That's right. He was also controlling. If we did anything that wasn't his idea to begin with, then he would make our lives miserable."

"Mom said that when you were eighteen, you went before a judge, told him everything, and got custody of her." My mother was fourteen when this happened. To the best of my knowledge, they haven't seen their dad since he was arrested for child abuse.

"When I first opened Ever After, I had a very serious boyfriend."

My eyebrows jump like that baby kangaroo from *Winnie the Pooh*. "I didn't know that."

She smiles softly. "You don't know everything about me, my dear. Anyway, I was just getting on my feet. Your mother had gotten a full ride to college, so I wasn't responsible for her

anymore. I had met Darrel about a year earlier, and it was instant attraction. We were getting pretty serious, but every spare second was poured into my new business."

She stops to take a deep breath. I can see this is getting emotional for her again, so I just wait quietly.

"I was working all the time, and I literally never saw him, barely spoke to him. I hadn't hired any help yet, and it was just overwhelming me to the point of breaking. We had a big argument about it one night." Aunt Jill stops and takes a deep breath.

She gets a faraway look in her eyes, and I know she is reliving it all in her mind. "He was upset, and understandably so. He said he didn't want me working like this anymore, and suddenly, I wasn't arguing with Darrel, but my father, and I panicked. I accused him of trying to control me just like my father. Of course, he knew all about my father, and the words wounded him deeply. In order to preserve myself, I went in for the kill. I broke up with him, saying he wasn't the man I thought he was. He immediately left. However, he called me to try and resolve the fight every day for two weeks. I ignored him."

"Wow."

She nods. "Honey, I let my fear of men like my father keep me from being with the only man I've ever loved. A man who was the very epitome of God's love. Fear is like the devil's arsenic. It kills faster than anything. I'm worried that you are allowing the same poison into your heart." Having recently been thinking about this, the irony that she listed arsenic is not lost on me.

I look away uncomfortably. "It's not the same thing, Aunt Jill."

"Not every man will betray you like Wyatt did."

"Maybe not, but Miles did."

She raises an eyebrow at me. "You work with him. You are going to need to resolve this."

I violently shake my head. "No, I don't."

She gives me a motherly look. "Yes."

"No, I mean I don't work with him, or at least I won't soon. I'm going to leave Ever After."

The shock on her face is almost comical. Her eyes are huge and her mouth hangs open and slung to the left.

"I have to," I say quietly.

"Have you prayed about this?" Her look transforms to youth pastor mode.

"Yeah," I lie.

"Sure you have," she says sarcastically. "You had better keep praying, girlie. I've never known God to tell us to run away in fear or abandon our friends based on an unforgiving heart."

"That's not what I'm doing." I stand up quickly, turning away from her, but she captures my hand before I can run away from her and into the safety of the guest room.

"Izze, you need to trust God and stop trusting only in yourself." She releases me, but before I can escape to the other room, she gets up. "I'll leave you alone for a while. Pray, Izze. Pray."

Quietly cracking the door open, I peek into the office. *Please, God, don't let Miles be here.*

I look around nervously and take a step inside. Miles is not at his desk. After listening for another moment, I'm convinced that no one but Lilly is in here. I can hear the furious typing on her keyboard, her telltale signature.

I've called out sick the last two days. Yes, it's been two days since Lilly and Miles fired Kaylee. I haven't even spoken to Kaylee. I can't bring myself to do it.

This is a dramatic, life-changing moment for me. I've thought a lot about my decision. Despite Aunt Jill's story, and her urging

that I don't go through with this, today I have come to quit my
job.

I have never felt so sick in all of my life. Not even the time in
twelfth grade when I was hospitalized for pneumonia.

I slowly walk to Lilly's cubicle. Every second feels like some
horrible dream. This is the point in the movies where you and I
would be yelling at the girl for being so stupid. "No, don't make
this decision," we would shout. "Work things out," we would
scream. Well, now I've lived it and now I understand.

Some things can't be fixed.

I step inside Lilly's cubicle and attempt to clear my throat. It
comes off sounding more like a cat hacking a hairball. "Lilly." She
looks up from her computer.

"Izze." She looks relieved to see me at first, but that relief is
immediately replaced with concern. "You look awful."

"Yeah, I've been better."

"I'm glad you're here. We've really need to talk about this."

"I'm not here about that."

She continues, not listening to me. "Izze, we had to do it. Kaylee
understood completely."

I can't even speak. My throat closes up again. "I understand
that. You are building a business, and you have to make cuts." My
voice is barely a whisper.

"It's not exactly like that."

I hold up my hand, enraged. I feel like letting out a lion's roar.
Now we have engaged the beast, ladies and gentlemen. "It's exactly
like that!"

"It's not!" Her own voice rises in defense, and she stands up
so fast that her chair falls backward. "There was no room in the
budget for this. Thanks to Miles, we are making money again, but
we need to hire another consultant. Unfortunately, that means
making tough decisions. You need to understand that if you are

going to manage this business one day."

"This business used to be about love and family and trust. You and Miles have made it all about money. Kaylee is like family, and you've left her high and dry." My nostrils flare and I thrust my jaw out at her.

"We did not leave her high and dry! Miles felt terrible, but this was the only—"

I hold up my hand, cutting her off. "No! Do not go there."

"Miles told me you broke up with him."

Something sharp stabs me in the heart just from hearing those words spoken out loud. All I can do is nod. Anything else, and I might fall apart.

"Izze, we need another consultant, and this was the only way to make that happen."

"You need two consultants," I say harshly.

The color drains from her face. "What?" Her voice is just a squeak.

"I can't work here anymore."

"But, I...Izze, listen to me..."

I shake my head, silencing her once again. Tears drip down my face. "I'm sorry for not giving you two weeks' notice. That's horrible of me, but I can't work here. Not with Miles. Not with all this." I gesture to the air between us. "This is killing me, and I am truly furious with you as much as I am with Miles. Not to mention that I've called out sick for the last two days. An employee shouldn't behave the way I have been and the way I know I will. So I need to leave."

"Izze, you can't leave." Panic consumes her voice. "You need to listen to me before you make this decision."

But I ignore her.

And I walk away. I keep walking until I no longer hear her voice, or see the store that used to be a second home to me. I keep

walking until I reach my car. I get inside feeling like this is just an awful dream.

Then, I drive. I just keep driving.

Chapter Seventeen

Since I'm still staying with Aunt Jill, I give her a quick call to let her know I won't be back for a while, and after assuring her approximately nine hundred and seventeen times that I am all right, I start my drive.

I don't listen to any music. I don't cry or pray. I don't even think. In fact, I'm hardly sure I do anything past basic motor skills.

If I had been thinking, I'm not sure I would have ended up here. I thought the devil's lair would have to freeze over before I willingly came back here.

I drove to the park where Wyatt left me that rainy afternoon.

I sit on the bench where we sat, staring past the same ancient oak tree and studying the same man-made pond to the right. I'm staring, but I'm not really seeing anything at all.

This was one of the worst weeks of my life.

Where have you been, God? I listen for an answer. I mean, I really listen for an answer this time, but still nothing.

Okay, now I'm angry.

"Where are you?" I shout and raise a fist to the sky. "Where have you been? Why does this keep happening to me? Why won't you answer me?"

I jump up from the stupid bench and throw my arms out wide in front of me. "Lord, answer me! Do something. Anything! I'm

still single, sad, and alone. I'm jobless, too. I'm a fool, and I hate how I feel right now."

How do I feel right now? I stop and really let myself feel everything I squashed down inside while I drove here. It comes at me like chunks of garbage being thrown at me over and over. Slowly, I sink into a crumpled heap in the grass.

I'll tell you how I feel. I feel guilty, and for more than just feeling like I've let Kaylee down. I feel guilty because of how I've acted ever since I found out. I feel guilty because I am fearful and untrusting.

"But it's not my fault," I whisper. "Wyatt was the one who broke me. It's his fault that I'm afraid and have a hard time trusting anyone."

I hear no audible voice, yet my soul hears something.

You don't trust Me either.

It's just a feeling, and it's gone as quick as it came, but it didn't come from me.

Come to Me.

How exactly am I supposed to do that?

My phone chimes from inside my pocket. Taking it out, I see a little envelope, indicating an unopened text message. Instead of reading it, I tap on the Bible App I have installed on my phone. I do a quick search for, "Trust in God."

I look at a few random verses until I come to one of my favorites in Psalm thirty-seven.

"Commit your way to the Lord; trust in him, and he will act."

"I trusted you. You never acted. Soon it became easier to trust myself," I say the words out loud, but the sound of crickets is my only response.

Keep reading.

I start over at the beginning of the psalm. The very first line makes me want to throw my phone into the man-made lake.

"Fret not yourself because of evildoers; be not envious of wrongdoers!"

I think about how much I've allowed Wyatt's seemingly happy life to consume me. I have indeed been envious. Already I'm feeling the holes being poked into my self-righteous balloon. This is not a good indication of the rest of the chapter.

Soon, I'm engrossed in the ancient prose. It's like this chapter was written for me. Every time it says "Fret not," I cringe. Every time I read about how judgment is coming for the wicked, I feel convicted. When I come to verse twenty-five, I can almost see the stories of David flashing right before my eyes. I see him go from the young man who defeated Goliath, to the old man whose own son tried to kill him.

But I never see him stop trusting in God.

I read the whole psalm, very slowly. I think about each verse before continuing onto the next one. Finally, I come to the last verse.

"The Lord helps them and delivers them; he delivers them from the wicked and saves them, because they take refuge in him."

Where have I been taking refuge?

In myself.

What a great and mighty fortress that turned out to be, eh?

I've known for a long time that I've only trusted in myself because of my fear, but it's like the implications of that have finally and fully dawned on me.

Wyatt's betrayal may have planted the seed, but I was the one who chose to water it.

It's ultimately my fault.

Before I have time to be lost in an ocean of self-loathing, verse twenty-seven leaps off the screen at me.

"Turn away from evil and do good; so shall you dwell forever."

Hot tears run down my face. Only this time, they bring a sense

of healing, not more pain. I can turn away from the evil. I can turn away from the fear and doubt and trust completely in God. There is an antidote for the arsenic in my soul, and it is God.

It's always been God.

"Hello, Miles."

The greeting froze the pen poised over the stack of paperwork on his desk.

Miles met the eyes of Izze's aunt.

His knees scraped the side of the rickety table as he stood up. His mother raised him to stand when an elder entered the room.

"Is this a bad time?" Warmth mixed with sadness filled her eyes.

"Uh..." How to answer? He had stacks of paperwork on his desk, tons of documents to go through on his computer, as well as an open e-mail with a deadline. Oh, and he'd rather not talk to anyone who had anything to do with Izze. "No, this is fine."

She smiled, crowfeet crinkling around her eyes.

"You don't hate me?"

"I came to see what was up. If you needed to talk. To see what was going on with the store where I poured my blood, sweat, and tears."

"I assume Izze told you what happened," he said coolly.

"Yes, but I wanted to hear your side."

"I've been going over the budget, studying ledgers..." He stopped when she waved her hand. "What?"

"I don't know about you, but I'm tired of hearing those details."

For the first time since this drama worthy of a teen soap opera went down, Miles smiled, relieved.

"Is this really the best decision?"

He nodded without hesitation. "Yes. I've been watching the

dynamics here for months. They need the help, and Kaylee can only work part time."

"Would she be interested in being a bridal consultant herself?"

Miles started to shake his head then realized that he had no idea. He had never thought of that. Why had he never thought of that? "I could lie, but honestly, I don't know."

Miles turned away from the intense, probing stare of the old woman and shook away the guilt. Miles had fixed the problem. He had done what was logical. Izze didn't like it. There was no further scoop to this news story.

"Izze is focused on one thing: thinking that I betrayed her. That's it. Dwelling and re-hashing everything won't change what I did or didn't do." Why was he so defensive? Jill was perfectly calm, trying to have a civil conversation, and he was the one getting riled like a grizzly bear. Maybe the fluorescent lights in the office were giving him a headache. Yes, that must be it.

Jill shrugged. "Izze's faced intense betrayal. While it's not my place to share, I think you need to understand that. Give her some time."

Miles felt his heart harden once again. "With all due respect, no. I'm done waiting for someone who refuses to trust me."

"Miles, I can tell that you care deeply for her. Just remember that it takes two to tango. She has her side and hurts, as do you."

Miles nodded his understanding, but he put a cold look on his face in a clear message. *Drop it.*

Jill sighed, dipped her head in a silent good-bye, and left. Miles sat back down, but an expanse as wide as the Grand Canyon separated his mind from his work.

Drop it, he told himself.

It's been almost a week since that day in the park. I've continued camping out at Aunt Jill's. I told her all about my experience at the park, and we cried and prayed together.

I've spent a lot of time praying since then.

However, not wanting to reintegrate myself in my sad reality yet, I've stayed with my aunt, so I could continue my soul searching and healing. After talking with Apryl, I gave her the directions to here so she could drop off some stuff for me.

I'm not terribly fond of wearing the same clothes every day.

I made her promise not to tell Kaylee. I know that soon I'll need to go home and face the messes I've made, but I'm not quite ready for that.

I'm afraid I haven't totally transformed. I'm still struggling with God about returning, but I'm getting there.

Baby steps, people.

I have the apartment to myself. I heat up some taquitos for lunch. I've got sour cream and salsa in little dipping containers. The oven timer goes off, and I dump the little baked rolls of tortillas stuffed with seasoned chicken and cheese onto my plate. I head into the living room, turn the TV on, and am literally about to take a bite out of the first stick when the doorbell rings.

Not cool.

I glare at the door. I had the thing in my mouth; I could have chomped down on it, but I didn't want to answer the door with my mouth full. Chances are it will be someone looking for Aunt Jill, and I will have to tell them that she's not here right now.

Aunt Jill doesn't have a peep hole in her door, so I leave the four chains locked and open it enough to make sure it's not a scary-looking dude.

No scary dude. However, there is a scary-looking redhead. My jaw drops.

"Kaylee."

"Time to talk."

"How did you know to come here?"

She waves her hand, like it's no big deal she just tracked me down after I've been avoiding her for over a week. "Please. Apryl can't keep a secret."

"Kaylee, I am so sorry."

She smiles gently. "Let me in, Izze."

I close the door, undo the chains, and throw the door open again, smiling nervously.

She sniffs the air as she steps into the apartment. "Taquitos?"

"Yup."

"The homemade recipe from your family?" I can nearly see her mouth starting to water.

"Yup." Every year, my mom and aunt make hundreds and freeze them. There are probably a couple hundred in her freezer right now. Perfect for a rainy day, which in my family is any day one might want to avoid cooking. "Want some?"

"You know it."

I set to work fixing her a plate and bring it out to the living room where she's sitting. We both start munching on the spicy goodness, before we talk.

Heart-to-heart talks always go better once you've eaten a proper meal.

When only a few crumbs remain on our plates beside half-eaten bowls of sour cream and salsa, I open the door to the conversation I have been dreading. "Kaylee, I am so sorry."

"It's okay, Izze. I forgive you. I was worried about you. My best friend just disappeared off the face of the earth."

"I know. I should have called you. I just couldn't bear it, knowing that I had let you down." I look at the floor, those feelings of guilt and self-loathing rising back up in an attempt to claim me.

"Izze, you didn't let me down. None of this is your fault. We've

both known I wouldn't stay with Ever After forever. It's not what God has planned for me. This new job is only temporary. God used this change to show me that."

Change. Urg. Have I mentioned that I hate change?

"It will be weird not working with you, but both stores are so close to each other, I really believe we will still see a lot of each other."

"What if you don't get the job at Sew Magical?" I stare at the nativity scene my aunt keeps on her entertainment center all year.

"They've already hired me. The application and interview process was a formality. When Miles told the manager about me, she told him that my reputation preceded itself, and she had personally seen a bustle I did on the gown for her best friend's daughter. The job was mine. I took it, but not until I had done some serious soul searching. My life doesn't lie in alterations, and it is time I start to figure out what God has planned for me."

I stare at the floor, thinking, trying to get all the heartfelt words I want to say lined up into a cohesive sentence. Something that makes sense. "Kaylee, you are my best friend. My non-blood sister. Finding out you wouldn't be there, that Miles had done this—it felt like someone took a tack and stabbed me in the lungs a million times. I'm sorry. I wish that things weren't changing."

Kaylee doesn't say anything. We've been Kaylee-and-Izze for so long, she recognizes that this is a big moment for me. Like, order your own brownie sundae because I'm not sharing *big*.

"I think that I've used my mistrust of people to justify my hate of change. But that's really stupid. God is always doing new things, bringing change into our lives. It's time I stopped loathing it with every fiber of my being. I'm going to welcome change now."

"Really?" she interjects. The raised reddish-brown eyebrow conveys disbelief.

"Welcome it, albeit begrudgingly." I grin. "I'm not going to

control things anymore. It's not my job. My job is to let God make alterations, both minor and major, to my life."

We talk for a long time, and I tell Kaylee everything. Hours pass, and Aunt Jill shows up from her unknown whereabouts.

She walks into the living room to discover us giggling like twelve year olds. "Nice to see you, Kaylee." She stoops down to give her a hug. "I see you managed to track Izze down."

"Yeah, finally."

She smiles and spreads her hands out. "After being a youth pastor for so long, I've come to enjoy my seclusion."

"I can see that."

Aunt Jill makes eye contact with me. "So what's next, Izze?"

"I think it's time for me to go back home. Thanks for letting me stay here, and for being here for me. I'm sorry for putting you out so much."

She pulls me up into a warm hug. "Kid, you are always welcome here, because I will always be there for you." She releases me and holds me out a little. "That being said, don't let the door hit you on your way out."

Chapter Eighteen

I am sitting on an uncomfortable stool in the manager's office. I shift slightly, cringing when the chair lets out a heavy groan in protest of my weighty behind.

I am interviewing for a position in the changing room at a ritzy clothing store in town. It would literally take me a year of saving in order to buy anything from this place. They don't just have things like Prada and Coach, but also brands like Citizens of Humanity in addition to that. The latest styles, and they are all at full retail. Crazy expensive. It makes the seven-year-old Coach purse I am clutching look like a joke.

I've been home about a week. Every day I tell myself I'm going to go apologize to Lilly and Miles, but every day I chicken out and hide in my room with the curtains drawn shut.

I also faced the reality that I do need to find another job. As the Bible says, if you don't work, then you don't eat. I've had to dip into my savings in order to put gas in my car and buy my eighty-nine cent dinners of Ramen Noodles. Chicken, shrimp, *and* beef, so I'm getting a variety.

The thin, wiry man across from me has been reading my résumé for the last fifteen minutes. There's not that much on there. This is what it consists of:

Bridal Consultant at Ever After Bridal Boutique

October 2009 to April 2016
Cashier at Burger Bud's Fast Food June 2007 to
September 2009

That's it.

I'm feeling very nervous.

Finally, he, the man known as Mr. Trill, looks at me from the top of his tiny glasses. "Well, you've certainly had several years of experience in retail and clothes. Why did you leave your last job?"

Ah, the humiliating part. "Honestly sir, I quit. There was a big drama, and I didn't think I could work there anymore with that drama." Oh, how I wish I could go take the minute hands on that metaphorical time clock and whirl them back to before I ruined everything.

He nods. After another ten minutes of awkward pauses and stilted conversations, Mr. Trill stands up from his leather chair and welcomes me to the team.

After shaking his hand, I head to the parking lot and climb into the car.

Ever After is not even three minutes from here.

I put the car into reverse and back out of the parking space before I lose my nerve.

It's a busy April day, so the traffic is thick in the downtown district of Keene. It's like the people have come out of their winter hibernation, and now they are claiming their summer territory. Some even fight for dominance.

The light turns green, and I drive by a strip mall where two women fight over a shopping cart while their children stand by and watch.

Soon I pull into the strip mall parking lot, and I can see Ever After's fancy filigree sign. My heartbeat immediately kicks up a few notches. Maybe I should have taken a stress test before coming here. I could have heart disease, and this kind of stress could be

life-threatening.

Are nerves heart disease?

Lord, help me get out of the car.

I push the door open and walk the very long walk into Ever After. I hear the familiar chime as the door opens. The first thing I see is the vintage bride picture that hangs in my bedroom. Despite the fact that I am no longer in the employ of Ever After Bridal Boutique, just being here makes everything in me shout, "I'm home!" The fact that I'm really not makes me ache all over again.

No one is in the lobby or at the front desk right now. The mannequins on either side of me stare as I slowly trudge to the front desk. Just then the office door opens, and Lilly comes out.

She stops short when she sees me.

"Izze." Her tone cuts like a knife.

"Um. Hi, Lilly." My mouth most be coated in sandpaper right now because my voice sounds scratchy and my tongue sticks to the roof of my mouth.

"What are you doing here?" Her expression is hard and her words are colder than the winter we just survived.

"I came to apologize."

She just stares at me, so I forge ahead. "How I acted was unacceptable. Truthfully, you didn't owe me any explanation. You are the boss, and you had every right to do whatever you wanted without my agreement or permission. You made a difficult decision, but it was one that has to be made in business sometimes." I let out a little cough. "I am so sorry. Really sorry. I hope you can forgive me."

She doesn't even flinch.

"Well." I smile nervously. "I don't want to bother you anymore. I just wanted to apologize for taking off, quitting, and for everything I said. It was wrong of me."

She nods a little.

"Well, I'm going to go now." I point my thumb toward the door. "Thanks for letting me speak with you. Have a good day." I awkwardly wave and dodge out the door.

                        ♥

"Can you bring me this in a smaller size?" The tall blond woman hands me the silky floral dress. "It's too big on me."

"Of course." I smile politely and wait until my back is to her before I roll my eyes. I wish I had that problem with clothes. Most of them are too small, and they are only getting smaller. All the stress eating I've been doing has produced a fabulous muffin-top belly.

It is my second day at my new job.

I have never missed the crazy brides at Ever After more. At least they have a reason to be crazy. The majority of women here are solely focused on the smallest size of clothing that they can tug onto their bodies.

I bring the woman the smaller dress and return to my station to help the next woman in line.

Lilly Marshall is the next woman in line.

"Hello, Izze."

"Uh."

Lilly flinches at my use of "Uh."

"Sorry. I just didn't expect to see you. Uh, sorry. Can I, uh, help you?"

Her face twitches each time, but she smirks. "Same old Izze."

"Hopefully not the same," I say softly.

"No. Hopefully not."

We stand there for a few very uncomfortable seconds.

This is so weird.

"So," I probe gently.

"I want to hire you back."

I inhale sharply. "What? Really?"

"Yes." She gives a definitive nod, the motion shaking her dangly ruby colored earrings.

My right hand starts nervously playing with my hair. "Even after all that I did?"

"Yes." She bobs her head again, which sends the brown bun of hair on top of her head bouncing back and forth.

"Even though I made a complete fool of myself?"

Her rose painted lips pull into a smile. "Yes."

"I'll need to give my two weeks' notice here."

She laughs, and I grin. Lilly is rather beautiful when she laughs. I'll have to make that my mission when I start back at Ever After.

When I start back at Ever After! No other words have ever sounded so beautiful.

"I'd expect nothing less," she says when she's done laughing.

"Okay." I'm grinning like an idiot now. God is so good!

She gives me one more Princess Kate smile before turning around. Her navy skirt swishes back and forth as she walks away.

I best go deliver the bad/good news to my current boss.

"I'd like the most flowery gown you can find in here," Melinda, an exuberant young woman roughly my age, says. "I'd like something with an open back like maybe a keyhole back, or an illusion lace back, or maybe something with a lot of little straps and lace work." She uses her hands to describe the possible details of each gown.

I love my job. It is so good to be back.

"I think I have just the thing for you." I point at her, grinning like the Cheshire cat.

"Awesome, bring that one first, and then we can go from there." She practically bounces into the closet sized changing room.

Melinda came to her appointment alone. It always makes me sad when a bride comes alone. This is supposed to be a memorable experience in her life. I know that when I get married, I'll bring, like, ten people with me to try on wedding dresses.

When? Maybe I should say "*If* I get married." The words are still painful, but not quite as much. Not as long as I keep putting my trust in God.

Back to the situation at hand. When a bride comes alone, I make it my personal mission to treat them like my best friend. I am going to make Melinda's experience unforgettable no matter what.

A few minutes later, I come back into the room with the dress that sprang into my mind while Melinda was talking. In my opinion, it is the most unique gown that I have ever seen.

The skirt of this full ball gown overflows with organza and tulle. The lace overlay is made to look like flowers and leaves, and the entire hem looks like it is made up of leaves. The bodice has little clusters of beads in the center of the flowers, and a pop-out, organza trail of flowers forms straps that leads up both shoulders. The back is a keyhole cut, but all of the lacy fabric surrounding the keyhole is illusion lace, so all you see is the flowery lace.

Melinda gasps when she sees it. "Oh, this is absolutely perfect." She fingers the organza flower petals on the bodice.

Once in the gown, Melinda can't stop twirling. "I look like a fairy-tale princess!"

I grin. "You sure do!"

"I don't want to take it off. Like ever." She holds the ends out and pretends to bow down before a prince.

I pat her hand. "Taking it off just makes it more fun to put back on later."

"I suppose that's true."

"Do you want to try on any other gowns? There are a few others that I think might work for you."

She raises both eyebrows at me and cocks her raven-colored head to the side. "Be honest with me. Do you really think it could get better than this? Because I don't."

"Neither do I."

"Then let's get this beauty to the cash register!" Melinda resumes her twirling and actually comes out to the front desk while still in the dress to place the order.

I perk up when we come out front. I've been back a week, and I haven't seen Miles once. I'm hoping that despite the empty desk in the corner, he's still working with Lilly.

I start typing on the computer, Melinda chatting a hundred miles an hour next to me, when the bell on the door jingles.

I type the same word three times on the order form. My heart races, but I will myself not to look up at whoever it is. A lot of customers have been on the receiving end of some very excited looks because I was hoping to see Miles instead of them.

A bald, sixty-year-old father-of-the-bride was particularly flattered.

A female voice comments on one of the dresses on a mannequin, and my heart plummets to my feet. Looking up, my eyes confirm what my ears have already told me.

It's not Miles.

The new consultant, a young girl by the name of Roxanne, comes out to greet the next customer. Candace works with another bride, and I will be leaving for the day after I finish up with Melinda. From work, I will be going to have dinner with my parents and supposedly my aunt Jill tonight.

Melinda leaves, in her regular clothes thankfully, a little while later. I wave good-bye to Roxanne and Candace and go grab my purse from my little desk.

Lilly comes out of her cubicle and attempts to put on her dress jacket while trying to open the door. I grab the handle for her and let her go through first.

"Thanks, Izze. Have a good night." She waves over her shoulder and heads for the front door.

I angle my head at Candace. "Is she leaving for the day, too?" Not that she doesn't deserve to go home for a change, but it's just that Lilly normally works twelve hour days. She's a bit of a workaholic.

Candace looks uncomfortable, and her newly crop-cut hair swishes as she turns to avoid my eyes. "No." After I stupidly quit, Candace went to Lilly and explained what she had overheard and subsequently told me. She apologized to Lilly profusely for her part in adding to the craziness.

I adjust my purse strap on my shoulder. "What are you not telling me?"

"I don't want to be a gossip."

"Then don't. But don't lie to me either."

She looks down at the floor. "She has a meeting with Miles."

"Oh." Just hearing his name makes my stinking heart flutter.

Candace sighs. "When Miles found out that you were coming back, he packed up his desk and arranged with Lilly for further meetings to be at his office."

"Okay." I try to shrug this news off like it's no big deal, but based on Candace's expression, she doesn't believe me. "It's really not a big deal. Anyways, I'll see you tomorrow."

"Have a good evening." Sympathy fills her voice.

Well, I'll try.

Chapter Nineteen

Three hours later, I arrive at my parents' house for dinner.

I unlock their front door, and the smells of barbeque sauce, pork chops, and peaches immediately assault me.

I should explain.

That's one of my mother's adapted recipes. It's some type of pork slow-cooked in sweet barbeque sauce, chopped onions, a splash of water, and canned peaches. It is so ridiculously good. She usually makes it with her famous chive mashed potatoes, dinner rolls, and buttered peas.

My stomach growls appreciatively in response to the delicious smells coming from the kitchen.

"Hey, Mom?"

"Hello, daughter. Come pull this pan out of the oven for me."

I go in the kitchen to see my mother rotating a blender in the mashed potatoes pot with her right hand and stirring the boiling peas with her left hand.

I slip on one of her floral oven mittens and pull the yeasty rolls of goodness out of the oven. "Everything smells great, Mom."

"Thanks, hon." She looks back at me, all while perfectly achieving the tasks she is already doing. "How are you doing these days? Everything still going all right?" I called my parents and poured out the whole tale after I left Aunt Jill's house. Needless to say, they were shocked, disappointed, and sympathetic all at the same time. That conversation lasted for several hours, but after hanging up with them, I felt so much better. Even more than I did after talking with Kaylee. Sometimes you just need your mom and dad.

I set the pan of rolls on the cooling rack Mom had set up. "Things are still going good. Work is good. I still haven't seen Miles, though."

"Give it time, honey. God will take care of it."

Time. Yup, giving lots of time here. Not necessarily by choice though. "Do you need help with anything else?"

"Jill should be here any minute. She said she was bringing a friend, so can you set the table for five?"

I pretend to gasp. "She has friends other than her dear family?"

Mom rolls her eyes. "She does have a life, you know."

"What friend?" I quiz.

"I don't know. She just said a friend."

I hold up a delicate flowery china plate and a plastic plate. "Fine china friend or regular plate friend?"

She splatters some of the milk from the peas onto the stove, and it hisses in protest. "The plastic plates. You never know who's going to walk through those doors when Jillian says she's bringing a friend. Last time she brought a friend, two of my china plates ended up broken."

"Hmm. Maybe this should be a paper plate night," I quip.

I grab the plastic plates with the blue and purple swirl designs on them and the silverware. Setting the table makes me feel like I've been transported back to my childhood. This was my first and number one chore around the house.

"Sandy?" My aunt's voice floats in from the entryway.

"In here," my mother calls from the kitchen.

"I don't know where here is," Aunt Jill quips.

"She's in the kitchen. I'm in the dining room," I yell loudly.

"Both of you come out here and meet my friend." She sounds excited.

At my parents' house, the entryway connects into the living room. The living room connects into both the dining room and the kitchen. My mother and I reach the living room at the same time, where we both abruptly stop.

Aunt Jill is standing next to an attractive, older man.

He has salt and pepper hair that is cut sort of like Patrick Dempsey's. He has very bright blue eyes, and a tall, muscular build. His arm is casually slung around Aunt Jill's shoulders, and she smiles at him like God bequeathed him with the responsibility of hanging the moon.

Suddenly my mind flashes back to my date with Miles at the theater. How could I have forgotten? This is the same man I saw her with that night! When my life got all crazy, I promptly forgot about what I had seen in order to focus on my drama.

Mom regains her composure and hugs Aunt Jill. "Is this the man responsible for your shroud of mystery lately?" Mom elbows her in the side.

Aunt Jill grins. "It is."

"Nice to meet you," Mom says to the Mystery Man.

I purse my lips. "All those phone calls?"

Aunt Jill nods.

My mom takes a step closer to Mystery Man. "I'm Sandy. And your name is?"

"Darrel MacLaran." Darrel the Mystery Man stretches his hand toward Mom.

"When you disappeared while I was staying with you? The guy at that movie theater outside of town?" I throw the questions at her.

"Wait, how did you know about the movie theater?" Aunt Jill counters.

"I happened to be on a date at the time. Walked into the lobby, and lo and behold, what do I see?" I wave my hand back and forth between the two of them. "You two."

They look at each other and shrug.

I smile. "Well, at least that mystery is put to rest."

Then Dad walks into the living room, apparently just getting home from work. He looks at all of us standing around in the living room, and then his eyes land on Darrel, who still has an arm wrapped around Aunt Jill.

His eyes widen in surprise, and he motions to Darrel. "What's going on here? Who's this?"

♥

"So you told me this big, dramatic story about the one who got away, when in reality, you two had already miraculously reconnected and started dating again?" I try to say this accusingly, but who am I kidding? I couldn't be more psyched for them.

Aunt Jill shrugs and smiles a multi-million-dollar smile. "That about sums it up, yes."

We are all sitting around the table, feasting on Mom's barbeque peach pork chops. Currently, Darrel and Aunt Jill have taken a short respite from holding each other's hands to shovel in the delicious goodness.

"Well, now I've heard it all," Dad says from the head of the table. "Please, no more family news for a while. I don't think I will be able to keep up with anything else."

"Well, actually," Aunt Jill begins with a smile on her face.

Uh oh.

I see Dad reach for his heart. My dad and I are similar in that we immediately think the worst case scenario. I can tell he's expecting them to announce that they are selling their homes

and moving to the backwoods of Alabama so that they can raise a million honeybees in preparation for a zombie attack.

Darrel smiles sweetly at my aunt, and she has the same dreamy look on her face that I see on all the brides at Ever After.

"Oh my goodness!" I jump up and squeal. She jumps up in return, and we hug and shriek over the dinner table.

"What is it?" Dad sounds even more worried now. I release Aunt Jill so she can share the news with her sister and brother-in-law.

"We're getting married."

They are completely silent for thirty seconds before they join in with their own congratulations. Everyone runs around the table, trying to hug the happy, reunited couple when Darrel speaks up.

"In six weeks."

"You can't be serious," Dad bellows, completely flabbergasted. He staggers backward, clutching his chest again.

"We are," they answer in unison.

"What? That soon? Where?" My mom stutters, her mouth hanging slightly agape in shock.

"We're having a small, potluck style reception at Darrel's church. The actual ceremony will just be close friends and family at the tramway in Franconia Notch, which is about half hour driving time from the church."

I shudder. "You're getting married at the tramway? That thing is terrifying." I hate heights. On a field trip in high school we went to the tramway in Franconia Notch, and the entire ride up and down I clutched the cabin floor moaning, "I don't want to die. I don't want to die," like Donkey from *Shrek*. Even on the top of the mountain I was terrified. All the trails were insanely close to the edge of one or more cliffs. For months after that trip I had nightmares where I was just falling and falling like *Alice in Wonderland*.

"Yeah. It's a metaphor for our relationship. We overcame our mountain." Aunt Jill beams as she says this, and it lodges into my

heart.

They overcame their mountain.

It is well past midnight at my parents' house. Aunt Jill and Darrel are getting ready to leave, and I give my aunt the look that clearly says *I need to talk to you.* She excuses herself, takes me by the elbow, and we move over to the furthest corner of the living room.

"What is it, honey?" Her hazel eyes are warm and inviting.

"Earlier, you said that you and Darrel overcame your mountain." I stop, unsure of how to ask this, but she nods at me to continue. "How did you do that?" I think back to the story she told me. She messed up, but now they are happy. I want to know how to do that, too.

She lets out a breath and looks to the right of my head. I turn to see what she's looking at, but it's just a picture of her and my mom when my mom was pregnant with me.

She looks back at me finally. "I struggled with it for a long time. I was always hoping and waiting for him to seek me out, but why would he? I was the one who pushed him away. I was the one who had caused the hurt. I was the one who needed to reach out and apologize. After many years of arguing with God, I did it."

I nod. It's scary how much this applies to my own situation.

"I got his address from a mutual friend on Facebook, and I sent him a very long letter with my phone number at the end of it. That night I ran out from dinner, well, he had just read the letter and was calling me."

I nod again, and Aunt Jill nails me with a serious look. "Izze, I can see those wheels turning in your head. You need to spend

some time praying before you do anything." She points to herself. "Don't pretend to be praying and really be arguing like I was. Make sure that God is telling you to go first. Don't just jump."

"Okay." She gives me a quick hug and goes to reclaim Darrel's hand. Mom and Dad follow them outside, leaving me alone in the corner.

Okay, God. What do I do?

Chapter Twenty

I sit by the door at Whipped Cream, dressed in all black, wearing sunglasses, a black trench coat, and a gray, wide-brimmed hat my mother had buried in her closet.

Miles should be here any minute. So far, he has resisted even being in the same room as me, not that I can blame him. So I've come up with a plan. I am desperate for him to hear my apology, and God made it abundantly clear that I needed to do at least that much. After weeks of getting nowhere, an idea popped into my head. All I needed was a place I could "accidentally" run into him, even though it was on purpose. So who do I turn to for help?

Grant Thurrs, my friends. I had to bribe him to help with his very own lobster dinner. My savings account is pretty much nonexistent these days.

I've been back at Ever After for three weeks and have not seen Miles once. He has definitely stuck to his plan to meet with Lilly at his office. Once a week she disappears and comes back the next day with all sorts of new ideas.

So here's the plan:

Grant called Ever After and asked for Miles's office number. Then he called Miles, and after making a point to say that he called Ever After first, says that he really likes what he's heard about Miles's company and would like some assistance of his own.

Obviously, Miles tried to arrange a meeting at his office, but Grant retorted, saying that he could not possibly leave the restaurant for that long. Miles knows Ever After's store hours, and knows that we are closed Sundays, and since Ever After is closed, this would minimize his chances of running into me. With that knowledge in the back of his mind, he set up the appointment for Sunday afternoon.

Just like I knew he would.

The appointment was set up for five o'clock. I got here at three fifteen just to be safe. I dressed in black, and much to Grant's dismay, rearranged the tables so that I could hide in the shadows.

It's a good thing we're cousins and he owes me for the time he chased me around the table with his pet snake at Christmas dinner.

This was four years ago, folks. Grown men should not chase a woman around with a nasty snake.

I scrunch farther into the shadows while I wait. He should be here any second. My pulse quickens. I've been praying like crazy for three weeks. The only sure thing I felt like I was getting from God was that I needed to apologize. Any cards He plans to play after that are currently being kept close to His chest.

The door jingles open, and I can see Miles's back as he walks to the front counter. "Grant?" He cranes his neck trying to see into the backroom.

Grant walks stiffly out of the storeroom, and he tries very hard not to look at me, but his eyes keep flickering over to where I am hidden. "Thanks for meeting with me, Miles. I sure would love your advice." His voice booms as he very obviously reads the words I wrote on the palm of his hand earlier this afternoon.

I don't have to see his handsome face to know that Miles has one raised eyebrow and already suspects that something fishy is going on here.

He turns around.

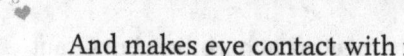

And makes eye contact with me.

"So that's why I'm here."

"I just need you to listen to me."

He snorts. "Funny. I remember saying that to you." He starts walking to the door, but I jump in front of it.

"You're right!" I yell and rip the ridiculous hat and sunglasses off my face. "I should have listened to you. I was a fool. A big, silly, stupid fool, and I am so sorry." My chest heaves as I shout the words at him. Probably not a good idea to yell at him right now. I need to tone it down a notch.

I can't take my eyes off his face. His eyes are unbelievably dark right now. It makes them completely mesmerizing.

However, he is attempting to look anywhere but at me. He looks at the floor, at the ceiling, at the pictures on the wall, and throws a glare back at Grant, who watches the whole scene from safely behind the counter.

Finally, he looks into my eyes.

I caused all that hurt. The full force of it makes me want to run away for good this time. I've been so scared about facing Miles again. I've spent weeks arguing with God about it.

"I don't think I can," I'd say, but then God responds with, *Sure you can. I'm with you. Trust Me.*

Arguing with the Creator of the universe is pretty much pointless. So, while I've been working on my trust and fear issues, He's been listening to the speech I've been preparing for exactly this moment.

Right, I had a speech planned. What was that again?

"I'm so sorry. I messed up big time. I should have listened to you. I should have trusted you, no matter what the situation was, no matter what the outcome. I miss you." I pause and suck in some air. I will need oxygen for this next part. "I think I was falling in love with you, and that scared me. I had another boyfriend, and

he cheated on me. It was a terrible breakup, and that experience left me untrusting of anybody. My first response is always to think the worst."

"I'm not like that, Izze."

"I know. I've been begging God for a good man for a long time, but never really trusted in His ability to do that after being burned by a man who was supposedly a Christian."

He taps his chest. "But I'm not like that, Izze," he says again.

"I want to get back together!" I blurt out and immediately clamp both hands over my mouth. I was not supposed to say that part yet, if ever.

His voice is hoarse. "I don't think I can do that."

I look at the floor. Tears sting my eyes. "I know." Lifting my eyes back to his, I wrinkle the hat in my hands. "I hope you can forgive me someday."

His eyes are moist, but he nods. "I will," he says.

"Can we be friends?" I look at him hopefully. This is such a lame line. We won't be able to be friends. Couples who have broken up never go back to being friends.

He nods again. "We'll take things from the beginning." Miles sticks out his hand, and I take it. He gives it a firm shake, completely lacking in anything romantic. "James Miles Clayton."

"Isabel Vez. Nice to meet you."

"Nice to meet you, too."

He lets go and moves for the door, but this time I don't stop him. "Good-bye, Izze."

"Good-bye, Miles."

"Nice meeting with you, Grant," he calls over his shoulder.

"Yeah, you too," Grant bellows awkwardly.

The door swings shut, and I just stare blankly after it.

"Are you okay, Izze?" Grant touches my shoulder, and I turn to look at him.

"God is in control."

He smiles. "That's right. God is in control."

I just need to trust Him. Miles may not be the man for me, and that's okay. Don't get me wrong. This totally stinks. But I'm learning how to trust God for real this time, and that means for a husband, too.

Miles trudged through the open doors of the restaurant. He had driven forty-five minutes to get here, telling himself that the rave reviews were the reason he wanted to come.

Not being in a radius where he could accidentally run into Izze helped make the decision though. It had been a week since she had cornered him in the café, and he had made it his mission to avoid her like the plague ever since.

"How many?" the young hostess asked him.

"Just one," he mumbled.

She nodded and scribbled something down before grabbing a menu. "Right this way please." Miles followed her through a maze of tables and sat down in the little booth that was clearly made for two. Instead of being cute and romantic, it just made him angry. He was about to demand another table, but she set his menu down, mumbled something, and scurried away before he could.

Miles perused the menu for a moment before snapping it shut. He looked around for his server. *Seriously, how long does it take?* He knew his mood was foul, but nothing was going to change that.

"How are you doing today? Can I start you off with anything to drink?" An older woman, probably in her mid-sixties, smiled widely at him.

"Yes. It's about time," Miles barked. Before he could continue with his order, the woman started wagging her index finger in

his face.

"Young man, I don't know who you think you are, or what kind of day you're having, but you never have the right to talk to a person God created like that. Do you understand?" Her pale blue eyes certainly didn't lack in fire.

His mouth just hung open in awe of her.

"Shut your mouth." The woman slid onto the bench seat across from him. "Lay it on me."

"Whoa. What are you doing?" Miles stuttered and held up his hands. His mouth was probably hanging even lower now. Who did this woman think she was to reprimand and demand such things from him?

"Son, I have been a waitress for almost forty years, and let me tell you, there is no bigger ministry. God has used me to minister to many a hurt, wounded, bitter, and deceived person in my time, and you need some ministering. So, lay it on me." Her silver-gray eyebrows rose in anticipation.

"I'd really rather order some food." A bounce of mocha colored curls grabbed his attention. Had his plan backfired? Every fiber of his being betrayed him as his breath caught in his throat, his palms started sweating, and his heart experienced tachycardia.

His waitress turned in her seat to look at the hair that had him frozen in place.

The woman turned around.

Not Izze. Good. That was a good thing.

Not Izze. His heartrate returned to normal.

Not Izze...

That's when he felt it.

What was this emptiness inside him? The hole where she had taken up residence, perhaps? Suddenly Miles found himself desperate to talk about her. To think about her. To fill that hole for just a little while.

"Uh...I...My girlfriend broke up with me. We work together, and I hurt her because I laid off her best friend. A week ago, she came back to me, asking for forgiveness. She said that she had a bad breakup several years ago and has had trouble trusting anyone ever since." Miles shook his head. He couldn't believe he was telling all this to a complete stranger.

"What happened next?" The older woman leaned forward slightly.

"She said she wanted to get back together. I told her no, and that I was still trying to forgive her."

She smacked her hand on the table, and several people glanced their direction. "You said what?"

What did this woman not understand? "I don't want to date her anymore."

"You prefer to sulk and make everyone around you miserable instead?"

Miles glowered at her. "No. Don't put words in my mouth."

"You may not be saying that, but your actions sure are. Actions speak louder than words, and your actions are screaming about how miserable you still are."

"What do you want me to say?" Miles raised his voice, and people stared, but he didn't care. "I loved her, and she trampled on my heart. Why should I open myself up to that kind of hurt again?"

The older woman held his gaze. "Isn't that what you did to her, in a manner of speaking?"

Miles just stared at her.

"Why haven't you forgiven her?"

"Because..." His voice trailed off. He was a church kid. He knew there was no reason good enough not to forgive someone.

"Did you pray about this situation?"

Ah, the proverbial stone in the forehead. The question smacked him. No, he hadn't prayed about this situation. In fact, he hadn't

even acknowledged God since this whole thing had blown up in his face. Nor had he been to church, or picked up his Bible.

He was boycotting God at the moment.

"I did pray, and I felt like God was telling me that our relationship was right, but apparently I wasn't listening to Him. It was my flesh and desires doing the talking."

"Why do you say that?"

He growled. "Because we broke up."

She shook her head, and her silver-gray hair bounced to the rhythm. "Nope. You think that because things didn't go according to your plan. I am also willing to bet that you haven't prayed since this relationship went south."

He remained quiet and avoided her piercing look.

"First of all, God says we need to forgive as He has forgiven us—Ephesians chapter four, verse thirty-two. Second, James chapter one, verse twelve says, 'Blessed is the man who remains steadfast under trial, for when he has stood the test he will receive the crown of life, which God has promised to those who love him.' Don't you think that if it was God's will for you two to be together, that the devil would try to ruin it? You've fallen into a trap, and now you are refusing to climb out of it."

He opened and closed his mouth. "What?" he finally sputtered.

"I'm saying you need to start praying about this again. If this isn't God's will, then He will make it clear to you. If it is, then you need to fight for what He gave you. Either way, you need to forgive her and start trusting God, or this will be like a poison in your soul. It will be like arsenic and completely kill your relationship with God."

Miles rubbed his face with his rough hand. Looking inside the door to his soul, a door he had been keeping locked shut ever since he and Izze broke up, he knew the waitress was right. He needed this heavenly kick to his soul.

But he didn't want to deal with this right now. He wanted to hold on to his anger.

The old woman stood up and took out her order pad once again. "Now. What can I get for you?"

"Uh, a shrimp kabob," Miles said. "To go, please."

She started to go, and Miles bolted upright. "Wait! What's your name?"

She turned around and smiled. "It's on my nametag." He saw "Lou" spelled out in all capital letters. Then she turned around again and walked through the swinging door to the kitchen.

Chapter Twenty-One

There are ten days left until Aunt Jill's big day. Needless to say, our lives are pure chaos as we try to prepare for this wedding. It has even started to affect my sleep. Last night I had a dream that we were stuck on the tramway car and couldn't have the wedding until I climbed onto the top of the car and untangled my scarf from where it had gotten stuck in some kind of mechanism.

Terrible dream.

I woke up wondering why my scarf was up there in the first place.

Pushing open the door to Ever After, I am holding one of those cardboard trays filled with drinks and balancing a bag of pastries on top of that from Whipped Cream.

"Need some help?" a sweet, feminine voice hesitantly asks.

I peek over the bag and see Roxanne standing about four feet to my left. She looks unsure of what to do. She sways forward and then takes a step back like she's scared of my reaction.

Yikes. I know I'm kind of cranky without my morning pick-me-ups, but I didn't think I actually scared anyone.

"Yes, please." I attempt to sweetly smile at her over the precariously balanced bag of goodies, but I think all she can see are my eyes. They must be creepy-looking, because her own eyes round slightly while she stares at me, unsure of what to do. After

pausing, she takes a tentative step to help me and reaches for the paper bag right before it falls out from under my chin, or worse, before I could smash all the fatty goodness into a little clump with my chin.

"Thanks so much, Roxanne!"

"You're welcome," she squeaks.

I set the drink tray on the front desk. There are currently no clients. Candace and Lilly must be in the office. "I texted Candace this morning, and she told me you like soy caramel lattes." To my credit, I do not gag as I say the word *soy*. "I grabbed one for you." I hold the coffee out to her. I haven't reached out to Roxanne very much since she started working here. I figure it comes with the job description of being a Christian. Does picking up the tab on coffee and pastries count as loving your neighbor?

She looks at me, looks at the coffee, and looks back at me before she takes the warm cup from my outstretched hand. "Thanks."

"So Roxanne, we haven't really gotten to know each other very much. Let's start off with your most embarrassing moment in high school." I slurp up the delicious mocha. "Okay. Go."

She just stares at me. I get this look a lot from people. This is the "she's-nuttier-than-a-can-of-assorted-nuts" look.

Suddenly, an idea hits me. When I first started at Ever After and was being really shy, Aunt Jill played a little prank on me. She called it the initiation prank.

"Anywho." I clear my throat and toss a lock of hair over my shoulder. "Say Roxanne, could you go get me some of the stick-on lace? I like to keep a roll or two in each room."

"The what?"

"The stick-on lace," I say causally. I sip my coffee again, before I address the confused look on her face. "You know, the stick-on lace. All the lace is basically glued to this plastic sheeting, and it comes in a big roll. When a bride has a plain dress, and she

wants to spice it up some, we use the stick-on lace. It peels off the plastic and sticks to the dress. It has some kind of fabric glue on it, because I've never seen it fall off a dress." I squawk at her like I am utterly aghast.

Roxanne slowly shakes her strawberry blond head. "No. No." At first her tone is sure, but the longer she studies my unwavering face, the more unconvinced she sounds. "No?" She finally questions.

"Yes. Roxanne, you need to know about this. Brides ask for it all the time. It's out back. I'd go familiarize myself with the different styles if I were you." I purse my lips together, partially to keep from laughing, and partially so that she thinks I'm annoyed. "I'll have to talk to Candace. She didn't do a very good job training you if you don't know about the stick-on lace." I shake my head and march into the office and firmly shut the door. Then I immediately whirl around and press my ear against the door. In eleven seconds flat she's bolted from the lobby and into the storeroom.

I lose it then, and collapse on the floor in a fit of giggles. I'm so happy I wore dress pants and my purple lacy sweater today. This would have been a bad landing in the pencil skirt I was considering wearing.

"Izze, what's your damage?" Candace stands over me and gives me a look I have also seen before. It's the "what-switch-got-turned-off-in-her-brain-this-time?" look.

"I got Roxanne," I whisper giggle. Just saying it makes me laugh even harder.

"What did you do to Roxanne?" Now Lilly is standing over me, and the worried look on her face makes me start to cry and laugh at the same time.

I wipe a couple of tears from both corners of my eyes, noticing the smeared mascara on my fingertips. "I told her about the stick-on lace."

Candace and Lilly exchange a look. Neither one of them is a stranger to the prank of the stick-on lace.

I start to giggle again, and moments later, they both join me. Candace extends her arm, and I grab her forearm so she can help pull me off the floor. "You're mean."

"Please. It's a rite of passage. I would be remiss if I didn't share this with her. I want her to feel like she's a part of the group."

"What happened to just buying her some coffee?" Candace grins at me, so I know that she is amused by my little charade.

"I tried that." I dust myself off. "She just kept staring at me. Not a big talker, is she?"

Lilly smirks. "Good. Makes things quieter around here."

"Hey! I feel like that was aimed at me."

Lilly is saved from having to answer the question as the door bursts open to reveal Roxanne. She looks at my teary-eyed expression, Candace's pinched-up expression, and Lilly's bemused expression. "The stick-on lace isn't real, is it?" She asks very slowly, and Lilly shakes her head no. Roxanne turns to me, her face a mixture of anger and disbelief that she had fallen for something like that.

I flash her one big, toothy grin. "You are officially part of Ever After. Congratulations. Your initiation is complete."

It starts off slow, but soon that sweet girl laughs along with us. "I can't believe I fell for that," she howls. "The whole time you were talking, I just kept thinking, 'This is ludicrous. Absolutely ludicrous.'" Her blue eyes shine from the sheen of tears.

"Well, I'm leaving for the day," Candace says. "I'll see you guys tomorrow."

One of the nice things about having a third consultant is that we've been able to expand our business hours, so we open an hour earlier and close an hour later. Candace and Lilly opened this morning, Roxanne came in two hours before me, and we will

both be closing today.

Lilly goes back to her desk, Candace grabs her huge leather purse, and the three of us attempt to walk out the door in a big clump.

"Bye, ladies." Candace gives a cute wave, grabs her green sunglasses from her oversized purse, and disappears through the front door.

I log into the second computer on the desk, check on shipping dates for incoming orders, and shoot off a quick e-mail to one of the designers we work with about the hem for a particularly short woman. I'm five-foot-two inches, but this petite little lady is four-foot-ten, with a baby face to boot. We commiserated on this little detail through the length of her appointment. Let me tell you, if I never hear, "You'll be thankful for that when you're older," ever again, then I will die a happy, baby-faced woman.

"So do you have any more pranks you're planning to pull on me in the future?" Roxanne asks from where she stands on the other side of the desk.

"I'm not going to tell you that."

She unclips her long strawberry blond hair, twists it up, and clips it back into place. "Super."

"There's a certain thrill in frantically searching through the stockroom looking for some made up item, isn't there?" I wiggle my eyebrows at her, and she rolls her baby doll blue eyes.

"You're mean." The door jingles open, and I turn back to the computer to finish my e-mail. "And you have a twisted sense of humor," she declares.

"Who has a twisted sense of humor?"

I freeze. I haven't heard that voice in weeks.

James Miles Clayton.

"Hi. Miles, right?" Roxanne smiles politely.

"Yes. Hello, Roxanne."

"Izze has a twisted sense of humor, and Lilly is in the office. She told me to expect you today."

I feel my eyes bug out a little at that piece of information. Whose idea was it to meet here, instead of at Miles's office? Lilly's? Miles's? What does that mean for us? Has he forgiven me for treating him like dog vomit?

I casually glance at his face, trying to figure out what this means, but I find no answers there. He's looking at me, but I can tell he's working to keep things away from awkward territory.

"Hi, Miles," I say quietly. I can do this. I broke his heart, he broke mine, and now we will move past this.

There's only one problem.

I can't stop thinking about him. I haven't stopped missing his goofy smile, the one he gets when he knows he's right about something. I can't erase his brilliant blue eyes from my mind. Based on my reaction when he walked in today, I still experience a spaz attack at the sound of his voice, and at the worst possible moments I catch myself thinking about his lips on mine.

I still love him.

He clears his throat, looks at me briefly, and redirects his focus to the office door. "Hello, Izze."

I nod. Oh my goodness. Why did I nod? I almost smack myself on the forehead like they used to do in those commercials for the V-8 drinks.

Miles must have noticed my internal struggle, because he smiles gently before going into the office. As soon as the door shuts, I slump against the front desk and moan loudly.

"What was that?"

I forgot Roxanne was right here, watching this whole exchange. Time to fill her in, I guess.

But first.

"I'll tell you if you tell me you're most embarrassing moment

from high school."

Roxanne and I bond over the stories we each share, the Miles and Izze saga from me and slipping on and landing in a pile of ketchup in a white sundress from Roxanne.

A bride and her two best friends came in to look at bridesmaid dresses and jewelry shortly after Miles arrived for his meeting with Lilly. It's been two hours, and the ladies are gone, but Miles is still here. That is, unless he climbed out the back window over Candace's desk.

I stare outside for the tenth time in the last five minutes. Roxanne went to put the dresses back in the stockroom, leaving me alone in the lobby.

I nervously tug at the skirt on one of the mannequins, straightening it. Is he ever going to leave?

The door swings open about three minutes later. Miles's broad silhouette appears in the doorframe. "Thanks for coming," Lilly calls after him.

I make a dash back to one of the mannequins and pretend to adjust the bodice as he walks through the lobby.

"Have a good night, Izze. Nice seeing you," he calls over his shoulder. I glance up quickly from the blush colored ribbon that I am untying and retying, but he doesn't turn back to look at me. My heart breaks a little in my chest. Apparently his coming here meant absolutely nothing.

The door opens and closes, and since his back is to me, I watch him go. As the glass door shuts, Miles turns and stands on the other side of the door, looking right into my eyes. He holds my gaze for several skipped heartbeats before he starts walking down the sidewalk. Even while passing the front window, he looks in

at me, but I can't read his expression.

And then he is gone.

Exhaling the breath that I had been holding, I rub my face. My eyes slide shut. "Oh, Lord," I moan out loud. "Please help me to get over Miles. He doesn't want to be with me anymore, not that I can blame him." The expression on his face swims into my mind's eye. "Please, Lord, help me to get over him and stop loving him."

What was the best way to ignore one's conscience? A bona fide method for drowning one's guilt? A foolproof plan for ignoring that nagging voice that sounded remarkably like Lou the waitress?

The television. Man's greatest invention.

Oh great. Miles was about to write a glorified sonnet about a box of wires. Did men even write sonnets today? He had never cared for poetry and whatnot.

He didn't even like this show. He just wanted the TV to run. The noise was more comforting than the silence.

The program switched to a commercial, and Miles took a sip of his soda, ignoring the man rambling about car insurance. He closed his eyes when the TV betrayed him.

Sweet music that sounded pink and tiara-like tinkled through the surround-sound system. Yes, the music really sounded that way. It made him want to smash his eardrums, but for some reason Lilly had thought it was perfect.

Miles slowly opened his eyes to see Ever After. His voice—was that really how he sounded?—filled his ears. He watched Lilly throw open the front doors, and nervous brides walk into the store. The commercial went through various scenes showing Candace and Izze helping them find a starch white dress. There was even a shot of Kaylee measuring one woman in her gown. The end

though, that was the killer. Miles watched as he passionately kissed Izze then heard himself say, "We believe in true love."

Cursed TV.

He smashed the OFF button and then threw the remote across the room. Why was that kiss a part of the commercial? It just seemed wrong.

He ranted and raved in his little apartment. Walking and pacing around in circles until finally his fist landed in the wall.

Stunned, he pulled his hand out of the cracked sheetrock. He stared at his hand, at the little white flecks and bloody, torn skin. This wasn't him. This angry, irrational man.

It was time.

"Fine, God. Let's talk."

Miles waited, expecting to hear a booming voice say, "Thou hast sinned."

Instead, warmth filled him. Love. Not condemnation. It gave him the courage to acknowledge what he'd been trying to ignore.

Yeah. He had messed up, too. He had hurt her, and then she had hurt him. However, instead of forgiving her like he had wanted to be forgiven, he held on to his grudge.

Miles had had the best of intentions. He had tried to help. For as long as he could remember, he'd been programed to think logically, with the expectation that that kind of thinking would always result in the correct answer.

Boy, had he been proven wrong.

"Lord," Miles croaked, "I spent my childhood trying to live up to a man who demanded perfection. I learned to think like my father, but that resulted in hurting the woman I loved more than anything. The woman I *love* more than anything." Miles had been so inconsiderate of her feelings. The realization hit him like a kidney punch from a professional boxer.

Even worse, he had responded like his father. Refusing to

admit his own guilt. That he had been wrong. That he had made a mistake. That he was indeed less than perfect.

Unlike his father, he was going to admit his guilt. He was going to ask forgiveness.

Starting right now.

Miles got down on his knees and put his face to the floor. The humblest position for a man who didn't like to be humbled.

Disgusting, too. He was not very good at sweeping.

"Lord"—his throat clogged with emotion—"I've made a mess of things. I'm sorry. I was arrogant, conceited, and, well, words that I won't speak in your presence. Forgive me." He continued to pray, feeling God's love and forgiveness wash over him.

Miles wasn't sure how long he stayed like that. All he knew was that when he stood up, he felt like a changed man. The drab apartment looked fresh and vibrant, thanks to his new eyes. Something was different; Miles was reformed.

Now he needed to talk to Izze.

Miles sat in his car trying to remember how to walk. How did one stroll into a room? Were arrogance and confidence the special ingredients, or was it all in the shoulders? More importantly, how was he supposed to stroll when he felt like a puppy with its tail between its legs?

"This is ridiculous." Taking a deep breath, he got out of the car and walked, neither strolling nor moving slothfully, into Ever After.

Izze typed something on the computer at the front desk, but he didn't miss the way her eyes brightened as he walked into the room.

She loved him.

The full impact of that realization felt like a cloak of love and responsibility. A cloak of knighthood that he should only don if he was prepared to win her heart.

And he was.

"Hi, Izze." Her eyes rounded, and Miles was grieved all over again for the way he had treated her. He would be kicking himself for that for years to come.

"Hey," Izze said tentatively.

He was about to ask if they could speak privately when he heard a shushing sound. Then he saw Candace and Lilly ducking back into their offices. Looking around for Roxanne, he saw her hiding in one of the changing rooms, despite the fact that her reflection on one of the thousand mirrors in this place gave her away.

"Um." How did he do this? Should he ask her to get back together? Just apologize? Maybe do a little dance? No, he wouldn't be caught dead doing any type of dance.

This wasn't right. This wasn't the right way to do this.

"Did you go mute?" Izze tried to joke.

"No, no. I'm in command of all my speaking faculties." A new plan started to formulate in his mind. He was the guy with the plan, after all.

Izze raised an eyebrow. "Okay," she said probingly.

She loved him. He loved her.

He had to do this right.

"I've got to go." He turned around and darted out the door.

Miles knocked on the door, and after a few moments of muffled voices and footsteps, it opened to reveal Izze's aunt Jill.

"Miles," she said in surprise. "Come in." She stepped aside, and Miles entered the warm house. She motioned with her hand for him to follow her and led him into the living room where an older man sat with his head in his hands, surrounded by bridal magazines. Jill introduced him as her fiancé, Darrel.

"Please, sit down." She gave him a genuine smile, and Miles marveled at the kind way she treated him after all that had happened and the rude way he had treated her.

They sat for a few awkward minutes. Miles shifted uncomfortably. How should he begin this conversation?

Jill broke the silence first. "So Miles, what can I do for you?"

"Well, ma'am. I need your help."

She raised an eyebrow. "Yeah? With what?"

"Well." Miles pulled at his shirt collar. Was it hot in here? "First of all, I need to apologize to you. You didn't deserve my rudeness. I'm very sorry."

"Thank you, Miles," Jill said. "Are you doing better?"

"I am. Thank you. It took a while, but God finally got through to me. Izze may have hurt me, but I also hurt Izze." He took a deep breath. "I was inconsiderate of her feelings. I shouldn't have just treated laying off Kaylee like it was the only logical decision, or that it wouldn't have impact. I'm ashamed to admit that when she tried to ask for forgiveness, I refused."

Jill nodded. "Why do you need my help?"

"I need to tell her how sorry I am and make sure she knows how much she means to me. I've got a plan, but in order for me to do this..." He paused for a fortifying breath. "I need some help."

Chapter Twenty-Two

My rose-colored, gauzy bridesmaid dress flutters in the breeze and tangles around my legs. Much to my dismay, Aunt Jill insisted that my mom and I wear full-length gowns. I mean, we are hiking through trails on the top of a mountain in order to get to their ceremony site. Why not at least put us in a tea-length dress? But no.

"What would be the fun in that?" my dear aunt had said.

If I were a gambling kind of girl, I'd be willing to bet twenty big ones—twenty bucks—that she didn't hike these trails in her bridal gown and white satin pumps.

A big black fly smacks into the side of my face. "Argh!" I yelp, and flail the shoes for the ceremony around like a giant bug-killing fan with my left hand while karate chopping with my right. In my mind I look like a ninja whirling around with nun chucks or something equally as threatening. In reality I'm sure I look like an idiot in a formal gown waving away the bugs with her ballet flats. Hence the reason I prefer to live in my imagination.

Mom looks back at me. "What is it, Izze?" The breeze has whipped strands of her light brown hair out of her clip.

"Stupid bugs are attacking me."

"Behave, Isabel." She rolls her eyes at me and turns back to watch were she's going. The trail curves to the left, and there is no longer a sweet, backwoods forest, but a deadly drop off the side of a rocky cliff. Fabulous.

I walk as close to the other side as I can without snagging myself on a branch. "The bugs are really coming after these bouquets."

"Yeah, they are. The ceremony isn't going to be that long though. The reception, on the other hand, is going to last forever."

I am so glad I brought ballet flats.

Mom lets out another huff at the thought of a long reception, and I smirk. Mom is hysterical about some things. Parties, receptions, cookouts, and graduations give her anxiety. "I never know when it's okay to leave. According to some etiquette books, the time directly relates to the type of social gathering." She fretted about this topic for two whole hours one night at dinner last year. My dad snuck the book to my car, and it's been hidden in my house ever since.

We come to a small clearing. A little tent stands on one end. Presumably we're supposed to wait there with Aunt Jill until the ceremony starts. On the other end of the clearing is a beautiful arch covered in red, white, and pink roses. Dad came early to help Darrel set up the flower arch. Now, they are both dressed for the wedding. Darrel's simple suit complements his salt and pepper hair nicely. However, Dad has ditched his suit coat somewhere and walks around in a short-sleeved dress shirt and vest.

Dad and Darrel are deeply engrossed in a conversation about the tramway and what it must cost to insure a business like this. There are about ten other people here, a few family members on one side of the rose petal aisle, several strangers on the other side, and one old man with a Bible taking a cat nap in a folding chair directly in front of the flower arch.

I walk to the tent. I'd rather hang out in the shade. "Aunt Jill," I call. "Care for some company?"

"Are they still talking about insurance claims?" Her voice is muffled.

"Yes."

"Be my guest."

Pulling open the tent flap, I step inside slowly, allowing my eyes plenty of time to adjust to the dim light. There is a card table, two folding chairs, and a cooler on top of one of the folding chairs. Aunt Jill half sits, half leans on a stool so she doesn't wrinkle her dress.

"Here comes the bride." I grin. She looks incredible. Lilly insisted that she come in on a Sunday so we could make it a family event. Aunt Jill tried on about a dozen gowns before deciding on the second gown she tried. The empire waist, with a gauzy skirt and adorable cap sleeves, suit her personality. There is minimal detail, just a tiny bit of pleating on the bodice. She's wearing a petticoat to make the skirt look a little fuller and allow it to swish with every moment.

"How do I look?" She fusses with the veil, and I quickly reach up and straighten it for her before she rips it out of her perfectly styled hair.

"Well, I helped you pick out the gown, so I'm going to say that you look like a million bucks."

"Thanks." She exhales and starts bouncing slightly. "What time is it?"

I open my matching clutch purse and pull out my cell phone. "We've got twenty more minutes."

Aunt Jill groans. "The waiting is the worst part."

The tent flap is pulled back, and a beam of light momentarily blinds us. It closes, and eventually I can make out the shape of my mom.

"Twenty more minutes until you become Mrs. Darrel MacLaran," she singsongs.

Aunt Jill groans again. My mom shoots me a questioning look.

"She's tired of all the waiting," I explain.

Mom nods and goes over to the cooler and removes a bottle of water from inside of it. "You're almost there, big sister." Mom looks so pretty in her gown. The rose pink is a lovely shade on her. She and I are wearing the same style dress. They are very similar to Aunt Jill's bridal gown with the gauzy skirt and pleated bodice. The only difference is that ours have a high neckline and are sleeveless.

"You guys need to distract me, or I'm going to go crazy waiting in here." The water bottle she clutches in her death grip pops and cracks under the pressure.

"I am afraid of bubble gum," I throw out for conversation. Mom and Aunt Jill both look at me like I'm crazy.

"Why?" Mom asks at the same time Aunt Jill says, "Are you crazy?"

Eh. I've been called worse than crazy.

I narrow my eyes at Mom. "Remember when I was eight and Grant and Miranda came to spend the night?"

"What about it?"

"Well, we were having a contest to see who could blow the biggest bubble. Miranda stank at it, so it was down to me and Grant. I was about to win when he blew a bubble into my hair."

"Is that why I came into the kitchen to find you cutting your hair with a steak knife?" Mom looks astonished.

"Yup." My school pictures that year were particularly flattering.

We keep talking about anything and everything until Dad sticks his head inside the tent. "Two-minute warning, ladies."

We scramble to pick up our bouquets and do last-minute touch ups as a guitar starts strumming outside the tent.

I smile sappily at my beautiful aunt and mom. Wow. So much has happened. It's truly amazing to see how far God has brought them, and how He has blessed them. Tears fill my eyes, and I loop

my arms around their necks for a last minute hug. "I love you guys so much," I whisper.

Quickly releasing them, I straighten my shoulders, breathe deep, blink away the tears, and step into the blinding sun. The aforementioned guitar player stands to my left. About twenty-five people stand on either side of the rose petal aisle. Darrel stands at the end of it, eagerly looking past me, trying to catch a glimpse of his bride. The flower arch looks breathtaking against the beautiful cornflower blue sky, fluffy white clouds, and jagged mountain peaks in the distance.

The breeze blows gently around me, the early smell of summer in the air. Confession: I have never been a bridesmaid before, so I'm pretty nervous. A walk down an aisle with everyone staring at you sounds like one of my high school nightmares. I imagine when you're the bride, it's not that big a deal because you are completely focused on your groom, but as a first-time bridesmaid, it's terrifying.

Slowly, I put one foot in front of the other and make it to the end without any new trauma to add to my résumé. I move to stand across from Darrel's two groomsmen. Next, Mom comes out, grinning from ear to ear. She shares a sweet smile with my dad and then stops next to me.

The guitarist starts to strum the wedding march, and Aunt Jill glides out of the tent. She looks radiant. She has the most serene, happy expression on her face as she walks down the aisle toward her beloved. As she comes closer, I can see her sniffling, and stray tears are wandering down her cheeks.

It's a good thing I insisted that she use the waterproof makeup.

Darrel takes Aunt Jill's hands and lightly squeezes them. His own eyes are moist.

"Good afternoon, everyone," the old pastor says, Bible in hand and folding chair nowhere to be seen. "We are gathered here

today to witness the union of this man and this woman in holy matrimony." For an older man, this pastor sure knows how to belt it out before the people.

He talks for a few minutes about the sanctity of marriage and then comes to the vows. The whole time the bride and groom just stare at each other teary eyed and mouthing, "I love you," back and forth. The pastor leads them in their vows. Aunt Jill cries through hers, and Darrel squeezes her hands every other word as he repeats his. They take communion, and then Darrel's best man passes him the ring.

"With this ring, I thee wed." His deep voice is filled with all the love and longing that was buried away for more than two decades.

Mom passes Darrel's ring to Aunt Jill. "With this ring, I thee wed." She pushes it onto his finger, and the biggest smile breaks out on both of their faces.

"It is with the authority given to me by God that I now pronounce you..." The pastor pauses dramatically. Based on the glint in his eye, this is clearly his favorite part of the ceremony. "Man and wife."

The small crowd of witnesses clap for Aunt Jill and my brand new Uncle Darrel. They hoot and holler, and someone starts whistling catcalls. Aunt Jill blushes about seven shades of crimson, and Uncle Darrel just waves at them like he is the Prince of Wales.

"You may now kiss your bride," the pastor announces in his big booming voice. Uncle Darrel frames Aunt Jill's face with his hands and gives her the most tender, passion-filled kiss I have ever seen. Everyone cheers again, and then they start the recessional. All the guests take the little pouches filled with flower petals and dump them on the happy couple as they pass by them. The photographer, a friend of Darrel's, snaps pictures at lightning speed as they walk under a shower of multicolored rose petals.

Aunt Jill and Uncle Darrel.

I just can't get over it.

"To the bride and groom!" I yell and thrust my bouquet into the sky victoriously. Today, true love won.

The lovely bride and groom talk amongst their family and friends. Pictures are done, and any minute we will be heading to the reception, which will have approximately five hundred well-wishers.

Yeah. I thought that was a lot too, but hey, that means a lot of wedding gifts.

I'm standing off by myself, down the path leading to the loading station for Ketchup and Mustard, the tramway cars.

Yes, those are the real names for the tramway cars.

I'm standing as close as I dare to the cliff, and I'm just gazing out at the breathtaking scenery. I love the mountains; they never grow old.

Taking a deep breath, I try to hear that still, small voice inside of me speak again. It's like He was calling me to this view, whispering, "Come see, daughter."

So I came, and while what I see is absolutely stunning, I think I'm missing the grand point God is trying to make.

"For I know the plans I have for you...plans for welfare and not for evil...to give you a future and a hope."

Jeremiah twenty-nine, verse eleven floats through my brain once again.

I look around, listening. A faint whisper of something else makes its way to my ears. *A beautiful headdress instead of ashes...* It's a phrase from Isaiah sixty-one, the verses Lou the waitress quoted to me when I hastily broke up with Miles.

Slowly, I raise both hands into the air, and just bask in the

presence of my Lord. I want beauty for ashes. I stand like that
for several minutes before an impulse slams into me harder than
that fly did when we were walking up here. Quickly glancing over
my shoulder, I pick my bouquet up from where I had dropped it
on the ground. Then I muster all the strength that comes from
one season of softball in fifth grade, and I throw it into the wide
expanse, into the arms of God.

"Make something beautiful out of it," I whisper.

I have on my chipmunk face.

My cheeks are puffed out big and round from all the smiling
I've done today. They must be swollen. Only I could accomplish
such a feat.

Uncle Darrel's church is about a half-hour drive from the
Franconia Notch Tramway, so about twenty minutes after tossing
my bouquet over the side of the mountain, everyone left for the
reception. Only my mom noticed that I didn't have my flowers.

"Where are your flowers, dear? Did you leave them at the
wedding ceremony?" she asked.

"Yeah, I did." Technically, this is true.

Mom clucked her tongue. "Well, we can't turn around now."

"That's okay," I said. "I'm honestly not sure where I left them."
Also true.

But back to the moment on hand. Uncle Darrel's church is a
beautiful big white building. A kitchenette and rest rooms occupy
the first floor, and the sanctuary takes up the second floor. At least
I'm guessing this is the sanctuary. According to Aunt Jill, all of
the church stuff was stored downstairs. Tables and chairs have
been set up everywhere, and the head table sits on the platform
where the worship team would normally be.

Big band music blares from the surround-sound speakers. This means that the dance floor is packed with couples of all ages swaying to the beat. That's where Aunt Jill and Uncle Darrel are now, along with Mom and Dad, and the rest of the wedding party. Thankfully, Kaylee, Apryl, and Courtney are here. Chairs have been pushed against the walls all over the room. We are sitting there, out of the way, talking.

"It's so beautiful in here." Courtney sighs for the thousandth time. She recently started dating someone from her college class, so she has that dreamy look in her eyes.

Even though it's simple, the room looks stunning. Honestly, it looks like something David Tutera from *My Fair Wedding* would have done, that is how awesome it looks. White and rose colored tulle hang from the ceiling, creating the illusion of a giant, gauzy tent. Someone even arranged the tulle over the floor-to-ceiling windows and doorways to look like old-fashioned drapes. Twinkle lights are hanging everywhere. The centerpieces match the bridesmaid bouquets. They are nice, short, and perfect for having a conversation with the people at your table. No one has to sprain their neck or fall out of the chair while attempting to talk to the person on the other side of the table.

Seriously guys, my second cousin's wedding was rough.

I nod and smile at another family member who I do not remember, but who expects me to remember them. I've been making Kaylee run interference for me. Every time one of them comes up to me, I take a quick sip of my sparkling apple cider. Kaylee jumps in and compliments the person on something, and then introduces herself. They always introduce themselves back, and then I jump into the conversation.

Thank you, but that is not my own brilliance at work. I learned that little maneuver from *Gilmore Girls*.

I've spent the majority of the night trying not to think about

Miles.

I've been failing miserably at this, in case you were wondering.

Somebody stops the surround-sound music and dims the lights. Craig, one of the groomsmen, taps the church's wireless microphone to get everyone's attention. "Everyone, if you could direct your attention to the wall behind the head table, Darrel and Jillian MacLaran have prepared a short video montage for you."

There is a roar as everyone tries to find their seats and the video starts. I grin at the baby pictures that have appeared on the wall. Some sappy love song plays in the background. This is kind of cheesy, but in a classically sweet way.

"Izze! Come here." I look up from my seat to see that Mom and Aunt Jill are both standing there. "Come with us."

I frown at them, but they don't see it in the dark. "Why?"

"Just come with us." Mom uses her stern, no arguing voice.

I spread my hands out before her. I am wedged between Kaylee and Courtney. Mom and Aunt Jill each grab one of my arms and yank them out of their sockets.

"Ow!" I yell. Someone hushes us from the table nearby, and Aunt Jill tells them that she's the bride and to mind their own business.

"Hurry up," Aunt Jill probes me.

"That really hurt." They don't listen to me whine, but instead they each take a hand and lead me out of the reception, down the stairs, and out the door.

Uncle Darrel stands outside with a camping lantern in his hand. He kisses my aunt before passing over the lantern.

"Come on," she says, and she and my mom start walking. I dumbly follow after them. It's a warm evening. The sky is clear and dotted with millions of little glowing stars. The full moon is to our backs, helping to light our path. Thankfully, the ground seems to have thoroughly dried out from all the melted snow. After a

couple of minutes, I realize they are leading me up the huge hill behind the church.

"What are we going?" I shriek.

"Hush, Izze." Mom uses her stern voice again, but this time I will not be swayed. I am an adult, and I have the right to know if they have both lost their minds.

I stop abruptly. "Where are we going? This is so dangerous. Aunt Jill, you are going to snag your dress on a twig or something."

"I'm carrying the hem," Aunt Jill says exasperatedly.

"Not very well." I point at her dragging hem and she moans. "You can't go up there."

She looks at my mom and shrugs. Mom shrugs back, and then Aunt Jill hands me the lantern.

"You need to go up there."

I start choking on air. "What?" I hold the lantern up so that they can see my bewildered expression. "I'm not going up there by myself." There is no way.

"Do you want me to go up there and snag my dress? Then it will be all your fault that I've ruined my wedding dress." She singsongs this to me, knowing that she's found an angle she can work.

"But...I—"

"Izze," Mom cuts me off. "Just trust us. There is something you need to see up there."

I look up the hill and sigh dramatically. "Okay," I mumble.

They start walking back down the hill, and I start the trek up the hill by myself.

The night air swirls around me, giving me goosebumps. This is creepy. I approach the top of the hill. What am I supposed to do now? That's when I see a slight glow coming through the trees.

Here are my options:

    1)   Assume it has something to do with the reason I
        was dragged out here.

2) Assume it is a serial killer and run back down the hill, waving my arms and screaming frantically.

I gulp and, against my better instincts, go with the first option. The light expands and gets brighter the closer I move toward it. I step around a small tree and into a clearing.

There are literally hundreds of little candles in mason jars everywhere. They don't form any type of pattern; they just dot the shortly cut grass.

Wait. Someone has been cutting the grass up here? Why?

Something starts to move on the other side of the clearing. I stop walking, frozen in place. My heart races, beating so hard I think I might be experiencing cardiac arrest.

It's a man, but not just any man.

It's Miles.

My hands fly to my mouth. He is dressed in a black suit, crisp white shirt, no tie. He walks into the middle of the clearing, flickering lights all around him.

I find myself walking toward him, and I stop about seven feet away. Feelings. So many feelings flow through me. I couldn't name them all if I tried.

"What are you doing here?" My words come out in a whisper, but he still hears them.

"I'm here for you."

A tear rolls down my cheek. "Why?" This is a dream—a terrible, wonderful dream.

"Because, Izze. I love you." He crosses the remaining distance between us.

I shake my head. "But you said—"

"I know what I said." He's standing right in front of me now. I'm having a hard time breathing. "You hurt me, and after that, I was scared. I did exactly what I accused you of doing. I ran and hid." He frames my face with those big, warm hands. Shivers

run up and down my spine. I keep watching his face, completely spellbound in the moment.

"I am so sorry. Please, my love, forgive me."

My mouths parts, but only a squeak comes out. He smiles, and his thumbs gently stroke my cheeks. "I forgive you," I manage to croak.

"God made it abundantly clear to me that I was being a fool. I love you, and I want you back. Forever."

Wait. Forever?

"Forever?" I whisper.

He nods, and with his blue eyes blazing brighter than all the candlelight combined, he drops to one knee. Then he opens a little velvet box.

"Isabel Vez, I love you and I want to spend the rest of my life with you. Will you marry me?"

I definitely feel like I'm in a dream as I listen to him say the words. The ring winks at me from the box, and a huge smile splits my face.

I throw myself into his arms. Wrapping my arms around his neck, I whisper my answer into his ear. "Yes."

Together we stand up. He kisses me firmly, and I melt into his arms. When he pulls away, he takes the ring out of the box and slides it onto my finger.

I gasp. "It's so beautiful!"

The ring looks like it has three separate bands, and there are two round cut diamonds on either side of another round cut stone, but it's not a diamond. It's glittering with all sorts of colors. I look at Miles.

He smiles. "I wanted you to have something unique. It has white, yellow, and rose gold. The two stones on the side are diamonds, and the stone in the middle is an opal."

I move my hand back and forth in the light, and the smile on

my face gets bigger. The opal has yellows, blues, pinks, and greens running through it. I have never seen something sparkle so much.

Miles looks at me intensely. "I love you," he says, and his husky voice shoots those shivers of delight all the way to my toes again.

"I love you, too." I reach up to kiss him. I think we may steal the World's Best Kiss from Westley and Buttercup. This moment is absolutely perfect.

That is, until someone breaks it. "Wahoo!"

I turn toward the noise to see a whole line of people standing on the side of the clearing that I had emerged from only minutes earlier. Kaylee, Apryl, Courtney, Mom, Dad, Aunt Jill, and newly appointed Uncle Darrel stand there clapping and letting out whoops of joy. They rush forward, and I am laughing and crying at the same time.

I point at Aunt Jill. "You weren't supposed to climb this hill in that dress."

"Right, like I was going to miss this little scene. I helped put this together."

I look at Miles, and he nods. "She and Darrel put together the video montage specifically so that they could get you out here without causing a big ruckus. She even insisted that I propose here instead of waiting."

She grins cheekily. "This is a day of love and celebration. It seemed like a perfect fit."

I laugh again, giving and receiving hugs, while showing off my gorgeous ring.

But in the midst of it all, I don't forget to send a huge mental hug and thank you to the One who truly orchestrated all of this.

Thank you, Lord!

Epilogue

"**D**oes it look all right?"

"I would hope so. There's no turning back now," Kaylee says dryly.

"Your unhelpful comments are not comforting to the bride," I retort. I try to keep a straight face, really I do, but as soon as I say *bride*, I start to giggle like a little girl talking about her crush.

I am getting married today!

Kaylee smiles, her green eyes shining against her fair skin. Kaylee, Apryl, and Courtney are my bridesmaids, and they all look absolutely radiant in lacy, fit and flare, sapphire blue dresses. Mom moves like lightning, attending to every detail imaginable to keep from blubbering. Aunt Jill touches up her makeup in the mirror, all the while telling my mom to take a breath.

Let me catch you up on what happened after Miles's amazing proposal.

The very next day, I bombard Miles with a list of things regarding our wedding and future. We spent a long time talking it over but decided to go with a yearlong engagement. I have never advocated a yearlong engagement, and after suffering through one, I can officially say I never will.

There have been a lot of changes in all of our lives. Miles picked up several other businesses, including Apryl and Courtney's antique shop. Oh, that's right. Well, that's a long story, and one that they'd probably want to tell you themselves. Anyway, business is booming for Miles. He actually had to hire a secretary.

Business is not booming for Kaylee. Her position at Sew Magical seems precarious at best, but again, that's something she'd probably rather be the one to tell you.

Six months ago, Lilly officially promoted me to the assistant manager at Ever After. I absolutely love it. I still get to work directly with brides every day, but I'm learning more about the budget and marketing. Lilly has even taken me to New York to help her pick out new gowns at the designer showcases. I can't wait for fashion week!

Oh, speaking of gowns! My dress!

How do you find the perfect dress for a bridal consultant who has the gift of helping other women find The Dress, but is not so good at applying this gift to herself?

The five closest women in her life lock themselves into a room with Wi-Fi and bridal magazines for five hours. And when one of them has personal ties with some major designers, good things happen.

Lots of lace and brilliant little beads cover the full, A-line style gown. It has this gorgeous sweetheart neckline, but there is beaded, illusion lace covering up that view, and bringing the neckline to a modest height. Beaded, illusion lace covers the back, but there are hundreds of little buttons going from the back of my neck all the way to the hem. I love that detail. There's actually a zipper under the buttons; they are strictly for look not function.

I adore my dress.

Anyway, where was I? Oh, right. Aunt Jill called in a favor with one of her designer friends, and they designed this dress for me from scratch based on the sketch she drew from their little powwow.

Kaylee fusses with my veil for a moment. My veil matches my dress. It doesn't have a blusher, and it sits on top of my head, flowing down and around my shoulders all the way to the floor. It is a cathedral-length veil, which is a fancy way of saying the veil is longer than the dress.

It adds drama.

"I'm just trying to position it so it looks like there is lace running across your forehead and framing your face." Kaylee says each word slowly and through clenched teeth. Her tongue sticks out of the right side of her mouth a little bit.

I wave her hand away after she almost pokes my perfectly made-up eye out of its home. "Kaylee, seriously. It's fine."

She stops fussing over me and takes a step back. "I'm so happy for you," she whispers.

"Thanks." I feel my eyes water. "Oh, my gosh. I can't cry. Not yet. Quick, say something to distract me."

"Uh, I think Oreos are gross, and I'm going to marry Luke Danes from *Gilmore Girls.*"

I hold up a hand. "Do you really think Oreos are gross?"

"Well," she starts.

"That's it. We can't be friends anymore. I'm revoking your maid-of-honor status."

"Well, at least I made sure your makeup was flawless before you kicked me to the curb." She rolls her eyes.

I lean in to give her a quick side-hug. "Thank you, dear friend."

"Oh, so we're friends again."

Now I roll my eyes. "Girl, if I haven't been able to shake you after all these years, I think we are in it for the long haul."

Dad sticks his head into the room, eyes clamped shut. "Father of the bride is here. I repeat, there is a man on the premises."

"Honey, open your eyes and stop it," Mom calls from the other side of the room.

Dad opens his eyes and grins at me. I am practically bouncing up and down, waiting to get this walk down the aisle started.

He kisses me on the cheek. "You look beautiful, sweetie."

"Thanks, Dad." I smile up at his weathered face and can tell that he is already trying to hold back tears.

Courtney climbs onto one of the stools in the room and claps her hands. "Okay, everyone. This is your ten-minute warning. Refresh your lipstick now, grab your flowers, and get into position."

Everybody rushes around checking their makeup, adding another layer of hairspray, slathering on the deodorant, and spraying the perfume one last time. My dad moves to a safe corner next to the door and just watches all of us. When the cloudy mist settles, he takes my arm and tucks it into the crook of his arm.

He shakes his head and mumbles, "I've been married for thirty-two years, and I still don't understand the need for all of that."

I snort.

One by one, my bridesmaids disappear out the door and down the aisle. Dad is on my left, and Mom is on my right. Together, they will walk me down the aisle. I recognize the beat in the music that we practiced over and over again two nights ago as my entrance mark. Pastor Dean said to step into the room, and the three of us were supposed to stand at the back for the space of five Mississippis.

I count and then exchange looks of love with my parents before taking that first step toward my new life.

I can't see Miles yet, but my heart and my mind are racing.

Oh, one last detail to share with you! Remember Lou the waitress from The Chow Man? Miles and I went to the restaurant to thank her shortly after becoming engaged. We walked into the restaurant, and there was no Lou. When I tried to ask the owner, the manager, and the regular wait staff, they all looked at me like I was crazy. They said, "Lou, who?" Then we went to the restaurant

where she and Miles talked—we'd just assumed she was holding down two jobs—and we got the same reaction. No Lou anywhere to be found.

Proof, my friends, that God will always send you what you need, when you need it. Period.

My parents lead me down the aisle. Friends and family surround either side, but I don't see any of them.

I only see the man waiting at the end of the aisle for me.

The crazy beautiful eyes that I love so much catch mine. They take my breath away. I'm going to wake up every day and see those eyes. The thrilling thought sends a ping through me that almost brings me to my knees. Once again, tears spring into my eyes as we approach the man of my dreams. A man who started off as the exact opposite. A man who was once known as Rude Guy to me. God changed all of that. Just like He took my stupid mistakes and my very own clumsy life—took it and changed it. Just like what the mysterious Lou said to me that fateful night so many months ago when she quoted Isaiah sixty-one, verse three to me, when she told me that God would grant to those who mourn a beautiful headdress instead of ashes.

As I take the last few steps to the man who is about to become my husband, I know without a doubt that God did this. He took my loneliness, and gave me true love. My dry, arsenic-covered ashes were traded in for a gown of lace. God took my mess, and He gave me a fresh start. All thanks to His minor alterations.

Author's Note

H ey friends!
      When I first started plotting this book six years ago, I was eighteen. I had started dozens of stories, but I had never finished a manuscript. I was determined this would be the one I finished. So I decided to set this story in my home state of New Hampshire. Why? Honestly, because *no one* sets a story in New Hampshire. At least not any stories I have ever read. I figured it would give me a creative edge.

I set *Love, Lace, and Minor Alterations* in Keene, New Hampshire. I visited Keene a lot during my teen years and thought this college town would be the perfect place. However, there are details in this story that resemble my hometown. Places like Ever After and Whipped Cream were completely made up, but the Franconia Notch is a real place. The tramway is a real attraction, and yes, Ketchup and Mustard are the real names of the tram cars. (Izze's first experience on the tram may have been based on my real life experience. Izze is braver than I, because I've never gone back!) Any inaccuracies about my home state are due to my lacking memory and/or getting carried away with my creative edge.

I'm amazed that a book I started writing six years ago, finished two years ago, and edited a few months ago could still be so personal, relevant, and convicting for me today. It's almost as if

God knew.... I hope that when you read this story, you laugh at the one-liners I rewrote fifty-two times, but most importantly, I hope you are touched by God. That trust blooms within you. That forgiveness moves you. That God's love speaks to you.

Ahem. Anyways....

If you enjoyed Izze and Miles's story, I beseech thee, please spread the word! Buy a copy for that person who claims they never have time to read, lend it to your best friend, or write a review. Thanks, my friends!

I'd love to connect with you! You can find me spending way too much time on Facebook, Instagram, and Twitter. I blog regularly at www.vjoypalmer.blogspot.com about books, life, and coffee. I also can be found on my devotional blog, www.snacktimedevotions.com.

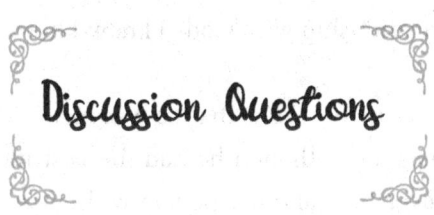

Discussion Questions

1. Confession. I love *Gilmore Girls*, and I definitely tried to infuse a Luke/Lorelai bantering element into Miles and Izze's relationship. Are you a fan of verbal kung fu? What was your favorite crazy, wit-filled battle starring Miles and Izze?

2. How did Izze's relationship change with her boss, Lilly? Did she learn how to respect Lilly as the person in authority?

3. Let's talk mushy! What was your favorite romantic moment?

4. Miles and Izze both have wounds from their past that have shaped and changed them. Do you have wounds from your past that have changed your view of the world?

5. What did you think of Izze's response to Miles's betrayal? I had always sworn to myself that I'd never write a scene where you wanted to scream at the character, "Do not do this!" Alas, I couldn't stop Izze. She needed to learn for herself.

6. Trust was a big issue for Izze. She had to learn to fully trust God before she could trust Miles. Do we sometimes allow our distrust to turn into a spiritual arsenic, killing our relationship with God? I know I have.

7. Miles came to realize that he was inconsiderate of Izze's feelings, even though he had the best intentions. Have you ever hurt another person without realizing it? Has someone ever wounded you without fully understanding the effect of their words or actions?

8. Miles and Izze had to forgive each other, but it took them some time. Has it ever taken you awhile to give your hurts or pride to God, and forgive someone? *Cough. What? I'm not avoiding looking you in the eye!*

9. I've made my fair share of messes. They aren't resolved overnight. Did it drive you crazy that it took so long for Izze and Miles to kiss and make up? Or was this a grueling, character-building process for them? Are these situation character-building moments for us? *Sigh.*

10. Aunt Jill told Izze about her difficult childhood and past failings in order to help Izze see the results of her own mistrust. How had Aunt Jill allowed the past to control her? What could she have done differently?

11. Jeremiah 29:11 is a big theme in this book. Is it sometimes hard to believe that God has a beautiful plan for us when we are in the midst of fire and ashes? What are ways that we can remember God's faithfulness and love?

12. What do you think the future will look like for Izze and Miles?

Acknowledgments and Huge Hugs of Thanks

There's really no way to thank all of you properly or enough. I could fill entire books and hundreds of libraries with all the ways you've helped me. I am so blessed to have such an amazing support system and writerly-minded family.

My Lord and Savior. I don't even know how to thank you! But until my last breath I will thank you for the gift of the written word. I will thank you for giving me this talent and desperate need to write. I will thank you for all the stories you have inspired me to write. I will thank you for your love and grace.

My Sam. You are the best husband in the world! You helped me plot, brainstorm, practice my pitch, and understand the confounding male mind, but you understand me because you have a writer's heart. Words cannot describe how much I love you, and I thank God for you. Your support and love on this up and down journey has earned you a lifetime supply of ice cream. ;)

Mom. You got me addicted to books and stories. You were the first person I shared this secret dream with, and it didn't surprise you. You got me writing books to strengthen my craft, and signed me up for classes. You watched my baby during countless hours of edits and fed me. You are so much more than my awesome, strong mother. You are my friend. YBB.

Rie. Thank you for always providing a place for me, for all your wise counsel, and for reading so many versions of this book. Aunt Jill was based on you!

Madeline. Sweet baby girl, you were the first person to celebrate my first contract with me—I just didn't know it! Sorry for falling down that day...I love you!

Emileigh. You are my writerly soul sister! Thank you for all your encouragement and for talking me off the writer's cliff when I was down and out. You are an amazing friend, and I love you to pieces! I can't wait to read your book!

Tanya. Thank you for saying, "Be Joy. Write like Joy."

Dad. Thank you for helping me go to my first conference. I love you!

Thank you to the rest of my sweet friends and family (A group far too large to name!). Teal, Christine, Sean, Bekah, Elisabeth, Sarah, my in-laws—Steve and Barbara Palmer—all the kids in the youth group, my church family, and my extended family. You were all so excited to read this story. You celebrated with me, begged me for details, and some of you even keep the preorder tab open on your phones. I won't name names.... ;) I am so blessed to have you guys in my life. Love you!

Thank you Roseanna and David White and all the staff at WhiteFire Publishing! Your editing and suggestions strengthened this story, and this cover is a thing of beauty. Thank you for welcoming me into the WhiteFire family, and for believing in this story!

Thank you Janice Thompson! You are such a funny, sweet woman of God. You were so supportive at my first conference, then remembered me two years later! Thank you for your help and advice, and thank you for believing in me and endorsing my story!

Thank you Cheryl Wyatt! You are so sweet and one of the most encouraging people I have ever had the pleasure of knowing!

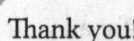

Thank you!

Thank you to all the sweet authors at WhiteFire Publishing. Rachelle Rea and Sara Goff, I count you as friends, and I've yet to meet you face-to-face! Thank you!

Thank you to my writerly friends! Peggy Trotter, Varina Denman, Abigail Wilson! I'm so grateful that I could come to you guys with questions.

Thank you to all my wonderful influencers! You guys rock!

Thank you to amazing authors like Erynn Mangum, Jenny B. Jones, Janice Thompson, Robin Jones Gunn, Melody Carlson, and the hundreds of other authors in my library for writing your stories! You inspired me!

Thanks to TLC for their show, *Say Yes to the Dress*. It was a huge inspiration, and the binge watching was excellent research.

Thank you to the cast, crew, and writers of *Gilmore Girls*. I aspire to infuse your level of wit into my stories. You are my Obi Won.

Thank you dear reader friends! You've helped make my dream come true, and I am eternally grateful! I love you, and God bless!